SEARCHING FOR DALI

ALSO BY ROBERT LANE

SEARCHING FOR DALI

A JAKE TRAVIS NOVEL

ROBERT LANE

Cover design by James T. Eagin, Bookfly Design.

Stronger than lover's love is lover's hate. Incurable, in each, the wounds they make.

—Euripides

Down by the river, I shot my baby.

—Neil Young

SEARCHING FOR DALI

PART I

THE EYES OF SOMEONE LEARNING
TO BEG

CHAPTER 1

VERONICA

Present Day

The cold breath of memory

Veronica Stafford had seven days left before the date on her phone calendar on which she had entered a single word.

Die.

She balanced a teacup in her hands as if it were the scale of justice. Veronica, she was Ronnie to her many friends, but considered herself to have only one true friend, had witnessed nothing in her life that resembled justice. She thought the single word on her calendar was as close to justice as she would ever come. But she was bone weary of thinking it. Of everything.

She'd never met the man sitting across from her until today. An urgency hummed within him. A simmering voltage of life that tingled the air. The tap of his heel. The effort it took to keep his eyes on her. Piercing eyes that sought all they could hold. Eyes unable to disguise his masked kindness, his shrouded vulnerabil-

3

ity. And you know what they say about eyes. Yes, she knew his type. The breed who woke each morning eager to scale the world yet fearful of slipping and racked with fear of failure. Veronica had always possessed the gift of recognizing herself in others.

She'd made her decision. She would pin her hopes on this battle king throned before her. He would harness his chariots. Be her victory beyond the grave. The dream of being more than ashes to ashes rested on him. But Veronica knew it was a fatuous dream. That even victory was fleeting, all of our works destined to be buried by the volcanic ash of time.

Was she leading him down a treacherous path? That was his problem. You've got to draw the line somewhere. Pragmatic in her constitution, Veronica held with Machiavelli's dictum that fortune is the ruler of half our actions and allows the other half to be governed by us. She'd blown her half. And fortune hadn't done her any favors either. Perhaps the man would fare better.

"When is the last time you saw your husband?" the man asked.

Her doctor had said her executive functions would be the first to slip away. Numbers. Simple facts. What you had for dinner yesterday. *What did I have for dinner yesterday?* Veronica Stafford was not a woman to second-guess herself until she second-guessed everything she'd ever done and, even worse, what she had not done. And she did. Question it all. Like a flapping stage curtain suddenly yanked aside, her whole life spilling sloppily into an empty theater.

"Ma'am?"

"Pardon me?"

"I wondered when was the last time you saw your husband?"

"Four days ago."

"Did you call his office?"

"Of course. Melinda, his new secretary, hasn't heard from him."

"And the painting you mentioned on your phone call?"

"I kept it in an upstairs closet. I looked after he left. It was gone."

"Maybe it's been missing for weeks. Months."

"No. He recently took it."

"But you don't know that."

"I know."

"Does it have value?"

"It is an authentic Salvador Dali. Do you know of his signature piece, *The Persistence of Memory?*"

"I do. It's a painting of melting clocks."

"Yes. Despite the Dali Museum being downtown, that iconic piece hangs at the Museum of Modern Art in New York. He painted it in 1931. The piece my husband took was painted in 1930. But instead of clocks draped over branches and a table, it's a human figure. A woman with a half-shadowed face you will never forget. His impressionist roots are evident in the painting. I find it more moving than *The Persistence of Memory.* A similar work he did in 1929, *The Great Masturbator,* also plays with fluid and surrealistic forms."

"Does the missing painting have a name?"

"*The Lost Body.*"

"Appropriate. Its size?"

"It's small. Barely two feet square. You'll know it when you find it."

The man's jaw tightened. He did not like games. But this was her play. Her production.

Her doctor had confirmed her fears: her mind was now an unwindable clock. Each progressive tick distancing itself a little further from the one that preceded it. Her doctor had tacked on this: "Your memory will become a cold breath." At first, it seemed an unnecessarily cruel comment. But then, she understood.

After that pronouncement, she'd asked her doctor, "Will I remember that which I have no memory of?" For this was Veronica Stafford's unspeakable fear. Her nightmare. Her living hell.

"What do you mean?" her doctor had asked.

"If I have a memory that is blocked, no recall at all, might it surface because of the disease?"

"It's possible," her doctor had conceded. "We don't fully understand repressed memory. But it's highly unlikely your brain erased a specific event. Rather, it's buried somewhere in your unconscious zone. And it may release it on its own accord."

If she'd ever had any doubts, that had settled it. She lived in a winter with no hope of spring. A night never to be rescued by dawn. Her doctor's comments had framed the remainder of her days. Her path was clear. She would not risk it. *Could* not risk it. She'd had the crawling dream again last night. Inching across the stone floor to the lumpy sheet. Her body had jerked awake before she got there. But she'd gotten closer this time. What if, one night, she actually made it to the sheet? Another reason to wrap it up in seven days. Shut this sucker down. She would act while she was still herself. Before only the cold breath remained. She would pick her time. Her instrument. She would do these things while she was still capable of doing so. She was Veronica Eileen Stafford. Goddammit.

And since her disease's glacier pace was barely measurable, Veronica had settled on seven days. Why not? After seven, they just repeat themselves. You've got to draw the line somewhere.

Her eyes wandered to her bookcases. She found solace in intimate, immobile items. Had lost all desire to challenge herself with unfamiliarity. When death is on the calendar, you spend an uncommon amount of time taking in the common.

The man said, "Ma'am?"

"Yes?"

"I said, it's really a matter for the police, is it not?"

He didn't say that, did he?

Veronica took a deep breath, trying to disguise her frailty from the man. She'd been nervous all day about meeting with him. This was strange territory for her, for in her corporate life, boardrooms shuddered when she marched in. She'd come to accept that every day was strange territory for her. Every day nervous.

"The police cannot be involved," she said. "They must never know."

"Why is that?"

"It's stolen."

"The Dali?"

"That is what we are talking about."

The man hesitated.

"By whom?" he said.

"That is not your concern."

"Are you looking for your husband, the painting, or both?"

"The painting. I have no interest in my husband. He outlasted his convenience for me. And me for him. He is fourteen years younger than me. His new catch is fourteen years younger than him. Do the math. He traded down twenty-eight years. I suppose one can hardly blame him."

"How long were you married?"

For heaven's sake, does any of this really matter?

"Four years. He was a mistake. I was never. . . good at love." She sat up straighter. Veronica Stafford could never lie without her body registering her false statement. "I thought that before it got too late, I should jump in. Perhaps learn by doing. I do not recommend that approach."

"And you're positive he has the stolen painting?"

"I am. Are you sure I can't get you something? Iced tea, perhaps?"

"That would be fine."

Veronica smiled inside and excused herself to the kitchen. The man had refused her beverage offer when he'd first come in. He was too polite to deny her a second time. She'd miss her natural ability to orchestrate her surroundings. To bend the world to her purpose. Like Dali's clocks. She always felt she was gifted in that area, although now the value of the gift escaped her.

While in the kitchen, she checked her notes. *Yes, I'm doing fine. Maybe seven days is too aggressive. No. Make a plan. Work the plan. Draw a line. Honor that line. What's his name? Jake Travis? No, that's not right. John? Shit. I should have written it down as well. I just won't address him.*

She returned with an iced tea in a slender glass. She handed it to the man. He was staring at a vase of wilted flowers. She'd been going to change them out, but why?

Or is he staring at the snow globe? Oh God, I hope not. What right does he have?

"Thank you," the man said, reaching for the glass. "This is the third cover of the song since I've been here."

"The Windmills of Your Mind" played over speakers.

"Yes."

"You do not tire of it?"

"You think I'm crazy?"

"If so, we'd have something in common."

"Are you insinuating that *I* think I'm crazy?"

"No." The man laughed, and she felt herself oddly endeared to him. "That we both are. Crazy."

"Well, you wiggled your way out of that nicely. It's not as bad as you think. Numerous artists covered the song. My playlist encompasses many of them."

"You play it every day, don't you? The same song. Over and

over."

Why wasn't Michael like that? Why didn't he throw me back at myself? Just because I conduct my life doesn't mean I know what the hell I'm doing. The light bulb, Michael. Did you change the light bulb?

"That's presumptuous of you," she said, struggling to stay in the room.

"You play it because you don't understand it," the man said, charging ahead, scorching her with a blaze of reality. "No matter how many times you hear it, you don't understand it. And you can't stop yourself from trying."

Just like that, he'd undressed her. Stripped her naked. Dropped her into a cauldron of boiling sexuality. She felt his fingers probe the skin between her ribs, her body begging, aching for one last, glorious climax. An eruption to remember in the long silence. A little something for her first share-and-tell in eternity. Her broken mind took it from there, creating a touchable vision:

A circle of newbies in heaven.

God: "Hello everyone. Continuing our introductions, please welcome Veronica."

Chorus of people (do they have wings?): "Hello, Veronica."

God: "Veronica, is there anything you'd like to share with us?"

Veronica: "I had the fuck of my life seven days before I died. Man did it with his words without ever leaving his chair. Took me down to my studs. You got anything up here that can run with that? Otherwise, what's the point? Oh, and coffee. There's coffee, right?"

"I play it every day," she said, conscious of the lapse of time. She did not want to be caught daydreaming again. "It's my evensong."

"I believe this is Noel Harrison, is it not?"

"It is. The original recording from the movie. You know it?"

"*The Thomas Crown Affair*. The remake as well."

"You're young to know of the original," Veronica said.

"I know about the Battle of Shiloh too."

"That's not the same. Who does your favorite cover?"

"Of the song?"

She nodded.

"Dusty."

"Why do you say so?"

The man paused before answering. "She crawls out of her skin with every note."

"Crawls, Mr. Travis? I hardly think so. She *rap*tures every note."

The man adjusted his weight, although his eyes never dropped from hers.

"Tell me about the painting," the man said.

A man in a hurry. And all that's waiting for me is a world slowly spinning backward.

"Not to sound pretentious," she said, "but do you know my name?"

"I am aware of who you are. The new cardiovascular wing of Bayfront Hospital is named after your parents. You donated fifty million dollars. That was generous of you."

Fifty, is that right? No, he's wrong. It was sixty.

Numbers first, her doctor had prophesied. And then all the yesterdays will roll back until only the mornings remain. No. We do not know why this is. In the end, you won't know the faces in front of you. *Half-remembered names and faces, but to whom do they belong?* Veronica found the whole predicament comical. She'd always relied on humor to sweep the disillusioned streets of her life. Hopefully, she had seven days of that magic potion left in the tank.

"It was my family money," she said. "I am but a steward of my father's good fortune and hard work. He was a wonderful man. My years running the company after his death and its eventual sale were made possible by his decades of dedicated work."

Oh, Ronnie. He doesn't give two shits about your elevator pitch. But I do. My parents' names will live forever. At least I nailed that. If this man is successful, Jamie, too, will have immortality. For true immortality lies in our children.

Immortality through children. That had been Veronica's theme ever since she read Doris Kearns Goodwin's biography of Lyndon Johnson a little over two years ago. The final pages. His frantic call to his young biographer days before his death. Telling her, imploring her, that immortality lies only in children. Everything else fades. *And he was president of the United States.*

The man's eyes slid to the bookcases. He can tell, she thought. By omission, he knew. He takes in so much more than he lets out. Yes, he is me. *Well, let's hope he's got better genes.*

She stood. "Let's move to the sunroom. It's delightful there this time of the day."

He started to follow her but stopped. He picked up a snow globe off a shelf. An outcast trinket surrounded by elegant glass vases and stoic books.

"It's lost its water," the man said, examining it in his hand.

Veronica's heart slumped against her ribs.

"It leaked out. Long ago," she said.

Don't ask. Don't ask. Don't ask.

He delicately put it back, as if putting a baby rabbit back in its nest, and she knew then that she had chosen correctly. They proceeded into the sunroom and settled on opposite couches. Slashes of golden sunlight came striding in the room through the partially closed blinds. The song started again. Now it was Dusty Springfield's turn.

"We were discussing the painting," the man said.

She took note of his erect posture. Her mother's instructions banged in her head. *Sit up, Veronica. Your back should never touch the chair. Well, for whatever it's worth, Mother would approve of him.*

"We were discussing—"

"I know what we were discussing. It was stolen from Rollins College nearly fifty years ago. One chokes evoking events from half a century ago."

"They certainly know it's missing."

"They are aware, but it is hardly something they broadcast. Who would want to gift something to an institution with such sloppy inventory control? The person who stole it didn't know what he had. When he realized he had a Dali, he was petrified by his deed. He never set out to steal it. But taking it back would be an admission of guilt."

"And so, he kept it. How did you end up with it?"

"The man who stole it—borrowed it, really—presented it to me. He wanted to return it, but without an admission of guilt. I agreed to keep it. To help negotiate how to return the picture without implicating him. But my husband, who was aware of the painting's presence in the house, packed it up with his razor. Whereabouts unknown.

"If I call the police and they find it, how would I explain how it came to be in my possession? I would implicate both myself and the man who originally took it. I will not have my family's name sullied."

"And you wish to protect the man who originally . . . borrowed the painting."

"I do. You will not learn his name."

"What is your husband's intent?"

"It is not as if we discussed the issue, so I can only surmise. But I am confident in his scent for money. He will sell it in the art black market."

"Do you know where, or to whom, he might turn?"

Veronica uncrossed her legs. "I'm sorry I cannot be of assistance. My husband, Nick Harris, we never married our names, has no knowledge of what he is doing. That is why there is urgency in my request. More than wanting the picture returned to its rightful owner, I need to protect my name in the event the history of the Dali is discovered, even years from now, and traced back to me."

"But you didn't steal it."

"That is irrelevant," she said like an insensitive teacher dismissing a daft comment by a student. "I knew of it."

"And you can't reach him?"

"It was a bad marriage. Must I explain more?"

"What if a transaction has already been completed?"

"Buy it back."

"How valuable is it?"

"In the current environment? Five? Ten million? Black market prices are usually a fraction of what auction houses get. I can afford it."

"I wasn't asking that."

Yes, you were.

The man took a polite sip of his iced tea. He placed it squarely on a coaster. He leveled his eyes at Veronica. The song had just ended and had yet to start over again.

"There are other people, Ms. Stafford, more qualified than me. Professionals who work for insurance companies who do exactly what you are asking of me. I suggest you contact such a person. Impress upon them your need for discretion."

"I will not."

"Pardon?"

"Engage someone else. You will do this."

They considered each other, a gulf of silence between them.

"Who recommended me?" the man finally said, the thinness of his patience leaking into his tone.

"I am not at liberty to discuss how I received your name. You are the man for the job."

"With all due respect."

Veronica Stafford had never exhibited due or undue respect for the desires of other people. She had no intention of starting now. She glanced at a piece of paper resting on the table. She'd placed it there, afraid she might forget the details. She never knew when her mind would break and become a song out of tune. Out of time.

"I believe you and your friend operate a refugee center," she said. "The Walter MacDonald Harbor House, correct? You provide shelter to abused women and working families who can't get ahead. You spent time in the special forces. You are also known to freelance for the CIA, working with Yankee Conrad—and no, he is not the one who recommended you. I haven't spoken to Yankee in years."

The man remained silent. His eyes unreadable.

She continued. "I think you are perfectly suited for this job."

She knew throwing out Walter MacDonald's and Yankee Conrad's names would pause him. Reveal her strength. Harbor House was gifted by MacDonald. It had been his home, his land. His endowment supported the operation. Not that it mattered. For when Veronica walked out of her attorney's office, it was all irrevocable. The man's fate was sealed.

Look at him sitting here, thinking he has free will. It has all been decided for him. God, I'll miss it all.

He stood.

"I'm not your man."

This surprised her a little. But it also reinforced her commitment to him. Not just in the painting but that other . . . stuff as well.

Do I tell him now? No. Make a plan. Work the plan. Wetzel can do it after I've left. He's better with details. The man will see the choice was never his to make.

She rose to her feet. Veronica Stafford was seventy-two years old. Every second of every day of every year contributed to her statue. Her presence. She'd always been proud of her height, although she knew she could claim no responsibility for that trait. She wore a tad too much makeup, for she never wanted to look into a mirror and search for withered youth. It was there. She knew it. She could feel the simmering ashes of the bonfire of her desires, the frustrated descendants of unspent lust.

She led him to the front door.

"I'm going north—tomorrow, Wednesday—for a week," she said. "To see the colors."

"Tomorrow is Friday."

"No, it's Wednesday. I've maintained a house in Ellicottville, New York. A cottage, really. It's from my father's days. I don't spend much time there, but the time I do spend is good time. Perhaps we can meet when I return."

"I'm not one to revisit decisions."

"I'm sure you are not. Yet I would like to meet again."

"Call me when you return."

The man wished her a pleasant trip. He started to turn but hesitated.

"It's one of my favorite songs as well."

She thought he might say more. He did not. She asked him, "Do you believe in alternative reality?"

Where did that come from? It's not in the script. Or is it?

"In what manner?" he asked.

"Do you think things we wish to be true are as true as the door? The glass? The trees?"

"I've always thought the sweet spot of life was a few degrees off reality."

Yes! Oh yes! The perfect man for the job.

"Have a pleasant evening, Mr. Travis."

She watched him stroll away, unhurried by the rain. She closed the door behind him, twisting the deadbolt with an audible snap.

She turned around.

Another man was waiting for her.

CHAPTER 2

VERONICA

Present Day

Promise me, Michael

"I only caught part of it," the man said. "I heard him decline. Did you tell him about the gift?"

"No. But he'll do it when Wetzel gives him the letter. I wanted to see first if he'd do it on his own."

"Does it bother you that he didn't?"

"It only amplifies his attraction."

"Wetzel will present it to him tomorrow?"

"Yes, Michael. Tomorrow. When he sees the money in escrow, he'll do as I wish."

"But what if not?"

"Then I've done all I could do. Promise me you'll have the strength to do it."

"I will."

"And that you won't follow me."

Michael stepped in to her. Confident, unlike in their absent middle decades. He enfolded her face in his hands.

"I'll take care of everything," he said. "You're sure of him?"

It did not escape her that he had not addressed her last concern, but she knew Michael Fredericks was incapable of word games. In this, Veronica Stafford was wrong.

"Yes. What time do we leave in the morning?"

"Eight," he said, lowering his hands to her shoulders. "I never should have brought it here. I should have just taken it back. Left it on a doorstep like a baby. It would have been fine."

"No. It's my fault. I should have hidden it better. Once Nick knew of it, that option was gone."

"You're confident? About the man?"

"He'll do everything. Jamie's name will live forever. We had good times with her, didn't we?"

"The best."

"What time are we leaving in the morning?"

"Eight."

"That's right."

Veronica touched his cheek. He was her height. His face kind. His soft eyes unmarred by the same years that had grayed his beard. He spoke and moved as if his voice and body were one. As if he had no parts, just the whole. The first time she saw his face, really looked at him, was at a student art show on a Broadway May evening of her senior year. An evening in which the sun, as if ignoring the almanac, had refused to set, lengthening the day beyond all reason. His face had reminded her of some instrument, but she couldn't recall which one.

She'd had no intention of going—art was not her thing. But it had gotten too tense. Too confusing. She had to get out. In that regard, she had Faye to thank for meeting Michael. She also had Faye to thank for destroying them, but she knew that was really on herself.

"We have a week," Veronica said. "And when we return, the painting will be where it belongs. Remember, I want you to do it while Dusty's singing. She does it best."

"We don't talk about it for seven days. That's no way to live."

"I promise, I won't. But Dusty, okay?"

"What if I can't? Do you know what you're asking?"

"You must, Michael," she said, frustration edging her voice. She thought about sharing the crawling dream with him. But to what purpose? It would only resurrect the pain. Remind them both of the horrid consequence of ignoring a mundane household task. Of her wretched betrayal.

"We've talked it through," she said, her mind dizzy with it all. "It's hideous. Ugly. Destroying me by the minute. I will not allow it. You can do it. And afterward, your memories will be of me. Of us. Not of some reduced form, simmered away until nothing is left. We always remember people at the end. The last pictures. The last words. If you don't do this, you'll remember me as mindless pounds of flesh. A gaping mouth with no words. You do it, or I will."

"I'll do it. But we have a week. No talk of it."

"And when it's done, don't follow me."

"Why would I do that?" Michael said with a nervous laugh.

"Promise me, Michael. I mean it."

"I promise. Now, no more talk of it. You hear me? No more. We have fall colors to see. Crisp air to breathe. Hills to hike."

"When we come back—"

"No talk of it."

Later, they both lay on their backs, her head on his shoulder. Veronica thought of Faye. It had been so strange to see her the other day. To have once loved her and now hate her and realize the hate was far greater than her love had ever been. Faye had taken advantage of her when she was weak. That wasn't love. That wasn't support. That was selfish. Mean. Narcissistic. To use another's grief for your self-centered emotions was a gross betrayal of the heart.

Did I tell her about the Dali?

She couldn't remember.

Veronica and Michael fell asleep tangled in each other's arms, as if they were trying to merge their molecules. The only light in the house was the lamp in the living room. The only sound the typewriter-clicking of the timer.

CHAPTER 3

I t was the fourth year of Joy's life and the beginning of the second trip around the sun for our younger daughter, Sophia. Since Kathleen and I had children, their lives have become the measuring spoon of time. The sun trekking north, then south again. The constellations rotating in the night sky. The shortening days of late summer, burdened by the constant vigilance on the seas for signs of forming hurricanes, were all waypoints. They were solely for the purpose of calculating the accumulative heartbeats of my daughters.

Those two hearts of mine nestled between my legs on a blanket cluttered with books. The late October Florida wind slept in the palm fronds that shaded us, the leaves spread like green fingers against the cloud-tufted blue sky. Both my girls were too young to have a lasting memory of the moment, although Joy was approaching that dawn. It is always my hope that in a manner beyond my comprehension, such moments would remember them. An implanted rudder to guide them through unnamed storms, low pressures already forming over distant waters.

Our home, south of Saint Petersburg, Florida, fronts Pass-a-

Grille Channel on Boca Ciega Bay. It faces east. The rising sun greets us every day, sparkling the bay as if some Liberace god had rolled a pail of diamonds upon the water. The moon beams dreams into our nights. I've rhapsodized about it before, but it's worth repeating: if you live on the water and face the morning miracle, you forfeit all rights to complaining. If it ever grows stale, it is only because it has entered my soul and is part of me, no longer an external stimulus.

I start every day running the beach in the dark. That morning, the theme of my predawn obsession had been common aphorisms. No clue what brought them on—every day's a wonder. I wrestled them for five hard miles. Their assumptive posturing. Their hoity-toity claim to universal truths.

Quit while you're ahead: But what if that point never presents itself?

Pride cometh before a fall: I've tripped plenty of times, and pride's not even in the room.

Play to your strong suit: What if you're dealt junk?

And my favorite: go big or go home. Many times, I've gone big *and* gone home.

I'm not sure, but I think that's what happened this time. Jury's still out.

But the puzzles don't puzzle me like they used to. Credit goes to the children's books that I read to my girls. For I've found comfort within those covers. It is there that my mind, which often has a mind of its own, is at peace. From a book yesterday: I wish you pause more than fast forward. And this: I wish you more treasure than pockets. Beats "go big or go home."

Why do I mention this? Frederick Douglass said it's easier to build strong children than to repair broken men. I'm trying to build strong women. It's a responsibility I tackle with a blank resume. No skills. No experience. Zippo references. None of that prevents me from possessing outlandish confidence in the task at hand. You'd be wise to question why. I am wiser not to explain.

As far as the broken man? Some might contend I am that man. Jury's still out on that as well.

I pointed and guided Sophia's tiny fingers over the textured pages. Feel the fur on a dog. The penguin's thick feathers. The scales of Mr. Fish. The smooth, shiny blue sky. Joy, who graduated from those books years ago, bolted up and stalked our cat, Hadley III. The cat stole low across the lawn, consumed by something unseen in the grass. Kathleen popped out of the house, gave each girl a kiss, added a peck to the top of my head, and dashed off. She taught English at a local college. She would arrive late. Kathleen doesn't get along with time. That's reason 157 why I'm wacky for her.

I had a full day ahead at Harbor House, a refugee center operated by my neighbor Morgan and me. Harbor House served the unfortunate, the poor. The "huddled masses." There's eight billion people on the planet and not enough luck in the universe to handle that load. We made special effort to help families who toiled relentlessly but never knew luck unless it came ugly. A vein of humanity never dealt a full hand, let alone a strong suit. We were adding yet another room, and I was serving as general contractor. Costs had skyrocketed. Business was booming. But we didn't have the capacity. The human capital.

A week ago, a car pulled onto the seashell parking lot. A man got out and approached me. He needed a place for his family to stay for a few nights. Until a room opened up at a relative's house. He had the eyes of someone learning to beg. One world leaving him. Another, once a horrid thought, now the gritty inevitable. As if he had dropped a level and knew he could not climb back without assistance. A man who used to wake up from a nightmare and who now wakes up every morning to a nightmare.

The man's children watched from the car. It was hot, the sun trying to burn me. I ached for shade. His wife joined him. Pleaded her case. Cried. Got on her goddamn knees. *Jesus, lady, stand up.* I told them they were welcome to sleep in the main room, but we were out of beds. Maybe in a few days. The man took the woman by her shoulders and helped her to her feet. They slumped away. I was trying to do good in the world, so why did I feel so worthless?

The man's eyes were still there when I went to bed that night. They'll be there tomorrow night. I'd gotten involved in Harbor House because I'd done some things in my life I wasn't proud of. Thought I'd make amends.

I left the army a decade ago and worked for insurance companies recovering stolen boats. One chase resulted in a gunfight on the high seas where I sent two drug runners to a saltwater grave. The press played me up as a hero. But I didn't like the publicity. The pats on the back. The free drinks at a bar. It was either me or them. Easy choice. Sorry, folks, no hero here. Check out your local kindergarten teacher, though. She might be the real deal.

After that, my friend Garrett Demarcus and I did freelance work for our former army colonel, Colonel Janssen. During that tenure, I killed a man named Victor. Here's what happened: I was protecting two young kidnapped girls. Victor had a gun. I told him to leave. Get out. He made a move. I shot him. But I realized as I pulled the trigger—*or was it a moment before?*—that he was taking my advice. He was leaving. Peacefully. That stuff happens when you carry. What also happens— and you never see this car crash coming—is that those moments own you. Your brain chucks up that memory whenever it wants. I never liked Janssen—he tolerated me just to have access to Garrett. I didn't like the positions he placed us in. I broke it off. Garrett never flinched in his support of my decision.

A few years ago, I met a man named Yankee Conrad when he summoned me to his office to discuss Elizabeth Walker. She was the ex-lover of an old army friend of mine, Andrew Keller. Keller had come to me for help, and I turned him away. He was dead two days later. Like Victor, you can't lose that luggage.

Conrad was a semi-retired CIA operative. Him, I liked. He exuded a class and professionalism to which I aspired. Especially during my parental-driven moods in which betterment of the individual was a solemn lesson to impart upon my children.

That's a lot. I know.

Back to the amends business.

After the police accused me of killing the man who allegedly kidnapped my sister while we were young—I was innocent, which was a shame as I would have loved to plug the guy who did it—I met Walter McDonald. More on him later. But my life did a hard right, and I am forever grateful to the man. His home became Harbor House. He named Morgan and me trustees of the endowment, and someone found a purpose, their green spot of life. It's not that simple.

Or is it?

Not to ignore the eight-hundred-pound gorilla in the room, and certainly not to refer to my wife as an eight-hundred-pound gorilla, but somewhere in that disheveled timeline, I met Kathleen. If you're looking for a show where a guy has lovers in four states, a pair of ex-wives he rarely speaks to, a child who doesn't know him from squat, and who searches for answers in the bottom of a bottle, you're in the wrong theater. (I do occasionally test the bottle theory.) That's not to say women don't trip me every day. A smile launched across the room, a touch of a finger, a casual, quiet glance—all thunder my heart. But I keep falling in love with Kathleen. Since Kathleen, I've obeyed Jake's First Dictum of Life: Do not enter the Den of Temptation. I have a Second Dictum of Life as well. That comes later.

Harbor House.

If I ever felt like a hero, it was there. Not that I care about being a hero, but since the arrival of children in our lives, I felt I should care about *something*, and "Here's my daddy. He likes bacon and kills bad guys" was not the introduction I wanted to hear on bring-your-father-to-school day.

Still . . . *But, yes, Virginia, someone has to fight the bad guys.*

Two days ago, a woman drove up in a salt-eaten Ford. Her boyfriend had expressed his ongoing disagreement with life on her face. One eye wouldn't open. Her upper lip was split. She wore one earring—a large looping heart on her left earlobe. Did she know she was down an earring? She didn't want to go to her parents or friends. He knew where they lived. This was not the first time. It had to be the last. She knew this. Again, we had no room. I offered the couch.

Morgan intervened. "Come to my house," he said. That was a hell of a thing Morgan did, taking someone into his house. Even if I weren't married with two young girls, that's not me. Perhaps I could contribute in different ways, play to your strength, right? But what would that be? What will the narrative of my life be when my children are sixty and placing flowers on my stone? When only ten characters edged in granite separate me from the masses of unknown dead. I don't know why, but that theme—my daughters' narrative of my life, to leave something more than traceless dust—had become the seasonless landscape of my thoughts. Feel the doggy's fur. The fish's scale. The woolly caterpillar. The effect of your father on your life.

My phone rang. I'd taken it off the "block unknown caller" setting as I was expecting a call from the city of Saint Pete Beach regarding a water leak in my front yard.

I didn't recognize the number.

"Frosty's Upside-Down Snowmen," I said. "Book now for the holiday season."

"Is this Jake Travis?" a puzzled voice demanded.

"Farmer Brown?"

"My name is R. Wetzel Brookings. I represent Veronica Stafford."

Joy skipped back to us with a gecko in her hand. I'd taught her, much to Kathleen's dismay, to capture the miniature lizards. She had a habit of sticking them in her pocket and forgetting to relocate them before entering the house. I swelled with pride when I saw one of the little guys in the house—Joy trying to capture it, Kathleen pretending to be upset with both of us. We didn't care. Not my little buddy and me. Joy giggled and—

"Mr. Travis?"

"What can I do for you, R. Wetzel Brookings?"

"Please, call me Wetzel. I wonder if I may impose upon you to drop by my office today. I'm in downtown Saint Pete."

"What's this concerning?"

"I think it best if we discuss it in person."

"I was at Ms. Stafford's residence yesterday."

"I know that."

"She wanted to employ me. I turned her down."

"I know that as well."

"Naturally."

"Can you be here in an hour?"

"In a bit of a rush?"

"I think you'll appreciate the early start."

He gave me his address.

"Will Ms. Stafford be there?"

"No. Veronica took off for western New York for a few days. I believe she indicated as much to you."

"You seem to be close to her."

"I look forward to meeting you."

He disconnected.

I handed the girls off to Bonita, our middle-aged nanny,

who made me feel like a visitor in my own home. Oddly, I didn't mind. She promptly chatted away to them in Spanish. Joy answered her. I'm not fluent in Spanish. That imbalance granted Bonita supremacy over me. As if I was the stodgy, immobile king of the chessboard and Bonita the swift and omnipotent queen. As I headed out the door, Bonita and Joy giggled from behind me.

I understood them, for I am fluent in giggle.

CHAPTER 4

A sweeping painting dominated the wall opposite the windows in Wetzel's paneled office in downtown Saint Petersburg. It was of a woman's bare back, an untouchable grandeur of skin and form. Her head was partially turned, her facial features never to be seen in full.

We took seats under the painting. Upon his asking, I rehashed yesterday's events, explaining that I'd politely turned down Veronica Stafford's request to pursue the stolen Salvador Dali painting. Wetzel had a runner's body and shag carpet eyebrows. He crossed his legs and smoothed his pants with his bony fingers. He spoke at a measured pace, a man unwilling to be rushed.

"Be that as it may," he said. "Veronica instructed that I present you a letter in the event that her attempt to persuade you was unsuccessful. She would have presented it herself, but as we discussed on the phone, she is out of town for a while."

"If it's so important to her, one would think she'd delay her plans for a day."

"She has a schedule."

"Or deliver it yesterday."

Uninterested in my reasoning, he handed me an unsealed envelope. I opened it and withdrew a letter.

Dear Mr. Travis,

I respect your decision not to assist me in searching for the stolen Dali. Your refusal, however, only reinforces my decision that you are the proper man for the job. Like many jobs, it may not always be what it appears to be. I am confident that you will excel in all endeavors of the pursuit.

I have instructed my attorney—and he will provide proof—to deposit ten million dollars in an escrow account. This money will be wired to Harbor House when the Dali is returned to me. I was a bit disingenuous with you the other day, as I had previously made arrangements with Rollins College to return the Dali. Which, of course, I cannot do now that it is missing. I will return it when you present it to me. The source of the painting will never be revealed. You will speak of it to no one. The money will be an unrestricted gift, although I do have one small favor to request. I am sure you will not object. Wetzel will disclose it at the appropriate time.

As we discussed, there is some urgency to my request. My husband, who has the Dali, no doubt is, while I pen this, plotting to dispose of it. Therefore, this request, and the subsequent gift to Harbor House, must be completed in seven days. Anything beyond that merely increases the chance of failure. I think you would agree.

If you appear without the Dali or fail to appear, the funds will be withdrawn from escrow and returned to me. Please track your expenses as I will gladly reimburse you. The world you are entering cares for little more than the weight of a man's wallet, the beam of a woman's purse.

I have the utmost confidence in your unquestionable devotion and ultimate success. I am, as I mentioned to you, vacationing this week and do not wish to be disturbed. There is nothing I can assist you with that Wetzel cannot handle. Perhaps more competently than me.

Thank you for your discretion, effort, and for the good work you accomplish at Harbor House. I look forward to our next meeting.

Respectfully submitted,

Veronica Stafford

I looked up from the letter to see Wetzel studying my face.

"Was this her plan all along?" I said.

"In the event you declined her request? Yes."

"She'd be better off hiring an insurance investigator. I told her this. It would also save her a considerable amount of money."

"The money, I should hardly think I need to point out, is going to a good cause. Outside of your expenses, you will not earn a dime. As far as your knowledge of the art world, you are dealing with criminals. Art is merely their currency."

I punched out my breath, stood, and strolled to the windows, legions above Tampa Bay. A sailboat keeled on the water. Its mainsail, like canvassed white wings billowed with wind and sun, pulling it forward. I yearned to be on it.

Seven days. Ten million dollars. One point four million a day. Six thousand an hour. Even while I slept. I thought of the man learning to beg. The woman on her knees. Their children in the car. Watching. Hoping. The hard, bad man who had turned them away.

What will my daughters know me for?

I spun around. "Where would you suggest I start in finding the stolen Dali?"

"Her husband," he said. "And anyone who might have come in contact with him during this past year."

"What can you tell me about the man?"

"We have been unable to reach him."

"Phone?"

"No answer."

"His office?"

"Not there."

"Yet you instruct me to start with him."

"If it were easy, you would not have been summoned."

"What was their relationship like?"

"I'm afraid I can't be of assistance to you in that matter."

"She indicated to me that it was less than ideal."

"I believed it hovered a notch above lousy. She was—is—a complicated person. One who reveals little of herself. I doubt Veronica ever tolerated a shapeless day. She stamped her will on the hours, crafted the weeks to her command."

"Like Dali's *The Persistence of Memory*."

He gave that a moment, his eyes not dropping from mine.

"I'll give you Mr. Harris's cell number. But, as I said, it has been of no use. David, my secretary, will also provide you with his office address and my card. You are permitted to present yourself as my emissary, one who is acting on behalf of Veronica Stafford."

"Tell me, Wetzel, how does this work? If I find the Dali, do you expect me to steal it back? What if it wasn't hers in the first place? What if the two of you are running a scam?"

"A ten-million-dollar deposit scam? I hardly think so, although I respect your vein of skepticism. Feel free to verify the funds yourself. As far as your question, I'm authorized to spend up to ten million dollars to purchase the Dali in the event that Nick Harris has already consummated a sale. That amount will not affect her payment to you."

"But if I purchase it back, whoever I buy it from could squeal."

"Unlikely, for doing so would expose them as someone who bought a stolen painting."

"They could cry foul. Say they knew nothing of the sort."

"If it were an easy job, Veronica would have picked a lesser man."

"I don't do miracles."

"We're not asking you to part the seas, Mr. Travis. Merely walk through her door in seven days with the Dali."

"Is Veronica of sound mind?"

"Pardon?"

"She was confused when we met. Didn't know what day it was. At times, she seemed distracted."

"I'm sure it was just a momentary lapse. She has a lot on her mind."

I wasn't so sure about that. We were quiet for a moment, and then, as if picking his opening, Wetzel said, "Think of the good you can do with that money."

"What if the picture has already been sold but I get it back without having to pay for it?"

A smile formed on his thin lips. "Veronica did not want to incentivize you to engage in an act you might be less than comfortable with."

"But?"

"But, should that be the case, her gift to Harbor House would double. Twenty million. This is not in writing for obvious reasons. You must take us at our word."

"That type of money could corrupt my morals."

"It was stolen in the first place. You would be returning it to its rightful owner."

"You're enjoying this, aren't you?"

He took in a deep breath. "She thought this arrangement might place you in a compromising position." He arched his bushy eyebrows. "I have no issue dangling that carrot in front of you. You seem to be a man capable of making his own decision."

I glanced down at the letter in my hand.

"What did she mean by 'in all endeavors of the pursuit'?"

"One's life collects . . . certain shadows. Illusions. When the time arrives, you will know what I speak of. Veronica and I are confident you will make the right decision."

His rambling answer made little sense. Veronica's reference to alternate reality came to my mind. Then, for an inexplicable reason, I thought of Joy and Bonita giggling at me.

I said, "Her letter mentioned a second, minor request should I successfully jump through your hoops."

"At the appropriate time."

"You're big on that theme."

He walked over to me, bringing a scent of aftershave with him. "Harbor House, through your efforts, will outlast you. Out-good you. You may think my statement is superficial encouragement. It is not."

"I need more than your good word, priceless as it may be."

"David will send you an encrypted email. In it, you will find all the proof you need that Veronica is good for the money. Unless I withdraw the request, the funds will be transferred to Harbor House the business day after you present her the Dali."

He paused before continuing.

"Nothing in my past qualifies me to give a man like you advice on such matters, but I urge you to proceed with caution. Billions of dollars in stolen art changes hands every year. By their nature, these are cash transactions. People will do anything to get their hands on the Dali."

"I need a name at Rollins College," I said.

"Pardon?"

"Your story is unusual. It comes with big money. Big risk. I need to verify."

"They are not eager for anyone to know of the missing Dali."

"A name or I'm out."

He went over to his desk and reached into a drawer. He handed me a business card. "Wayne Gibson is the comptroller of Rollins. You may speak to him freely. I will let him know that you will be contacting him."

I asked him if Gibson knew Veronica was behind the effort to locate the Dali.

"I believe she addressed as much in her letter to you. Without admitting or denying, Veronica impressed upon the college that she may be able to return the Dali, but only if no names were involved. No accusations. Ms. Stafford had been waiting for them to make the next move. They have the more difficult task: how to assimilate it back into their collection without admitting they'd been hiding its absence for fifty years."

"How will they accomplish that?"

"Ask them."

"I will. One more thing. You indicated Veronica had not been married long. Was there ever a previous marriage?"

He hesitated. "She was married when she was young. It lasted but a few years."

"To whom?"

"Does it matter?"

"That's my call."

"The man's name was Michael Fredericks."

"Was? Is he dead?"

"Not that I know."

"Do you have contact information on him?"

"No. But I should think you could find him on your own. He also attended Rollins College."

"Did he ever remarry?"

"I wouldn't know."

I nodded at the painting on the wall. "It's a beautiful piece."

"Thank you. I had it commissioned. It's of my ex-wife."

"You keep your ex-wife's picture in your office?"

"She died of cervical cancer seven years ago."

"My condolences."

A sadness shadowed his face, although he had not impressed me as a man prone to sentimentality. "Sometimes I imagine her turning her head, searching out over the water. She was fond of that." He shifted his eyes to me, for he'd been looking at the painting. "The painting has grown to unsettle me. For I do not know whether she is at peace not being able to search or trapped in a hell for the same reason."

"Why do you keep such a perplexing piece in such a prominent position?"

"I still believe in answers, Mr. Travis. Foolish. But I do."

CHAPTER 5

S even days.

Fine with me. More time meant trails got colder. More time meant greater opportunity for something to go wrong. More hours to doubt myself. Seven days. Seven nights. Sleep could take the week off. I would telescope myself into a singular act: find the Dali.

I marched out of Wetzel's office and grabbed a cup of coffee and a cherry Danish at the Kahwa on Second Avenue North. I secured an inside table by a window, sat on a cushionless chair, and started punching my phone. Veronica had been president and chief operating officer of Stafford Pharmaceutical, a midsize distribution firm founded by her father. Theodore Stafford suffered a fatal heart attack on the tee box of the 174-yard par-three at the Vinoy golf course. The obituary pointed out that his playing partner quipped at the funeral that Ted died of indecision. He could never decide between a nine iron and an eight. Veronica, an only child who had worked at the company, ascended the throne. She sold the business eight years later. Her mother had passed, and she gifted fifty million to the local hospital, which is more impressive than a plaque on a tee box, in return for the cardiovascular center being named for her parents. After that, she disappeared from the world without a whisper.

As she had belatedly admitted, she married Nicholas Harris four years ago. She kept her maiden name. Harris, divorced with no children, was an investment adviser who had jumped between various firms before hanging out his own shingle. Harris looked like the man you'd see in a television ad hocking diamond jewelry. Well dressed. Coiffured. A Crest smile a shade too white. Greased hair a shade too black. I recalled what Veronica said about not being good at love.

I needed to keep my eye on the prize. Find the painting within seven days, and Harbor House would be the recipient of ten million dollars. Maybe double that. That money could make a big difference in many lives. A live-in facilitator. More meals for hungry families. More rooms for battered women. Such acts can be a life ring. "Hard work pays off" is a handy single-ingredient recipe for the American dream. But it's only another oversimplified aphorism that keeps us from wrestling with inconvenient truths. Everybody loves a butterfly, not so much a worm. But neither has any more choice in what they are than a person born into poverty in some shit-ass country who would rather die trying to leave than perish without ever getting a chance to live.

We would always turn people away. Perhaps even more, once the word got out. Jesus supposedly said, "The poor you will always have with you." But that was no excuse, no reason not to do what we could with the opportunities presented to us.

Play to your strength.

Despite the money, I had to marshal my thoughts from resenting Veronica Stafford's unsolicited intrusion into my life. I'm not fond of someone pulling my strings and dictating my days. A strong part of me wanted to walk away from the game for that sole reason. But I couldn't ignore her generous offer any more than a cat can ignore an opened can of tuna. Nor could I stop myself from admiring her gambit. Nicely done, Veronica. Nicely done. Besides, how nasty can the art world be?

I went to take a bite of the cherry Danish, but it was gone, and for the life of me, I couldn't remember eating the last piece.

CHAPTER 6

Nick Harris's voice mail was full. I headed to his office in the 700 block of Central Avenue to see what I could learn about the man. A woman behind the desk glanced up when I marched in. She was of indiscernible age and wore a headset with a thin wire curving around to the front of her mouth. Double monitors rested in front of her.

"Yes, Dr. Bronstein. The check left your account three days ago. Yes, mail. You know how that is these days. That's right, a three-legged pony. Two? Oh, that would just be sad. What is a three-legged cow called? I don't know. Lean beef. Oh, that's cute. No legs? Tell me. Ground beef. Yes, I get it. Listen, Dr. Bronstein, I can't put a stop on it. Not until seven days. You should get it any day now. Okay, dear. Bye-bye." Her eyes flicked up to mine. "May I help you?"

A nameplate on her desk read MELINDA VARKER. Next to it rested a tea caddy with a soaked tea bag in it.

"Nick Harris isn't in by chance, is he, Melinda?"

"No. He hasn't been here for days."

"Do you know where I can find a stolen Salvador Dali painting?"

"Pardon me?"

I repeated the question. Who knows? Maybe it was that easy.

"I have no clue what you're referring to. Is there something I can do for you?"

I introduced myself. I handed her my business card as well as Wetzel's card. I explained that I'd been retained by Veronica Stafford to find Mr. Harris. That her attorney had been unable to locate him.

"I'm aware of all that," she said tartly. "Ms. Stafford called looking for Nick. I told her I had no idea where he went. Her attorney called a day later."

Melinda's blouse was spotted with cats and dogs, like something a veterinarian's assistant would wear—only because they had to. Her round face was coloring-book-paper white. The wall to her right held two shelves upon which she'd stuck pictures of her life. Crude crayon drawings leaned against the wall. An opened box of Twinings English Breakfast Tea sat among greeting cards of some sort. She spent her days tethered to a machine while, from her right flank, her life pantomimed for attention.

"You've certainly heard from him," I said.

"Certainly have not. Did you call his cell?"

"His voice mail is full. But you already know that."

"Actually, I don't. When I call him, if he doesn't pick up, I hang up. He calls me back."

"And has he?"

"What?"

"Called you back."

"Just told you I haven't heard from him."

I nodded at the pictures. "Is that your family?"

"It is," she said warily.

"My wife and I just adopted our second daughter. How many do you have?"

"Three boys, all in their twenties. I always wanted a girl, and I finally got them as grandbabies. Three so far."

"They live nearby?"

"They do. Keep me hoppin'."

I picked up a brochure on annuities. It was on a table with other brochures, all from life insurance companies.

"What kind of business does Mr. Harris engage in?"

"You done buttering me up by asking questions about my family?"

"How'd I do?"

"You barely passed. You could do better."

"You sound like my ex-teachers."

She smiled and nodded. "I hear you."

"Your business?"

She tilted her head. "Well," she said with mock pride, "we are a full-service investment firm. Know what that means? We sell annuities. Need income? Buy an annuity. Save money for the kid's education? Let's talk annuities. Looking to pass wealth on to your heirs? Stamp that ticket with an annuity. Fearful that you'll live forever? Let me introduce you to income riders. Got the picture?"

Her forgettable taste in clothing gave her no defensible claim to style. But the joyful rhythm of her voice, her singsong personality, made me consider that, just perhaps, I'd been too harsh with my earlier judgment of her clothing. Why am I always in such a desperate hurry to judge people?

I said, "Why the laser focus?"

She shrugged. "Make money?"

"Did he tell you where he was going?"

"No. He didn't show up last Friday. Called, said he'd be out a few days. That was the last I heard from him."

I asked if she knew when he might return.

"Day after never?"

"That's a long time."

41

"It is. Why the nine-one-one in finding him?"

"I'm working for his wife, and—"

"The one who's losing her mind?"

"Excuse me?"

"Nick said she was slipping."

My mind rewound a few scenes. Veronica's hesitancy. Her troubled eyes. Her confusion with the days. Wetzel had defended her. But I'd already decided he wasn't showing all his cards.

I asked her what exactly Nick had said about Veronica.

"Just an offhand comment he made. Nothing I should repeat. I'm sorry—I interrupted you."

I explained that I was searching for a lost, and possibly solen, painting by Salvador Dali. I was careful not to indict either Veronica or Nick. I was taking a chance blabbing about it, but I was gunning for a quick score. Maybe wrap this whole sucker up by dinner. How cool would that be? Eat your heart out, Nero Wolfe. Take a back seat, Lew Archer. Pull up anchor, Travis "Busted Flush" McGee. In your dreams, Philip Marlowe. Stand down, Sammy Spade. Ten million big ones. Smoked all you boys slaving away for some long-legged blonde with a flirtatious smile and a lipstick-soaked cigarette dangling from her mouth—or, in the case of Wolfe, another extravagant meal.

What's your rate, Mr. Travis? Ten million a day, honey, but, for legs like yours, I might consider eight. Oh my, that seems—

"Mr. Travis?"

"Excuse me?"

"I said, I don't see how this affects me."

"It eventually will."

"Oh, the suspense."

"How long do you think until your paycheck bounces?"

She leaned forward in her chair, bouncing her head along the way. "You thinkin' that's where this train's a-headed?"

"On a downhill track."

She blew out her breath. "Geez, what a breeze of sunshine you are. I knew this job was too good to be true. Just sit here and answer the phone, he said. I mean, the man's wife was loaded. What did he need all this for?" She scrunched up the left side of her face. "Problem is, I believe you. I don't know why, but I do. Here's what I got: I heard him on the phone before he left. Said something about 'I got it. See you soon.'"

"Got what?"

"Dunno. I'm worried about him."

"How so?"

"I haven't known him that long, but how shall I say this? He's sweet. Considerate. Has rose-in-the-teeth good looks. But he doesn't seem comfortable with himself. It's like he sews on different versions to see which fits. And not to pile on, but I'm not sure he's the sharpest tool in the shed."

"You mean his elevator doesn't go to the top floor?"

"He's not cooking with gas."

"Are you telling me, Melinda, that he's not playing with a full deck?"

She smacked her lips. "That's the word, hummingbird."

He couldn't be too dimwitted if he had the good judgment to hire Melinda. I asked her who she thought Nick was talking to on the phone call she overheard.

She hesitated, as if assembling her thoughts. "Carrie Crowlings, the woman before me. I could tell, you know, by the tone of his voice."

"Tell me about Carrie."

"Sure. She was his previous girl Friday. She trained me. Also did all his personal business. Pay bills, stuff like that. He keeps his old client files in the closet—everything's on the computer now—and it's locked. She and he have the only two keys, like they don't even trust me. When I hired on, she said I wouldn't be doing his personal stuff. That she would still perform those functions. I thought that a little"—she crinkled her nose—

"weird. They must have had a thing, you know? But I didn't—don't—want to know."

"Is Carrie about fourteen years younger than Nick?"

"I see you know her."

"How long did she work for him before you came aboard?"

"Hey, I got another one."

"One what?"

"He got off the bus too early."

"Uses the wrong end of the toothbrush."

"Ohhh, that might be the best one yet."

"How long did—?"

"You imagine that? Using the wrong end of the toothbrush? She was here about six months."

"Not all that long to trust paying bills."

"I'm with you there. Nick might push annuities a little hard, but in his core, he's a decent man. But that woman?" She shook her head. "She's out for herself. I could smell it on her. Not that I'm an expert on such things."

I asked her to describe Carrie.

"She knew that I knew she was working him, know what I mean? But she wasn't afraid. Women like her discard women like me as if I didn't even exist. Tall, to answer your question, and proud of it. Never saw her without heels on. She always has her auburn hair over her right shoulder. Like she looked in the mirror one day, liked it, and decided to go with it twenty-four seven."

"Do you—?"

"And in a hurry. Like she's in a mad dash to get somewhere, and everyone's in her way."

"Do you know what she did before she worked here?"

But Melinda Varker wasn't done venting.

"She spent two weeks training me. We sat side by side for eighty hours. You get to know someone pretty well like that." She nodded at the pictures of her life next to her. "I mean, how can someone sit here and never ask about my grandkids? My family? You led with it—your comment was mainly designed as a door opener, and that's fine—but her? It was like she wanted to show that she didn't care. That she was superior to me. She's smiles on the outside, knives on the inside. And her language. She'd make a sailor blush, although I give her an A for creativity."

I asked her if she had any more information on Carrie Crowlings, a variation of my previous question, which she had not answered.

"Well," she drew out in a playful tone. "She was in the restroom one day. She'd left her phone on the desk. It rang, so I peeked at the caller ID. It said *Sunshine*. She'd told me she was expecting a call to get a new dishwasher installed. You know how they give you a two-hour window? Said she'd have to skedaddle if she got the call. I picked it up, thinking I was doing her a favor. I mean there's Sunshine Irrigation. Sunshine Plumbing. Sunshine Locksmith. Sunshine Colonoscopy. Everyone in Florida sticks *sunshine* in their name and, in the latter case, up your you-know-where.

"A curt woman demanded to know who I was. When I told her, she hung up, I told Carrie when she returned. She was pretty pissed. Told me not to answer her phone again. Actually, I believe it was 'Don't pick up my frickin' phone' again, toad face.' Toad face. That hurt. She took her phone outside. Came back a few minutes later, snatched her purse, and dashed out. Said she had to get home. That her dishwasher was being delivered. Next day? I asked her how her dishwasher installation went."

"Did she remember?"

"She was puzzled for a second. Score one for toad face."

"You have a pretty face."

"It's too round."

"You have a pretty round face."

She cocked her head. "Thank you."

I asked her if she happened to remember the phone number.

"Numbers stick to me like Velcro, for whatever that's worth. I can reel off half our clients' social security number and account numbers. Right after Carrie bolted, I checked the cross directory—learned that when I worked at the DMV. The number belonged to Sunshine Escort. Got a web page and all. Girls and guys to accompany you to dinner. The theater. Wherever."

"What possessed you to take that leap?"

She shook her head. "There is no reason to put other people down. Make them feel bad."

"What do you think's going on, Melinda?"

She leaned back in her chair. "Well, Jake, I've given that some thought. My bet? She targeted Nick. Can't imagine why, it was his wife's money. But maybe bimbo Carrie didn't get the memo. You'll keep me apprised, right?"

"I will."

"You think this all ties into your missing painting?"

"I do."

"Is it valuable?"

"It is."

"Thousands or millions?"

"Millions."

She let out a low whistle.

"That'll make your hair stand up and your socks fall down. And that's definitely the type of money that would put Carrie's nose to the ground. Betcha you find her, you find your Degas."

"Dali."

"Right. Dali."

CHAPTER 7

I left Melinda Varker and drove to Veronica's home. Veronica had departed that morning, but I wanted to see if any neighbors could be of assistance. Her absence made the job easier.

A light rain, just enough to activate the windshield wipers for a solo swipe, misted the air. A small leaf took the trip with the driver's side wiper. After I climbed out of the truck, I reached over and plucked the leaf from under the blade. But I didn't drop it. I held it for a moment. Massaged its texture. Fingered its veins. Marveled at its glossy green finish before letting it flutter to the ground where it looked so lonely. Must be those children's books.

I knocked my knuckles raw. My opening line was that I'd been retained by Veronica to look for Nick Harris.

"We never really saw her much. Him, never."

"Sorry. I'm busy right now."

"Don't know anything of either of them."

"Hey, there, long and tall. Why don't you come in from the rain? Wasn't that a song?"

"Ms. Stafford? I talked to her a few times. Pleasant in a

distant sort of way. She was never out much. I mean we'd have block parties, football tailgates, you know, things like that. But they never made an appearance. Probably an age thing."

My accumulated knowledge was this: despite living there for over thirty years, Veronica was rarely seen on her grounds. I did learn that while she was active in the corporate world, she'd used her home for business functions, but most of those guests were not of the neighborhood. Many of the houses, including the one to her left and two directly across the street, had turned over in the past ten years.

No one answered the door to her immediate right. I googled the house. No sales records. It was owned by Barbara Langford. She'd likely been Veronica's neighbor for decades and I made a note to check back in a few days. I drove three blocks to Beach Drive and got lucky on a parking space. I approached the hostess stand at Mangroves and requested a high top on the sidewalk, pointing at the one I wanted. The hostess informed me it was damp. I countered that I was a wizard with napkins. I dried the chair and ordered an iced tea and burger, substituting a salad for my side. Joe Healthy here. When the waiter delivered the salad, I caved and tacked on an order of fries. Joe Hungry here.

I asked for the chit so I could pay and leave on my own schedule. Here's a little quirk of mine: I don't do waiting. I'm working on it, but really, the rest of y'all just need to speed up. Self-checkout lanes have added years to my life.

I called Detective Rambler, a friend—that might be engaging a broad definition of the word—in the police department. I told him I was looking for Nick Harris, no foul play suspected, and asked him to keep me informed if he heard anything.

"What's really going on?" he demanded.

I explained I was searching for a missing painting. I didn't hold anything back.

"That's not your wheelhouse," he pointed out. "They should hire an insurance dick."

"That's what I told them."

"Too bad they didn't listen."

We disconnected, although his parting remark stuck around.

Next up was Wayne Gibson, the comptroller at Rollins College and the name Wetzel had provided me. He told me he'd been expecting my call. I asked if I could drop by around noon tomorrow. Even though tomorrow was Saturday, he indicated that was fine. Rollins College was in Winter Park, a glitzy suburb of Orlando. It was about a two-hour drive.

My final call was to Sunshine Escort. I arranged for an escort the following night for when I returned from Rollins. I wanted to see if I could find someone who knew Carrie Crowlings. Maybe someone at Sunshine could point me in the right direction. Before I left the restaurant, I returned to the hostess station, made a reservation for my escort dinner, and indicated the sidewalk table I wanted. Another quirk: I'm picky about restaurant tables and abide by a simple rule: it's okay not to have the best available table in a restaurant, but it's not okay to not ask for the best table in a restaurant.

THAT EVENING, KATHLEEN AND I sat on the screened porch as the sky faded to a deep bruise. Both girls were asleep, leaving us tired, a nearly exhausted bottle of wine between us. The tendril from a solitary candle flicked the air. It resembled the flaying arms of a ballerina whose feet were welded to wax. The meditative bay showed no signs of disruption from either man or nature. I thought of dropping another record on the 1961 floor-model Magnavox but hadn't the energy. I'd just finished telling Kathleen about the Veronica Stafford affair, concluding with how I resented being a marionette.

"Buckle up, cowboy," she said. "For ten million, you forfeit all claims to your puny feelings."

"Puny?" I took a sip of wine. Like a priest taking sacrament, I pined for it to be so much more than it was.

"You heard me. For that cash, you enter a dance marathon. What's your next move?"

I explained to her that I was going to Rollins College in the morning to meet with the comptroller. I wanted to make sure the school's version of the Dali was the same one that had been preached to me. If not, I was out.

"Also, I won't be home for dinner," I added.

"It's only a couple of hours, isn't it?" The flame, small as it was, brightened her face.

"I'll be back. It's just that I have a date with another woman."

"Is this payback for *puny*? Wow, that was swift retribution. Or was the meat loaf overdone? Oh, please tell me, darling. I know I can do better."

Kathleen needed a GPS to find the kitchen. Once there, she would pass through it, a disoriented traveler in a foreign country, mildly interested but eager to return to a five-star hotel. Reason 158. Or was it 36? As for meat loaf, she likely thought it was a cow playing a video game. I wondered if Dr. Bronstein had thought of that one.

As the sound of blowing dolphins broke the night, I told her that I'd contacted Sunshine Escort and requested a date. That we were having dinner at Mangroves. That I was looking for Carrie Crowlings as a road to finding Nick Harris. Maybe someone at Sunshine Escort knew Carrie.

"You're taking her to our table at Mangroves?"

"I didn't say to our table."

"You won't sit at another table."

"I will."

"Incredible. You already booked it, didn't you?"

"Maybe."

"What are the odds that one escort would know of another?"

"I need to start somewhere."

"How does it play out? You spend the next seven days taking women to dinner—maybe squeeze in a lunch or two—all in the name of fundraising for Harbor House?"

"Have I ever failed to support *your* career?"

"Do they have male escorts as well?"

"You know I don't swing from that tree."

"If we hit two people in one night, we double our chances of finding someone who knows Carrie Crowlings."

And that's how Kathleen and I ended up on Beach Drive, downtown Saint Petersburg, on a lovely autumn evening, our backs to each other, having dinner with someone else.

That back-to-back part? That was her game. Little vixen.

CHAPTER 8

Rollins College's picturesque Mediterranean-style campus rested on manicured lawns dissected by a spider network of sidewalks. Live oaks draped with Spanish moss shaded the grounds that partially bordered Lake Virginia. A Parisian art student would never find a more worthy setting.

It was alumni weekend. Banners from every five years ago —up to seventy years—welcomed back the youth who once traversed her hallowed grounds. After a ten-minute search for a parking spot, I capitulated and squeezed my truck into a tight space two blocks off campus. I trekked back to the college and made my way across the crowded grounds. Everyone was festive. Everyone young again.

Gibson's office was on the second floor of the scantly inhabited main administrative building. His door was open, and he sat behind a desk studying a monitor. Probably porn. I knocked on the wide trim. He glanced up as I stepped in and introduced myself. He rose and strode over to greet me, his hand leading the way, pumping air before our hands interlocked. The room had sky-high ceilings with large windows. Those windows overlooked green lawns dotted with white tents.

"Busy weekend," Gibson said, peering over his glasses, which were halfway down his nose. His nose was slightly askew, so it did not serve as a straight demarcation line between the left and right sides of his face. "It's always a joyous occasion to see so many of our alumni returning to the fields of their youth."

"It is an illusion of those who have lost youth that youth was happy," I said, mauling Somerset Maugham.

Gibson smiled at me appreciatively. "I couldn't agree more," he said in a buttered voice. "But we encourage such illusions. Passion for their bankrupt youth keeps our coffers full."

I asked him to tell me about *The Lost Body*.

"Perhaps Dali named it knowing its fate." He extended his arm toward a sitting area. "Please."

We settled in opposing chairs. Gibson crossed his legs. He wore blue socks with a gold *R* over an anchor. I'd opted for beige pants, a pale blue shirt (robin's egg, Kathleen had corrected me), and a dark blue blazer Kathleen had recently purchased. She buys me a new blue blazer every year, saying the style changes. They all look the same to me. Want one?

"The painting's disappearance took place well before my time," he explained. "Fifty years, give or take. Likely sometime in the early seventies. We are, somewhat embarrassingly, not even certain of the exact date. The painting was last inventoried by the art department in the late sixties. Ten years later—there is no mention of it. Those who occupied these halls at that time were not eager—nor can I fault them —to accept that it had been stolen. Only after years of searching did we face the truth. It had been swiped from under our noses."

"And the knowledge that the college ever had it?"

"Few know. It was deemed not just self-incriminating but also blatantly irresponsible to come forth and say it was missing. That we didn't know how long it had been misplaced, and that, furthermore, we had no path by which to pursue its repossession."

I asked him how the college first received the painting.

"A gift from Margaret Carnegie Miller, the only child of Andrew Carnegie. Rollins was fortunate to be the recipient of massive grants from the Andrew Carnegie Foundation. Carnegie died in 1919, leaving his estate to his daughter. She gifted it to the college, among other artwork. From what I understand, she owned a great many pieces of art. Our first library, finished in 1908, was named for him. That building has had numerous uses since then. Tour it if you'd like. It houses some administrative offices and classrooms at the present time."

"When was the gift made?"

"In 1948. It had some value then. Nothing like today, of course. And not just because of inflation. Salvador Dali was not the success then that he is now."

I asked him to tell me about Veronica Stafford. He hesitated, searching for words.

"She has been generous to the college over the years." His tone conveyed more of what he didn't say than what he did.

"But."

"She has, or purportedly knows the whereabouts of, the Dali. We had been negotiating with her for the return of the painting. We didn't want it until we had a plan to assimilate it back into the college's inventory without her name being involved—a request of hers that we pledged to honor. That delay, if we are to believe her, cost us. Ms. Stafford, through her attorney, now claims she can no longer place her hands on the Dali. We've been negotiating with him. Mr. Wetzel Brookings. I believe you've met him."

"He's cloudy on a lot of points."

"An overcast virtuoso."

"And if it is returned?"

"Lucky me," he said. "Going forward, it will be my job to absorb it back into the college's collection without bringing attention to it."

Going forward.

Not many phrases curl my spine, but *going forward* does the trick. Versus what? Going backward? Like there's a rewind button in our lives? If you're not going forward, you're dead. Is there any sentence that is materially changed by adding *going forward*? Why even—?

"Mr. Travis?"

"Excuse me. How do you plan—going forward—to absorb it back into the collection?"

"We will likely sell it. Say it was an anonymous gift, deflect questions, and move on."

"Certainly others will trace its ownership back to Margaret Carnegie Miller."

"Not as easily done as you may think. We will say it was buried in the vault. Because its disappearance was a half century ago, the current administration is absolved of sloppy management. To the contrary, we will be the good stewards who found it after all those years."

"If I find it."

"I and the few others who know of this are rooting for you. The Dali will bring in a good bit of money. Your success will be appreciated on more levels than you can imagine."

"She told me someone—not her—found the painting. He or she took it, not knowing what it was. They never set out to steal it."

Gibson said, "We got that line as well. Did she give you a name?"

"No. Does it matter?"

"I suppose not. Oh, I'm curious as hell, but I don't want that curiosity in any manner to interfere with our objective." He tented his hands, fanning out his fingertips. "Not all agree with this approach. Some of my associates wish for the whole matter to be turned over to—and I mean no disrespect—a professional. One who does this sort of thing for a living. But Ms. Stafford insisted on you. As I said, she is a generous donor. It's her fiftieth reunion this year. I checked the RSVPs. She's not attending."

"And you?"

"You have my full support. Although, if you fail, going forward, we will pursue the painting on our own agenda. I'm sure you understand."

When I failed to reply, he continued. "If you don't mind my asking, what are your arrangements with Ms. Stafford?

"She gave me seven days to find the Dali. If successful, a refuge house that I help operate will be the recipient of ten million dollars."

"That's a lot of money."

"It is."

"And for you?"

"Nothing. Who else knows about the history of *The Lost Body*?"

"The president. Chairwoman of the board. One or two others."

"And they kept it a secret?"

"Absolutely."

"You know what Ben Franklin said about three people and a secret?"

"It's safe if two are dead. But killing two out of three is hardly a civilized approach. Are you driving straight back?"

"I am."

He stood and went to his desk. He opened a drawer and handed me a yellow ticket with today's date on it. "Have lunch on us. It's the least we can do. You can present this in the cafeteria or any of the alumni tents. The cafeteria has a greater selection, but all the tents are catered as well."

I thanked him and asked him for directions to the cafeteria.

Halfway there, I had a better idea.

CHAPTER 9

Veronica Stafford's class, the class of 1973, camped out on the Georges Seurat shore of Lake Virginia. The first cold front of the season with any muscle had blown through during the night. The heartland breeze, combined with the canopy of blue sky, created the sense of suspended time indigenous to college campuses in the fall. Students, some lugging backpacks, wandered along the sidewalks that hugged the lake. Gibson/Maugham were right. Youth is a hell of a product. Especially when viewed through the rose-tinted memory mirror.

I presented my ticket to a young woman sitting behind a table outside the tent. Her hair was parted down the middle. The left side was pink, the right side blonde. I liked it. She also had a pierced nose—but that particular piece of body art has never punched my ticket. The tent was bulging with people in their early seventies. More were scattered on the benches by the lake, some sitting on lawn chairs. The women were thin, and the men East Coast uniformed in linen pants, crisp shirts, and designer sports jackets that they probably updated every three months. And expensive shoes. Each person had more money on their feet than the man who was learning to beg had to his name. What I could only surmise were a few grandchildren scurried around, spicing the air with giggles and reminding anyone who bothered to pay attention that hope is born every day.

A buffet table ran across the back of the tent. I curved my way through the crowd. Neil Young's "Down by the River" played from speakers on the ground.

"You sure you have the right year?" a woman inquired of me. She had silver hair, an orange headband, and a matching scarf that flowed down her side, stopping just short of her tight-at-the-top, flared-at-the-bottom jeans. "If you graduated in seventy-three, I want your doctor's name."

"I'm not an alumnus," I admitted. "I was hoping to run into Veronica Stafford."

I knew she wasn't there. But I thought it might be beneficial to meet someone who knew her.

"Veronica Stafford," she said, granting distinct weight and tone to each syllable. "That's a name that hasn't come with a face in a long time. She shows up on the donor list—not the nickel-and-dime stuff either. But I don't believe she's set foot on campus since the day they kicked us out."

"Did you know her?"

"We'd pass—small campus and all. But that was about it."

I asked her if Veronica was active in school.

"Active? Let's see. Class vice president. Water ski champion. Tennis team. Girl about campus, if that answers your question. I was more into the anti-war-pro-Jesus movement. Species don't always mix."

"Did you run—?"

"I worked on the school's paper, *The Sandspur*. I made sure the running tally of war dead was always placed next to the tennis scores. Wow, look at me changing the world. Rattling my sword. Why are you searching for her?"

I told her I was in town and wanted to go over a few things with Veronica.

"You certainly have her number. Call her."

"I'd rather see her in person."

"You're going to have to do better than that."

My orange headband woman wore a name tag.

"I can, Colleen. I talked with Veronica last week. She hired me for a peculiar job. Before accepting, I thought it would be advantageous to meet people who knew her."

"And you're starting with fifty years ago?"

"This particular request is best met by meeting those who knew her while she was a student here."

"I see. Particular and peculiar."

"Specific and strange."

Colleen sucked in her lower lip.

"Can you help me?" I lobbied her. "Perhaps steer me to someone who knew her?"

She waited a beat before answering. "You should probably talk to Faye."

"Is Faye here?"

"Did you ever see *The Thomas Crown Affair*?"

A tingle ran up my spine. As if a corner piece of a thousand-piece puzzle had dropped into place. Problem was, I didn't have the box cover. No clue what the picture looked like.

"I have."

"It was big in the late sixties. Came out when we were in high school. Faye Wilkinson looks like Faye Dunaway. When she was alive, of course."

"Faye Wilkinson is dead?"

"No. I was referring to Faye Dunaway."

"She's still alive."

"Really. I just assumed all our idols were gone. A totally selfish assumption. You see, I'd rather they die young and not age. That way, I, too, stay young."

60

"Little harsh, don't you think?"

"The price of fame."

I asked her if she could point out living Faye to me.

"To answer your earlier question, she just left. Said she was going to visit some of the old haunts. The chapel. Classrooms. Those sentimental tugs that really do you no good. I find it hard to visit the past without being dragged into it."

"Yet here you are."

She canted an eyebrow. "Here I am."

"Where do you suggest I start?"

"Try Carnegie Hall. When these grounds were ours, and for us only, it held classrooms. No idea what it's used for now."

She kept her eyes on mine, as if trying to see someone—or something—that wasn't there.

"Anything else?" I prodded her.

"There was a boy," she said, her voice taking her back half a century. "He was two years ahead of us. Michael someone. I doubt he'd be here—not his five-year mark."

"Michael Fredericks? I believe they were married briefly. What about him?"

She looked at me as if startled that I was still there.

"Oh, I don't know. Nothing, I suppose. It's so long ago, it's like a different life. The three of—" She stopped, her mouth open. Whatever she was going to say got censored in her throat. "Best of luck to you."

She turned and slipped into the crowd, her orange headband marking her movements. I grabbed a hot dog, squirted mustard on it, and marched to Carnegie Hall. Halfway there, a streak of mustard dripped from the dog onto my shirt. I tried to clean it but only made it worse.

CHAPTER 10

A woman sat in the back row of the third empty classroom I poked my head into. I don't know why, but I knew she was Faye Wilkinson. She stared at a chalkboard where someone had scrawled Euripides's quote: "Stronger than lover's love is lover's hate."

"Faye Wilkinson?"

She looked up. Her face was vulnerable. Her eyes, at first lost, became cold and focused. Sometimes you look in someone's eyes and see truth. Other times you see eyes that don't believe in truth. Faye's were the latter.

"Yes?"

As with Melinda, I decided to go for the quick close.

"My name is Jake Travis. Veronica Stafford hired me to find a stolen painting."

"You have mustard on your shirt."

"I know."

"It looks as if you tried to get it out and made it worse."

"That would be an accurate assessment."

"Am I to believe you are pitching that line to everyone you see today?"

"No. I met Colleen. She suggested I talk with you."

"Colleen? What did that tree hugger say about me?"

"That you look like Faye Dunaway and you knew—or know —Veronica."

She stood and strolled over to me. She looked like money and smelled like Wind Song. The perfume smacked me back to a girl who wore it. The salty kiss when I told her I was leaving.

"What if I don't feel like talking?" Faye said, her voice dripping with tease.

I forced myself back to the present. "Perhaps you can help me get the mustard off my shirt."

She took a step closer. She purred. An honest-to-God rapturous vibration of her vocal cords that shrank me by a good six inches.

"I'd rather get the shirt off the man than the mustard off the shirt."

Let's pull over for just a minute and allow me to tell you about Faye Wilkinson. For this wasn't my first trip to Winter Park.

She was seventy-two, working hard for forty-two, and had to settle for sixty. Her face was professionally reconstructed. Her body lithe. She hadn't eaten bread in twenty-five years. Her casual-looking clothes cost the gross domestic product of Uruguay. Faye was on a first-name basis with the first growths of Bordeaux. She'd gained ten pounds since college and had long ago surrendered the battle of ever shedding those ten. Eighteen, she'd belatedly come to accept, while permanent in mind, was transitory in body.

She shopped Restoration Hardware like most people shopped Walmart. She never brought groceries into her house, her maid did that through the side door. She greeted her friends enthusiastically with double air kisses and pretended to listen while never hearing a word. Men were easy. Beguiled by her bedroom smile, her sex-soaked eyes, her lusciously roped body, they were rendered powerless, doomed the moment they entered the honey-soaked realm of her attraction.

Such attributes did not add to her individuality but rather allowed her to blend in unnoticed on Park Avenue, the town's look-at-me promenade, where Rollses and Bentleys battled for parking spaces, and people strutted dogs like runway models. Dogs that came with papers. Ancestry.

None of that helped me as I fruitlessly searched for a sharp retort. Faye reached out and anointed my shoulder with the tip of a long gray fingernail. "You want to know about Ronnie? Buy me a drink." She stepped past me and then swiveled her head. "Don't worry, Jake. I don't bite. Hard."

She sashayed out the door, leaving me scrambling to keep up with someone several decades ahead of me.

WE SETTLED IN THE ground-level bar in the student center, which was ripped out of a Ritz Carlton hotel. A glass wall gave view to an Olympic-size pool and Lake Virginia, where ducks paddled and bobbed, their little duck-butts sticking up in the air. The polished mahogany counter was nautically decorated with thick ropes wrapped around corner pilings. A song—I couldn't remember who performed it—played over the speakers. I was ticked that the artist eluded me. Had the alcohol started killing off irreplaceable good brain cells?

Faye ordered rum on the rocks. "Little twerps today have no idea how lucky they are to have booze on campus," she said. She took a sip as if it had been forever since she last had a drink, and that told me she hit it every day. "We spent the better part of our youth hunting alcohol. What do they do now that that game's over?"

"There's always chasing skirt."

"To chasing skirt."

She dipped her tumbler toward my beer mug. She crossed her slender legs, putting her ageless part out there.

"Tell me about Ronnie," she said.

"Ronnie?"

"Veronica was Ronnie to everyone who knew her. Well, all but one."

I glossed over my meeting with Veronica.

"You're searching for a painting," she said.

"I am."

"Care to share some details?"

"I can't."

"Or won't?"

"Same thing."

"So, this is a one-way street?" she said.

"It is. I'm at your mercy."

"Handcuffed to the bed, so to say."

"Begging for help."

"And nothing to offer me."

"Only the satisfaction of putting me out of my misery."

"Do you talk to all women like this?"

"I thought it was your language."

A smile formed on her lips. Her lipstick was the shade of faded strawberries. Ones you regret sinking your teeth into, but you'll do it again and again.

"My remark about getting the shirt off you was strictly old school. Ronnie chose you for this top-secret government mission?"

"She did."

"She wants the painting back?"

"She does."

"Bad?"

"One could say that."

"Any leads?"

"None," I admitted.

"Certainly something?"

"I wish."

"And you didn't know each other before you accepted this assignment."

"We did not."

She shook her head. "Good to know she hasn't changed."

I asked her if it had been a while since she saw Veronica.

"Forty-nine years. Does that count as a while?"

"It's a start."

"What's that cat up to? I don't mean her pharmaceutical business, which she sold. Give me some juice."

I told her about her marriage to Nick Harris. Faye claimed to have never heard of him. About how Nick ran off with a younger woman. I related how Veronica said she'd never been good at love, so she thought she'd jump in and give it a try and that she didn't recommend that course of action. I surprised myself and rambled, telling her about the song "The Windmills of Your Mind." How it played over and over. About her generous gift to Harbor House, if I came up with the stolen painting in the allotted amount of time. How she knew who stole the painting, but it was not for me to know.

Why did I dump all that on her? I was on the clock. Had to push the envelope. I wasn't sure the path I was on led to the Dali, but the more I knew about Veronica, the better my chances. As I got closer to the Dali, I planned to position myself as representing a buyer. But I wasn't remotely close to that. And unless I took some chances, embraced occasional recklessness, that day might never dawn.

Toward the end of my monologue, Faye drifted away. Her eyes grew vacant. Her once-erect spine betrayed her years. Her fingers massaged the sweating tumbler. A boisterous group of four settled next to us and lassoed the bartender. They acted as if they'd just crashed a house party where they weren't invited and didn't care. One of them belched out a donkey laugh.

Oblivious to them, or because of them, Faye stared out the window. The bartender served the celebratory party. They relocated their battling voices outside.

"She said that?" Faye said.

"Said what?"

"That she was never good at love?"

I thought it an odd piece to pick up from everything I'd just laid down.

"Something like that."

She placed her hands in front of her lips as if she were praying. She let her breath out, squared her shoulders, and placed her hands on the mahogany bar.

"Little bitch."

"Excuse me?"

"She lied."

"Why do you say that?"

"Because I never met anyone more in love, and she was damn good at it."

"You know this?"

"I do."

"Any person in particular? Colleen mentioned a man— Michael. I believe she was married for a short time to Michael Fredericks. I assume he's the same person."

She let out a low whistle. "For a man with mustard on his shirt, you move pretty fast."

"Tell me about Michael."

She didn't reply. I took a stab at it. "Did you like Michael as well?"

"Me?" she snorted. "You've got it all wrong, mustard man."

"Right me."

She shoved her drink away, stupid thing that it was.

"Fine. He stole her from me."

"Michael?"

"That is who we're talking about."

"I don't follow."

"Oh, for God's sake. What do you do over there in Saint Pete? Raise chickens?"

"Were you and Veronica—?"

"Ronnie and I were lovers. Michael fucked it all to hell."

CHAPTER 11

Faye turned her face back to the window. Our eyes met in the glass. I shifted my glance toward a great white egret coming in for a landing on the reedy grass shore of the lake. The bird went from flight to ground without ever breaking grace. A nearby duck paid it no attention and buried its head in the water searching for food.

"It started as a fling," Faye said without prompt and speaking to her reflection. "It's what you do in college. A true liberal arts education." I leaned in to hear her better. She turned to me. I instinctively drew back. "This was the early seventies, remember. You didn't stroll across campus cupping each other's ass like they do now."

I wasn't really interested in the sexual flirtations of Faye's youth, but my calendar was clear until my evening date with a Sunshine Escort. I might as well play PI and hang around and see what I could pick up.

"How serious did the fling become?"

"I'll take another," she said to the bartender, disgusted he had not anticipated her need. She shoved her glass forward. He glanced at me.

"I'm good."

"Are you married?" Faye asked me.

"I am."

"Do you think you love each other equally?"

"I can't imagine anyone loving me as much as I love her."

"Christ, you ride a white horse?"

"Tell me about you and Veronica."

She skipped a beat before coming in. "It started as an experiment. For a notch on our belts. How do you know unless you try, right? But it became serious. Real. Then Michael busted in. Baptized by boy-love, Ronnie ditched our girl-on-girl experience. Said she surrendered all passion. Have you done that, mustard man? Surrendered all passion?"

"I'm in debt. I surrendered passion I don't even have."

"Well, goody for you," she said with a bite. "Ronnie dropped me like a ropeless anchor. You know what I've been doing for fifty years?"

"Searching for your Michael? Or Michelle?"

"Touché. Or, as we said back then, no shit, Sherlock."

Faye possessed a nasty streak not far under her surface. Something sinister, as if the River Styx coursed her veins. I wanted to avoid that part of her and guide the conversation back to my pursuit.

"Do you think Michael knew anything about the Dali?"

But Faye Wilkinson wasn't interested in what I was interested in.

"What do you think?" she said. "I entered a bar, but he left a minute earlier. I thought of saying something to her, or she to me, but a meaningless phone call interrupted our destiny. After a while, you get the message. It won't happen for you. There's no snake oil cure for being unlucky in love."

We were quiet a moment. I wondered why Veronica had lied to me about love. Or had she? It was possible that Michael, whoever he was, was long gone. It was likely that he had nothing to do with the stolen Dali. But loose ends are not to be ignored.

And someone snatched the Dali.

I tried a different door. "They married, didn't they?"

"They did."

"What happened?"

"Do you think that all people who fall in love stay together?"

I thought her question rhetorical and waited for her to continue, but she did not.

"No," I admitted. "Why didn't it work out for them?"

"She got pregnant."

"Pardon me?"

"Knocked up. You're familiar with it, right?"

"Veronica is childless."

"I suppose that's the official version."

"Are you telling me otherwise?"

"I'm not telling you anything. I lost track of her." She leaned back on her stool. "I don't know how any of this will help you find some stolen painting. When was it stolen?"

"About fifty years ago."

"From where?"

"I can't say."

"From the college?"

"I can't—"

"We both know it was. Any leads?"

"You asked me that already."

"I forget your answer."

"None."

"Anybody else looking for it except for you?"

"Not that I know of."

I thought she was going to continue her pelting questions, but instead she took a meaningless sip of her drink.

I took a final swig from my beer and worried about the

traffic on I-4 heading home. I had a date with my escort at seven. Kathleen had also booked an escort for the evening. Between the two of us, we hoped to learn more about Carrie Crowlings. She was my ticket to finding Nick Harris.

Faye glanced at her watch, a thin diamond-studded strap on her wrist. "It's been lovely, Jake. I'm hosting some classmates at my house this evening and need to attend to a few things."

I asked her if she'd ever married.

"Why are you asking me that?"

"I don't know."

She paused, then blurted out, "Twice."

"But you said—"

"That love eluded me? It has, but that didn't stop me from the game. A woman can get a lot of miles off high cheekbones and long legs. Build a considerable nest egg."

"Did you ever have children?"

"God, no." She punched her breath out. "Want the Cliff Notes? Husband number one owned storage units and land to build more. I took equity in his business in lieu of support. You'd never know it, but I'm the storage queen of Orlando. A city, I might point out, of stellar growth over the past fifty years. For my fiftieth, my girlfriends hired an ABBA cover band for a party. They changed the words of "Dancing Queen" to "storage queen." I liked it. Even changed the name of my company to Storage Queen Properties.

"Husband number two was a three-year mistake. In between was a woman who might have worked. We were in New York to see *Phantom* when it opened. She tripped on a curb and got clipped by a car. I was talking to her, and then I was looking down at her body in the December slush, wearing a beautiful brown plaid jacket she bought at Bendel's earlier that day."

"Who stole the painting?" I said, for I was eager to bank one in from half-court and sensed that she was holding back.

She stood, and I did likewise.

"I haven't a clue. Enjoy your stay in Winter Park. Are you spending the evening?"

"I think I'll saddle up and head back to the egg farm." That earned a smile, but it didn't fool me. Faye Wilkinson came with a warning label.

"Good luck with that shirt. I'd give you a tip, but I don't know a damn thing about getting stains out of shirts. Or life."

We exchanged phone numbers, an act that bored her. She wrote hers on the back of one of my business cards. I recognized the handwriting. It was the same that had been on the chalkboard in the classroom. Faye had written Euripides's quote on the chalkboard. She had then taken a seat and stared at it.

I said, "You wrote it, didn't you? Euripides's quote."

Her hollow eyes rested on mine.

"What of it?"

"You left off the second line."

She gave me an expressionless look and then cat-walked away. Nothing in the world worthy of her.

AS I STEPPED ONTO onto the side street where my truck was, a man sidled up beside me. Another maneuvered behind.

"May I buy you a drink?" my new companion said. He was thick with a low center of gravity. More bowling ball than man.

"I'm fine, Boris. Thank you."

"It's Karl. You really think two against one is good odds?"

"Good point, Karl. I suggest you get reinforcements."

"I have." He pulled open his jacket, revealing a gun. "We'd like to discuss our mutual friend, Mr. Dali."

"Now that you mention it, I am a bit thirsty."

CHAPTER 12
VERONICA

1972

Midnight Confession

A cello. That was the instrument his face reminded her of. Veronica was walking across the campus to the students' art show, the late May sun refusing to leave the stage. A woman with a cello cradled between her legs sat under the giant oak tree in front of the newly built Ward Hall. Void of contemporary volume, her instrument filled the air with the siren song of a grief-struck angel. The sonorous music rolled over the campus, a seamless transition of notes from a stately instrument that looked to Veronica like a large golden grain.

She entered the spacious hall. Tall opened double-hung windows allowed the warm, creeping edge of summer into the room. Students mingled in front of paintings and sculptures. Music played from a stereo system on a folding table. A table-cloth on the table came up short on both ends.

She saw him, and in his face, she saw the golden grain of music. She wandered up to him.

He stood beside his prized painting, clumsily shifting his weight from one foot to the other. But it was his cello face that transfixed her, not his artwork. Certainly not his footwork.

"What do you think?" he asked.

Veronica studied the painting. The canvas was a storm of color. Red, blue, black, and gray. All globbed together with no attempt at form, no evidence of design. A faded white line ran down the middle. A feather protruded out of the clump of colors.

"I like it," she said.

"Why?"

"I don't know."

"Yes, you do."

"Oh, do I?" she retorted playfully, which surprised her. "What makes you say that?"

"I heard you sing freshman year, before you dropped out of choir. You have a beautiful voice. Anyone who sings like that knows why they like a painting."

"Hmm. That seems like a stretch to me."

He scrunched his face. "Best I could do on short notice."

"It's peaceful. Tranquil. It calms me, which is a mystery, for it also seems . . . violent. Is that enough?"

"You nailed it."

She hadn't planned to attend the senior art show, but she and Faye had a scuffle. That whole thing was getting too serious. Faye tugging them forward. Deeper. Veronica resisting. Veronica needed fresh air. To clear her head. Faye said go. Get out. It'll be good for you.

She'd seen Michael around campus. He was two years ahead of her. Her classes were business, and he was fine arts. She always caught herself staring at him. His beard. His Christ-like presence, as if he had a permanent role in a passion play. He never seemed rushed, and she wondered how that could be. Veronica was always dashing from one class to another. Prepping for one worthless academic challenge after another. One more peak to summit only to start all over again.

They had never spoken. Until now.

"I'm Michael."

"I'm Veronica."

"I know. Why did you drop out of choir, Veronica?" he asked.

Because I don't like my voice.

"I didn't have the time. I double majored in business and accounting."

"I didn't even know the school had business and accounting. The show closes in less than an hour. Wanna grab a drink somewhere?"

"Maybe." She toyed with him. "Tell me about yourself."

"Sure. Let's see: I'm a surprisingly strong swimmer but a lousy runner. I love Pop-Tarts. Cry at movies. I'm way too pragmatic to believe I can ever support myself by painting, and I have a thing for 'Midnight Confession.' It's a song by the—"

"Grass Roots. I know it. And have you?"

"Have I what?"

"Confessed to the world at midnight that you love someone?"

"No, have you?"

"Not yet."

The universe stopped its expansion. All the gods were quiet. Michael, in a voice distant even to himself, said, "Would you like to grab that drink now?"

"Sure."

Two days later, he confessed he'd been working up the courage to ask her out for over a year. Then he said that was a lie. He'd wanted to ask her out the first day she walked into the choir room her freshman year. In that damn checkered brown-and-beige flannel shirt.

"You liked that old thing?" she asked.

"Oh, sweet Jesus" was all he could muster.

Three days after the art show, Michael kissed Veronica with every color he'd ever known.

Five days after the art show, in response to her questioning, he still refused to tell her what inspired his colorful painting. He just kept asking if she liked it. She assured him she did.

Six days after the art show, he wrote her a poem. He liked tinkering in poetry. She thought it was corny. Oozing with junior high emotionality. She read it again, this time fighting back the tears.

What the fuck?

She thought she was expanding herself with Faye. Finding herself. But now she knew that all she'd done was to confuse sex with spirituality. Her feelings for Michael shattered her constitutionality. Rechartered her heart.

One week after the art show, on a Saturday night after pizza and Italian wine on Park Avenue, they made love. Afterward, he got out of bed and put *Simon and Garfunkel's Greatest Hits* on a Philips RF835 radio/record player he'd recently purchased. (Three watts per channel. Sapphire stylus. Six-inch dual-cone drivers.) He turned the volume low. They wrapped arms and legs around each other, pressing as much skin as possible. Veronica fell asleep listening to "The Boxer." He did not. A man does not sleep when destiny lies in his arms.

They made love again the following morning, never bothering to come out from under the sheets. Michael said he was out of coffee. Would be back in a jiff. He returned ten minutes later with two large cups and the Sunday *New York Times*. They spread the paper out on the bed. Michael dropped some records on the turntable.

She devoured the Business section. He got buried in Arts. After reading a section, Michael folded it neatly, returning it to its original form. Veronica laid waste to whatever she touched. They discussed Crosby, Stills, and Nash. Judy Collins. Linda

Ronstadt. Nixon. Joan Didion—Michael had read her, Veronica had not. Dylan. The Black Panthers. Eldridge Cleaver. Columbia. Nam. Archie Bunker. Michael's crunchy carpet: "I recommend keeping shoes on at all times."

The Stones' "She's a Rainbow" came on.

"I love that song," she said. "What's it called?"

"You're my rainbow," he said, altering the title. For Michael had found his rainbow.

They discussed relationships.

"I'm in one," she said. "Sorta."

He put down the paper. He'd been reading an article on a University of Michigan chemistry professor who was reinstated after being relieved of his post for showing antiwar slides during organic chemistry classes.

"Oh?"

"It's not serious. I'll end it. But it's different. You should know."

"Different?"

"It's with a girl."

"Faye Wilkinson?"

"The fuck? Does everyone know?"

"The seven-thirty club, you know."

Veronica swung her head. "Unbelievable."

The seven-thirty club. You could tell who was sleeping with whom when, in the morning, you would see people leaving dorms or apartments they didn't live in. An observant person would note that the clothing was the same that the guilty party had worn the previous day.

Veronica situated herself so that she faced Michael, her legs crossed under her. She picked up a pillow and plopped it on her lap.

"It's nothing," she said. "An experiment. Know what I mean? I don't regret it. There are no apologies. But that life-style, that . . . desire is not who I am. I know that now. I don't know if I needed to find out, or I was just bored. Does it matter?"

"Are you done with the book review?"

"I'm serious."

"It's been on your side of the bed all morning, and you haven't touched it."

She brought the pillow up to her chest.

"Does it matter?"

"No."

"You're just saying that."

"Okay. It does matter."

"Does it?"

"No."

"But in the future."

"Are you asking me if I fear losing you to a woman someday, or if I'm upset you had a relationship with a woman?"

"Both. I think? We don't want either over us."

"Don't worry about it. I'm fine."

"You sure?"

"She's pretty hot. Stuck up as hell, though. Hey, you guys didn't do any pictures, did you?"

"It's not funny, Michael."

"It's not that serious either."

"You sure?"

"I am."

"I need to tell her. Today. It means more to her. Know what I mean?"

"Is she in love with you?"

Veronica scrunched her face. "I think so? I don't have those feelings for her. But I don't want to hurt her. I don't want to hurt anyone."

"You'll tell her today?"

"I will. Can I stay here tonight?"

"Only if you promise."

"Promise what?"
"To stay every night."
"Promise."
She told Faye that evening.
It did not go well.

CHAPTER 13

My new friends and I settled on the Wine Room on Park Avenue. It was my pick. I lobbied that if I was being unwillingly corralled, at least I should get to choose the place. They had no interest in wine, a clear indication of an unfulfilling relationship. They sauntered to the bar in the back while I stopped at the front counter.

No cash. You bought tokens and then roamed around feeding them into hungry Enomatic machines—they had over 150—selecting one of three pour sizes. The wines ranged from bottles that retailed for as little as thirty dollars to others that came with a home equity application. Feel free to sit wherever you wish.

"And the food?" I asked the pleasant woman behind the counter, who had just explained all that, including the home equity quip.

"You don't need tokens for food or to purchase bottles of wine. Just for the Enomatic machines." She paused and tilted her head. "Would you like me to demonstrate? I'm off in fifteen."

"I appreciate it," I said, "But I'm good."

"Drinking alone is good?"

"I'm joining the two fellows I came in with."

"They didn't strike me as . . . our usual clientele."

"Perhaps I can enlighten them."

"Fifteen . . . if you weary of your mission."

I bought fifty dollars of tokens and found a 2016 Grand Cru Saint Emilion. The machine charged an indictable offense for four ounces. I joined my new playmates at the rear bar. The man who had spoken to me, Karl, sat to my right. On my left, an empty stool separated me from the other man. He had a flat top haircut and hard-not-to-stare-at tiny ears.

I took a sip of the Right Bank Bourdeaux, savoring the musty, grainy, and smoky liquid. The foul yet irresistible seductive taste of grapes. Drinking wine is like having oral sex with the earth.

"What's on your mind, Karl?"

He didn't answer but stuck up one finger.

"I'll take a beer," he told the bartender. "Anything on tap. Do you have a charcuterie board?"

"We do."

"Please." He pivoted his head to me. "I need to know what you told Mr. Gibson or, more importantly, what Mr. Gibson told you."

I was followed?

"How do you know I saw Mr. Gibson?"

"We have our sources. The college is missing a Dali painting, *The Lost Body.* What is your interest in it, and why are you concerned with its history?"

He spoke as if his mouth needed oil. Each word, each syllable, laboriously pronounced. But unlike the hollow Tin Man, Karl impressed me as a black hole, so dense nothing could escape him. His block shoulders rendered him neckless. He wore a long-sleeve silk shirt with no T-shirt.

I said, "Dali's missing his body? Good thing he's a surrealist."

"I asked you a question."

"Two, actually. Pushing three."

"I hope you don't persist with this unacceptable level of cooperation."

"I hope you don't persist with expecting me to cooperate."

"What did Mr. Gibson tell you?"

"He told me to go forward."

"Pardon?"

"He's big on that."

"I'm trying to be polite."

"I'm sure that's hard for you."

"And we can make it painfully hard for you."

I scrambled to figure out how he knew I saw Gibson. I made Karl to be muscle representing someone interested in the Dali. That meant he, or his boss, must have run into Nick Harris.

I played that card.

"What did Nick Harris tell you?" I said.

"I don't know that name."

"You don't know that name because you're lying or because you don't know him?"

"Why don't you tell me about this Nick Harris."

"I would. But since you don't know him, I won't waste your time."

He gave me a smirk. The bartender presented the charcuterie board. Flat Top leaned over and attacked it like a Cajun Catholic coming off Lent.

"It would seem to me," Karl said, "that if you were interested in this piece of art, you would keep a low profile."

I settled on a story that would keep the conversation going. Forward, of course.

"I informed Gibson that I represented a collector who was considering gifting paintings and sculptures. I slipped in that it had been rumored that the school once had a valuable piece that had gotten away from them. It unfolded from there."

I thought it a good cover. Karl was not convinced.

"I think not. That's too much risk."

"Sure, it was. But not as much as blindly pursuing a painting without knowing the original owner's intent on recovering it. My client isn't interested in buying trouble."

"About this client. How does he know it's on the market?"

"We have our sources."

"I think you can do better."

"You didn't," I pointed out. "Are you fencing it for Nick Harris, or did you steal it from him?"

Karl took a slice of carpaccio and dabbed his mouth with a napkin. His fingers were thick, swollen pasta noodles.

"We may be in a position to obtain it," he said. "We have others who have expressed interest. You are an unknown. We like to know who we deal with. There's a thin line between competition and customers."

"You didn't answer my question."

"A habit I picked up from you." He snapped his fingers at the bartender. "Another board, please." He turned his attention back to me. "I represent a man who is not to be denied. We welcome you as a potential customer, but you should think twice about being a competitor."

"Karl, I struggle with thinking once. Last chance. Do you know of Nick Harris?"

"No."

"Does the name Carrie Crowlings ring a bell?"

"Nothing."

"How about Santa Claus? A white beard? Jolly cheeks?"

"May I offer you some advice? Suggest to your buyer that there are other, more suitable paintings for him to pursue. Your aggressive approach has dampened any enthusiasm we might have developed for you. Your active interest in its ancient history is somewhat disturbing."

"But we've just begun to get acquainted."

"There's little reason to pursue our relationship. You see, I don't trust you."

"How did you know I was meeting with Gibson today?" I asked for the second time, which did not escape Karl.

"We covered that already," he said. "We know much about you, Mr. Travis. Your history in the special forces. Your years recovering stolen boats for insurance companies. Your association during those years with numerous deaths is most bothersome, although you seem to have exhibited more self-control in recent years."

I pivoted on the stool so as to directly face him. "Here's what I think, Karl. You don't have the painting, and you don't want competition. I'm not surrendering my pursuit because you don't like me or my résumé."

"I never said I didn't like you. I said I don't trust you."

"Karl?"

"Yes?"

"You don't trust anybody."

The left side of his lip curled up. I sensed that Karl operated at two speeds. One slow and ponderous and the other in which I was not eager to experience.

"Let's save each other a lot of time," I said. "If you find the Dali, allow me to view it. I might be your best discreet buyer. If it's not what it is purported to be, our time here, the fine charcuterie board notwithstanding, is for nothing."

"And if you find it first?"

"Perhaps we can split the spoils of war."

Two women took the stools on the other side of Flat Top. They chatted away with glasses of white wine in front of them.

Karl stood and leveled his eyes on mine. "We'll be in touch. Or not."

He and his friend loitered out the front door.

I presented the second charcuterie board to the women. The bartender presented me the check.

I DIALED GIBSON ON the way out.

"You got a leak," I said when he answered. "They knew I was seeing you today."

"Who?"

"A man named Karl. He came with a side unit. Who else knew I was here today?"

"As I told you, only—"

"Who keeps your schedule?"

"My secretary. Shona."

"Tell me about her."

"She's new."

I asked him if his schedule mentioned the Dali.

"No. Just your name and time. But she may have overheard conversations I had with others. Did you mention it to her when you called to arrange an appointment?"

I replayed my conversation with Gibson's secretary in my mind.

"Not by name. Only that I needed to discuss a painting with you. She asked what painting. I said you would know. I believed that was the only ticket I needed. You're not missing more than one painting, are you?"

"We are not," he said testily. "Should I question her going forward?"

"That's your decision."

"What if it wasn't her?"

"Then we're back to killing two out of three."

I meant it as a humorous retort, but it didn't come out that way.

I drove back to Saint Pete, wondering if I'd learned anything that would lead to the Dali. And, if I had, was I smart enough to see it, or would it only be in hindsight that I realized what was so clearly in front of me? I didn't think that was the case, but one never does until hindsight kicks in. Still, I felt good about my momentum. I'd ruffled a few feathers. Brought the players out—I had no doubt that Karl and I would meet again.

The next step was finding Carrie Crowlings, and that kicked off in three hours.

CHAPTER 14

M y escort rounded the corner and scanned the tables. I raised a finger. Her eyes settled on me. I'd taken off my wedding ring and stuck it in my pocket where it felt larger than it was. For I'd untethered myself from that which I paid little attention to, and its momentary absence was so much greater than its presence had ever been.

As she approached, I stood and pulled back a chair. She wore a white dress, her hair the color of a mustard field in September. We shook hands—is that what you're supposed to do? We introduced ourselves. Asked questions. She was well poised and a gifted conversationalist. Her eyes never left mine. No quick glance at the sidewalks teeming with people. No nervous glance at her watch, a delicate band of gold that encircled her freckled wrist. Her world was me and me alone.

Where are you from? (I lied.) What do you do? (Said I was in town for business and didn't want to eat alone.) What music do you like? Do you like to travel? Where have you been? A man can get a lot of satisfaction sitting with a beautiful woman whose entire world revolves around him. I batted the same questions back at her, but like an accomplished fencer, she slipped each one and came at me again.

Her name was Stacey Remington. Any passions she had, she bottled up before sitting down. My hope of winning her confidence before asking about Carrie Crowlings and revealing my mission was fading fast.

I'd just asked her about her day job. My second pass at it.

"I'm a sales rep for Four Hundred Central."

Four Hundred Central was the latest in a string of high-rise condo buildings to be erected downtown. I told her I was familiar with the building and asked her to tell me more about it.

Stacey Remington started in on her sales pitch. I held up my hand.

"Stacey?"

"Yes?"

"I'm not a potential buyer. Tell me why *you* like it."

She hesitated, as if aware of breaking rank. I gave her a nudge.

"How did you become interested in real estate?"

The floodgate opened. She told me her father owned two four-family buildings. How, as a child, she would accompany him as he did odd jobs. Later, he introduced her to cash flow analysis. Net operating income. Depreciation. Building wealth through OPM: other people's money. She had an encyclopedic knowledge of the downtown condo buildings. Cost per square foot. By floor. By view. By location.

When you find someone's passion, you find the person.

"I want to be a realtor of downtown condos. The whole lifestyle that entails. If I could get one listing, others would follow, but that first listing is hard." She abruptly stopped. "You said you were in town for business."

"I am."

"Then how do you know about Four Hundred Central? And the other buildings?"

"Because I lied to you."

She shot me a smile that she kept in her quiver for such occasions.

"There's no need for dishonesty," she said with a mirror-practiced tilt of her head. "Discretion is part of the job."

"Do you know the name Carrie Crowlings?"

"I don't think so."

I was about to plow into my script and describe Carrie when, lo and behold, Kathleen and her escort took the empty table next to us. The plan had been for her to go to a different restaurant. Kathleen, never one to shy away from harmless play, had manipulated behind the scenes to place us at adjoining tables. What a catch. She makes everything fun. Reason seven. Or should that be number one?

Kathleen selected a chair so that our backs were to each other. She draped a shawl over her chair, theatrically fluffing it so that it brushed me.

"I wonder if they have meat loaf," Kathleen said, two notches above her normal conversational setting. "It's so tricky to do it just right. What do you think, *Bentley*? Do you like meat loaf?"

"Meat loaf? Sure," her date said. "One of my favorite wolf-down foods. Maybe an appetizer beforehand?"

As Kathleen and I chatted to our respective Sunshine Escort partners, the panorama swirled around us. Children climbed the banyan trees across the street in Straub Park. Royal banners draped the Museum of Fine Arts. Cars choked the street, and people flowed around the sidewalk tables like water coiling around rocks. On the far side of Straub Park, Tampa Bay lay readying itself for the night, its saltwater mist perfuming the air.

Time to scoot the evening along.

"You've never heard the name Carrie Crowlings?" I said to Stacey. Our plates had just been cleared. I had red snapper, and Stacy had ordered spaghetti. She had managed to eat it without creating a mess, her freckled wrist and hand in full command of her fork.

"No," she said. "Why do you ask?"

"She works for Sunshine. A friend recently had dinner with her. He wants to get back in touch, informally, not through Sunshine. But he misplaced her contact. You don't use different names, do you?"

She scrunched her face. "No. Why would we do that?"

"Really? Stacey Remington?"

She curled up a corner of her lip.

"White."

"Pardon."

"Stacey is real. My last name is White. But only because my grandfather immigrated from Poland where our name was Wisniewski, and that didn't fly in Cincinnati in the 1920s. Remington helps me differentiate between my day job and night persona. Like a pen name."

"My friend said Carrie was tall, with long hair that she favored over her right shoulder."

"That sounds like Mary Ann Simpson."

I scooted my chair back so that I was partially even with Kathleen. "What can you tell me about Mary Ann Simpson?"

"I don't really know her," she said warily. "I met her once. If it was her at all. Sunshine doesn't really hold many company events. Sorry."

I cranked my neck toward Kathleen. She'd been conversing with her escort, but their words had been unintelligible.

"Dead end. You?"

Kathleen twisted her head toward me. "Bentley says you can use your real name, or you can pick your own and he chose the former. But I don't believe him."

"That you can pick your own name?"

"That his real name is Bentley."

Stacey: "Hey, why are you talking to her?"

Bentley: "Do you two know each other?"

"And Carrie Crowlings?" I said.

"Bentley says she's a gold digger."

"Bentley's useful."

"Great hair."

"I noticed."

Stacey: "Excuse me?"

Bentley, raking a hand through his hair: "Thank you."

"Tell me more," I said to Kathleen.

"That's as far as we got. But I think Bentley's got potential. He's made for the job."

"Not Stacey. She's big on real estate."

Bentley: "What are you guys talking about?"

Stacey: "What about real estate?"

"Switch?" I said.

"On three."

"One, two . . ."

Kathleen and I popped up and switched chairs.

"Hi," Kathleen said. She extended her hand across the table to Stacey, who reflexively accepted it. "I'd like to apologize for the confusion. Jake and I know each other."

I kicked my chair out so that I angled myself to participate in both conversations. I introduced myself to Bentley. He looked like the guy on the box for a men's hair-coloring product.

He bobbed his head a few times. "Okay. Okay. You and April are a team, right? I like it. A little kinky, but I'm in."

"April?"

Kathleen craned her head back. "Forgot to tell you. I'm April tonight."

"April?" I said for the second time.

"In sixth grade, her boobs popped out first. Honey, we *all* wanted to be April."

"How did I not know this?"

"There's a lot you don't know."

Stacey: "Someone tell me what's going on here."

Bentley: "I dated a girl named April once. Wouldn't mind doing it again. I dig older women."

"Hey, buddy," Kathleen said, blasting him a look. "I'm not that much older than you."

Stacey stood. "Someone tell me what's going on, or I'm leaving."

"Bentley and you both work for Sunshine," I said.

"How do you know April?" she demanded of me.

"We're married."

"You and April?"

"Yes. Me and Kath—April. How about if we take a stroll down the pier? I'll spring for ice cream cones. You both deserve an explanation."

Stacey gave that some consideration. I wasn't worried about Bentley. He was game for anything. But I felt responsibility toward Stacey.

"Sure," she said, cocking her head. "I love ice cream."

Ten minutes later Kathleen (April), Bentley, Stacey, and I walked out of Cassis Bakery, each with our own cone. We settled on the seawall, our legs draped over the side. It was a challenge to stay abreast of the sea breeze that attacked the ice cream with the same gusto as we slurped it.

I was fortunate that I had talked Kathleen into coming. (That's how I remember it.) For it was Bentley—the most painful, the most methodical, the most anal ice cream cone slurper on the west coast of Florida—who delivered.

"Oh yeah," Bentley exclaimed. "I know Carrie. Whatdaya want to know about that babe?"

CHAPTER 15

Bentley studied his ice cream cone, granting it the intensity of a general planning a military campaign. Stacey—in opposite treatment of how she approached spaghetti—licked hers with joyful childish abandonment. This was the lineup. Bentley, chocolate. Kathleen, salted caramel. Me, vanilla. Best damn flavor in the world and you know it. Stacey, strawberry.

Strawberry. And spaghetti. Who knew they made girls like that anymore? I wanted to take Stacey home to Mom. But I already had a woman, and my mother passed years ago, so that fantasy never even got cleared for takeoff.

"Most of the time she went by Mary Ann Simpson," Bentley said after he finished a tepid bite. We were discussing Carrie Crowlings. "But she liked changing it up. For a while, she went by Mattie Walker."

"Anyone go by Ned Racine?" I said.

"Not that I know. Why?"

"Just asking."

I explained that I worked for Veronica Stafford and that I was searching for her husband, Nick Harris. That I had reason to believe that Nick Harris had met his former secretary and

94

possibly current girlfriend, Carrie Crowlings, through Sunshine Escort. Kathleen (April) tacked on that it was her idea (okay, fine) that we doubled our chances if we spoke to two people instead of one. No harm. No foul.

"Sunshine had a party little over a year ago," Bentley said. "You know, get to meet each other, swap stories. We don't do that much, so I made sure to go. I ran into Carrie there. We got pretty looped. She was totally in the business to find a man with money. And I don't mean the first guy to show up in some leased Mercedes. She wanted serious dough. Had the patience too. Said if it took years, that was fine with her. She wasn't one to pick the first Christmas tree. Studied prenuptials in her spare time."

"And Nick Harris?" I said.

"Maybe help you there, maybe not." He cocked his head at a different angle. He went in for a lick, withdrawing before any damage could be inflicted upon him. "We kept in touch since that evening. Nothing constant. A text here. A drink there. She was fun. I mean, totally dangerous to a guy, but . . ."

"But you're gay," Kathleen said, "and so you never felt threatened by her."

"I'm me," Bentley proclaimed, cocking his feathers. "I don't subscribe to this whole . . . letter thing. I'm. Just. Me."

"Go on, Me," I said.

He rotated his cone and attacked with the tip of his tongue. A stream of melted ice cream dribbled down his chin.

"Damn," he said. He wiped his chin with a napkin. "Carrie was relentless. Got every job she could. Her motto was 'You're not going to catch a fish without a line in the water.' About six, seven months ago, it was right after Gasparilla, she texted me. Two words: Got one!"

"Did she give you a name?"

But Bentley's mind had become untracked. He tilted his

head at Kathleen. "That loud comment you made about meat loaf when we sat down. Was that some sort of signal?"

"We were supposed to go to separate restaurants," Kathleen confessed. "But I know what table he likes at Mangroves. I arranged to have the one next to it. He also swoons over my meat loaf."

"Cute."

"You didn't know she was going to be here?" Stacey asked me. She bit into the top rim of her cone. Stacey Remington was the first to storm the castle. It did not slacken her commitment but rather, like breaching a fortress wall, rallied her cause.

"I did not."

"Please," she said. "Don't tell me you're both as happy as you appear."

"We got two kids and a cat," Kathleen said. "We're thinking of adding a hamster. Maybe even sea monkeys."

"I had sea monkeys when I was a kid. They were ugly . . . whatever they are."

"Tell us about Carrie's catch," Kathleen said to Bentley. "Was it our boy, Nick?"

"Tell me about Nick."

"Married to Veronica Stafford," I said. "Around fifty-eight years old. Solo operator of a financial service company."

"Nothing yet," Bentley said.

"Lives in the historic district, a few blocks north of downtown."

"Sorry, guys. She didn't give a name. Just said he was married. But supposedly, this guy had a ticket to ride not related to his wife's money and beyond the reach of a prenup. Said it was right up her alley."

I asked him what alley that might be.

He combed his hand through his mane. "Carrie works for art studios. Rumor is she runs with a fast crowd. A crowd that doesn't care about authenticity. There's a lot of money flipping a twenty-dollar print for a grand.

"After that text, we hooked up for drinks. She said she might score enough in one deal to set her up for life. Said her guy had a piece of art worth millions, and he was free to sell it. Discreetly."

"Discreetly?"

"You know, like it was hot. Stolen."

"She wouldn't fence it herself, would she?"

"Our girl's too smart for that. And she knew this piece was too rich for her regular channels. She had to make new connections."

I asked Bentley if he had the name of the art dealer she hooked up with.

"She dropped the name of someone she was told who could fence something big, but I can't remember it. A single name, you know, like the singer Pink. Or Sting. But not a color or a bee's butt. Sorry, I can't think of it."

"Did she tell you anything about the painting? Name? The artist?"

"Nada."

I asked him where I might find Carrie.

"She hangs out at Repose Gallery in Clearwater. Invited me to a couple of shindigs there." He shrugged. "She acted like she owned the place. She could be a boastful little bitch when the mood hit her. A real manipulator."

Kathleen said, "Aren't you in the same business?"

"Do *not* drag me down there. I'm strictly aboveboard. If a woman has taste, great. If money, even better. Essential, really. Same way with a man. But I don't fake feelings. I was pretty excited about April. Style. Personality. Plus, older women usually come with a dowry."

"One more crack like that," Kathleen said, "and I'm planting this cone in your face."

"Just pushing your button," Bentley said with a playful smile.

"How old are you?" Kathleen asked him.

"Twenty-nine."

"That's a hard sell, buddy. You need to jump to thirty-four for a while."

He gave a reproachful glance at his cone. "I don't really like these. They're so . . . primitive. You're probably right. It's about time for an age adjustment, but to where? I'm too old to be young and too young to be old."

"Can you get in contact with Carrie for me?" I asked.

"She's not returning my texts. I'm dead to her. I was just another stepping stone. Demos. That's the name I couldn't remember. You know, the guy who could fence it."

"Boy, was that good," Stacey said. Her cone was gone. She licked her fingers and then rubbed them on a napkin. She held the soiled napkin, unsure of what to do with it.

I opened my hand.

She cocked her head. "Thanks." She dropped the soiled napkin in my palm. "Well, it's been interesting. Some of my friends are meeting at the Canopy. You birds mind if I split?"

"I appreciate you putting up with me," I said.

"It makes for a good story. Hope you find . . . whoever you're looking for. Give me a call if you ever think of selling or buying."

She gave me her business card, and I texted her my number. I asked her to call if she heard anything. That left Bentley, Kathleen, and me.

"So," Bentley said. "You *birds* want to catch a drink someplace?"

"We appreciate the offer," Kathleen said. "But we turn into parents at midnight."

Bentley shrugged. "Whatever. Thanks for dinner." He

looked at me. "I'll let you know if I hear anything else. You going to check out Repose Gallery?"

I told him I was.

"They don't keep regular hours, but they have an open house twice a month. You're lucky. It's tomorrow night. Suggestion? Pretend you're loaded but don't know much about art. They *love* people like that."

"Do you have a job tomorrow?" Kathleen said.

"I do."

"What color will your hair be?"

"Why?"

She grimaced. "It's crooked. Just a tad."

"Damn." He ripped off his Elvis pompadour, revealing a shining bald head. "I can never keep these fuckers straight."

"Oh God," Kathleen gushed. "I love bald men." She fluttered her hand over her face. "Is anyone else hot?"

"Get out of here."

"It could have been us, Bentley, all along."

"I'm getting too old for this gig. I'm going back to my gardening."

"Oh, come now," Kathleen said. "You? Garden?"

"Mm-hmm," Bentley said with a teasing smile. "I'm president of the club: Fruits of the Earth."

"Get out of here."

CHAPTER 16
VERONICA

1972

I don't love you

It was Sunday evening. Faye Wilkinson, shoeless and braless, stood in the kitchen of her off-campus apartment wearing a pair of shorts and a tight Tars T-shirt, eating an orange.

A half-full cup of cold coffee, the mug stained down its sides, sat on the counter. Black crumbs, the remnants of an over-toasted piece of bread from Faye's new two-slice Toastmaster, littered the sink. A bottle of Ivory liquid sat on a dirty windowsill under an opened window. The night air slithered in, carrying the tinny chords of a song from someone's stereo.

Veronica came out of the bedroom, suitcase in hand.

"Going somewhere?" Faye said. Veronica had been quiet and noncommittal when, earlier, Faye had inquired about her whereabouts the past few days.

"I'm going back to my apartment."

Faye put down her orange. She wiped her hands on a dish towel. "This is how you do it?"

"Apparently."

"What's his name, right? The guy you've been sneaking around with the last week."

"Michael."

"Did you fuck him?"

"Faye."

"Of course, you did. What is he? Mr. Right? Johnny Wonderful? Jesus, Ronnie, you hardly know the guy."

Veronica stood motionless, not knowing what to say. How to talk without hurting her.

"It's not for me, Faye."

"It? Did you really just say that? Oh, this is getting rich."

"I didn't mean it that way."

Faye walked up to Veronica. She placed her hands on her shoulders.

"Ronnie, you're scared. Frightened by what we have. Don't you see? You're running from it. From us. That's all he is. He's anti-me. Anti-us."

Veronica had given that line of reason a lot of rope the past week. Vented it every way she could. She feared nothing except the unexamined life. And so, she had examined hers. Embraced her feelings. Embraced Faye, a woman she felt as deeply for as anyone she'd ever met. But Michael blew past those introductory emotions. Vaulted her into the heavy literature of love. It was that simple. And if it wasn't, Veronica Stafford was wise enough at twenty-two to know that sometimes you need to turn off the blathering noise in your head. You need to trust your intuition.

Veronica squeezed the handle of her suitcase. As if it reinforced her decision, its mere presence a supportive friend. She glanced around the room for something to look at other than Faye. Her eyes rested on the black-and-white photograph Faye had taken of her. The right side of her face was shrouded, her left eye wide and innocent. Her thin lips parted. Faye loved the photograph. Veronica thought it made her look haunted. Spooky.

She forced herself to look at Faye.

"I have feelings for you, Faye. But it's different with Michael. It's who I am."

Faye released her and stepped back. "And what of us? What was *it*—recess? Playtime for you?"

"No."

"Then what? Tell me what we did in bed wasn't real. 'Cause it was real to me, and I know it was damn real to you."

"It's not that, Faye."

"Then what?"

I don't want to spend my life with you. I love Michael. I want children.

"Don't confuse sex with love," Veronica said.

"Oh, for God's sake. You hardly know him. You're afraid, baby, don't you see? Let's blow this place. Take a trip. It's too small here. Everyone knows. It will be good for us."

"No."

"Come on, babe," Faye said, her voice cracking. She reached out again and touched Veronica's shoulder. Veronica flinched.

Faye withdrew her hand for the second time. "Really? My touch is poison, now?"

"I'm sorry, Faye."

Veronica started walking toward the door.

"Don't leave me. I need you, Ronnie. You know that."

Veronica turned around. "Please, don't make this hard."

"I love you, Ronnie."

Faye's statement hung in the air like a Sinatra note. So big. So simple. Yet everything. The world suspended in the duration of a single pitch. There was no place for it to land. Go there today, if you can find the apartment, and gather in a deep breath. You will breathe in Faye Wilkinson's unclaimed declaration, for unrequited love has no half-life.

"I'm sorry."

Faye waved her hand. "Go to your fucking Adonis. You'll be back."

Veronica again started walking toward the door, which seemed to have moved farther away.

"Oh no," Faye said. "Not before you say it."

Veronica kept walking. Three more steps to go.

"Goddammit. Have the guts to say it," Faye demanded. "I did."

Veronica halted. She spun around. Her voice was firm. Her words clear.

"I don't love you. I love Michael."

She marched out the door. But that is not to be confused with marching out of someone's life.

CHAPTER 17

The following morning, there was still no response at Veronica's neighbor's house. Next stop was Yankee Conrad's office. Veronica had indicated that she knew Conrad, although she insisted she'd not seen him in years.

Here's more on Walker McDonald, the man who started Harbor House, I promised earlier.

It was Yankee Conrad's wife, Constance, whose father, Walter MacDonald, had gifted his home after MacDonald and I formed an uncommonly quick and deep friendship. My father drank himself over the edge after my older sister was kidnapped from our lives. I don't know if Walter MacDonald, in the brief time that I knew him, became a surrogate father, for I have no basis by which to judge. I suspect he did. He'd left a modest endowment to operate his home "open to those in need" and, in a transformative moment in my life, named Morgan and me as cotrustees. Morgan and I rechristened MacDonald's home the Walter McDonald Harbor House.

Why did he choose me?

I think Walter MacDonald saw more in me than I ever saw in myself, and everyone can profit from having someone like that in their life. I mention this only because of what I said earlier. I was beginning to consider what type of father I would be. What picture would I leave? Not just for my daughters, but what would make Walter MacDonald proud of me? Hard as I tried, my witless ambitions were still a trackless waste of disjointed words and blurred imagery. Nothing had yet taken form. What if it never would? Life is full of possibility, they say. What if nothingness is a serious contender?

I squeezed my truck into an empty space behind Yankee Conrad's office in south Saint Petersburg. His office, a converted bayfront home, had a deep front porch indicative of an era that did not know air conditioning.

Today's bow tie was yellow mermaids in a sea of blue. I'd never seen the man in anything other than unimpeachable clothing. Every step he took, every word he spoke, dripped with exquisiteness. Yet, like a cavalry man from the age of Tennyson, I had no doubt that for the right cause, he would lead a suicidal charge across a muddy and foreign field.

I told him about Veronica Stafford's opening gambit. It was a long shot that he could help. But with the clock ticking, I needed to cast a wide net. Yankee Conrad indicated that he knew of Veronica through social functions but had not spoken to her in some time. He was unaware of any missing painting.

"Constance and Veronica used to talk occasionally, although I'm not sure how much recently."

Constance also had ties to the CIA as her father had worked for the agency's predecessor, the OSS, Office of Strategic Services. In a totally sexist thought, when I'd first met her, I assumed she worked for her husband as an assistant. I later learned that she held the power.

"Where is Constance?" I asked. She'd not been at her post when I arrived. Her desk was in the parlor of the house. In stark contrast to the well-lit parlor, Yankee Conrad's somber office was cut from the planks of his great-great grandfather's sailing ship.

"A girl's trip," he said. "Maine. She'll return in four days. Would you like me to call her?"

I told him I didn't think it was necessary at this time. My phone buzzed an incoming call. Detective Rambler. I let it go to voice mail. I asked Yankee Conrad if he knew anything about the underground art world.

"I assume it is no different from any other criminal enterprise. People will do anything to protect and advance their economic interests. Perhaps one small difference."

"What would that be?"

"They dress better."

I thanked him for his time and left. On the way to my truck I returned Rambler's call. He gave me an address ten minutes away and instructed me to meet him there. Before I could ask why, he hung up.

A clown pedaled a bike toward me down Beach Drive. He had orange hair, and I thought of Colleen and then of Faye Wilkinson. The clown clanged his bell, although there was no one around him. I've said this before and will take it to my grave: clowns don't fool me. They are the mutated dead dressed to walk among us. The last time I'd seen one, he'd bled out in my arms, the victim of another clown. I looked away. When I glanced back up, he was gone, leaving me to wonder if my senses had deceived me.

CHAPTER 18

Detective Rambler stood in an alley dominated by an overflowing dumpster against a filthy brick wall. Nothing good happens in alleys, and I sensed this would be no exception.

A white crime lab van and two police cruisers partially blocked the entry. (Another clue to my highly trained eye that something was amiss.) Rambler signaled to a policewoman standing at the entry, and she let me pass. Each step I took clung to my feet. The rancid air smelled like sour laundry with a catfish carcass tossed in, and don't ask why I know that smell. One side of the alley was in full sunlight, the other side in shade. The odor knew no boundaries.

"A kid dumping trash called it in," Rambler said when I pulled up beside him. "Time of death still uncertain, but likely toward the end of twenty-four hours ago. They roughed him up a bit. I've seen worse. In the end, a single shot appears to have done the trick."

"Appears?"

"Autopsy's always the final word."

"Who is he?" I asked, but I had a pretty good idea who I was looking at.

Rambler rested his weary eyes on mine. Eyes that reached their capacity for man's inhumanity to man long ago but still answered the alarm every day.

"Your boy. Nicholas Alexander Harris. Know how I can contact Mrs. Stafford? We've been unable to reach her."

"It's *Ms.* She's out for the week with a 'Do Not Disturb' sign."

"Let me be the first to congratulate you for once again getting involved with people who should never have been born. Any clues?"

"I had the pleasure of meeting a bowling ball named Karl yesterday."

I explained my meeting with Karl.

Rambler said, "Did he give any indication that he was looking for Mr. Harris?"

"He did not. But this looks like something he would do."

"You said you just met the guy."

"I know the breed."

"You ever question the line of work you're in?"

"I'm not in a line of work."

"If you insist. How's the baby?"

"Growing up. Is your new girlfriend still tolerating you? I'm sorry, what's her name again?"

"Carol. Hard to believe she can't do better than me. For a while, she struggled with my good relation with my ex, but as the ex is planning to marry the woman she lives with, she's coming around." He dipped his head toward the body. "His wallet was still on him. We always appreciate it when the killer does that."

I asked him if he thought robbery was a motive.

"Possible. No credit cards. No cash. Either he didn't have those, which is unlikely, or the killer took them."

"But he left the driver's license. How do you see this?"

"The single, close range shot screams professional. The driver's license? Our killer's arrogant. Telling us he's not afraid. He's killed before. He'll kill again. Lack of blood on the pavement indicates he may have been murdered elsewhere and carted here. We'll know more later."

I gazed down at the body of Nick Harris. "Things didn't work out like he thought they would."

"Makes our bumps look pretty small." Rambler had been looking at the body as well. He raised his eyes to mine. "Watch yourself. Children need parents."

I was going to ask him if wedding bells were in his future, but he lumped away toward the white van, calling out to a man who had been taking pictures.

I trudged around the corner and called Wetzel. I gave him the news of Nick Harris's death. He informed me that Veronica had given strict orders not to be interrupted. He said he would contact her and leave the decision of whether or not to talk with the police up to her. I suggested that her cooperation in the death of her husband might aid my search for the missing Dali.

In a tone too cool for my liking, Wetzel said, "His death should impress upon you the perils of your mission."

I returned to the alley and conveyed that exchange to Rambler. He was powerless. He could not force Wetzel to reveal where Veronica was. I gave him Wetzel's contact information as well as Veronica's number. I glanced down at what was once Nick Harris. Rambler was right. The bullet was his friend. I wondered what they wanted from him. What they got from him. At what point he realized he'd made an irreversible error. That he should have stuck to annuities.

Melinda Varker cried when I informed her that her boss was dead. I was pretty sure that wherever Veronica Stafford was, whatever she was doing, when Wetzel gave her the news, she did not shed a tear.

With the death of Nick Harris, the Vegas line had moved against me. I had to find Carrie Crowlings. Fast. Before she, too, ended up in an alley where the odor knew no boundaries.

CHAPTER 19

VERONICA

1972

Everyone has a thing for Doris Day

L ate October. Another hallelujah Sunday morning. Another *New York Times*. Coffee in bed. Crosby, Stills, and Nash on the turntable. Linda Ronstadt's "Long Long Time," which Michael played every Sunday. Veronica: "It's sappy." Michael: "It's beautiful." Veronica: "Fine. Beautiful and sappy." Another day half gone before it started, and those are the best days. Veronica said she wished every day was a Sunday. Michael countered that if every day was a Sunday, then no day would be a Sunday.

While autumn in Florida is no match for the lordly death of northern deciduous hardwoods, the season still trumpets its arrival. The air not cold, but fresh. Lengthening nights that are so advantageous for academic and inward pursuits. On this fall day, they exhausted the newspaper. Michael reconstructed it to its original form while Veronica made a Rubik's puzzle out of what she'd read. After the coffee had gone cold and the hour hand of the clock had started its downward descend into the single digits, they ventured out to the streets. They were surprised at the bustle beyond their nest. Nothing shrinks the world more than two people newly in love.

"What's the backpack for?" Veronica asked Michael as they rounded the first corner.

"I was a scout once."

"Meaning?"

"Be prepared."

"For what?"

"You'll see."

They ducked in and out of clothing stores with embarrassing prices. Michael insisted they go into a Christmas store that she'd always thought looked cheesy. It sold trinkets. Reindeers. Santas. Angels of white with wings of gold. They came across a snow globe of a grove of half-bare trees. They turned it over and over, mesmerized by the glitter of tiny snowflakes, some falling to the ground, others getting stuck in leaves of gold and red. Michael bought it.

They ventured into a hardware store.

"Why are we going in here?" Veronica asked.

"I need a hammer."

"Why do you need a hammer?"

"I don't know. But I think I'm at the point in life where I need a hammer."

"I see."

They shared an éclair. It augmented the sesame seed bagel they'd split in bed. The bagel had left a grainy litter in the sheets that Veronica worried about. They grabbed an early dinner of Swedish meatballs, buttered noodles, and a delicious yet forgettable bottle of Badia a Coltibuono chianti, which, contrarily, Veronica would recall years later. They strolled across the street to the park adjacent to the train tracks. The trains had been hauling people from the Northeast to the land of no winter for longer than their lifetime. When passengers left the Northeast on the night train, they went to bed in a gray world and woke up in a green one. Florida was never the same.

An outdoor movie was just starting. *Pillow Talk.* Families were gathering on the lawn, setting up chairs, and spreading blankets. People on a stopped passenger train peered out the windows. Veronica thought they looked like a picture from a children's book.

"Let's watch it," Michael said.

"*Pillow Talk,*" Veronica said. "Doris Day? Rock Hudson? Are you serious?"

"Have you seen it?"

"God, no."

"Come on. It will be fun."

"I don't know. I've got to study. And it's cold."

Michael opened his backpack and pulled out a blanket and a sweater.

"You planned this?" she said.

"I considered the possibility."

"Really. You got a thing for Doris Day?"

"Everyone has a thing for Doris Day."

"Just like everyone needs a hammer?"

"You're catching on."

"I don't know. It was a relic the year it came out."

"Let's give it a shot. Who knows? Maybe they were on to something back then."

Veronica put on Michael's sweater. They settled on the checkered blanket. As the temperature fell, she snuggled deeper between his legs, his arms wrapped around her.

At the end of the movie, Rock Hudson's character, Brad, learns that he is to be a father. He takes the news in Hollywood 1959 fashion: He drinks. He's excited. He's scared. The movie ends. The world is good. Michael was right. How can anyone not like Doris Day?

"What do you think?" Michael said as he folded the blanket after brushing off lawn debris.

"I didn't expect it to be so funny."

"Dated?"

"Absolutely. But it makes you wish more things were."

"And the ending?"

"Fifties Hollywood. Fall in love and have a family."

"What do you think?" he said again.

She paused, sensing that Michael had orchestrated the entire day to lead to this point. This grain of time.

"What part?" she said, forcing him to show his hand.

"About having kids."

She chose her words with care. "I wouldn't necessarily say that part is dated."

"We never talked about it."

Veronica was about to blurt out that they hadn't had a one-month anniversary yet, but something in his tone slowed her.

"Are we talking about it now?" she said.

"I think so."

What if he doesn't want them?

"Do you?" she said. "Want them?"

"I do." Then, as if fearful of scaring her, he rushed out, "But certainly not right away."

"God, no. But after grad school. You know, get a job first."

"More than one?"

"Job?"

"Kid."

"Sure."

Veronica Stafford wed Michael Fredericks a year later in a stained-glass cathedral. She had to belatedly admit that it made her feel like a fairy tale princess. The ceremony was followed by a lavish reception at the country club. She didn't want the Cecil B. DeMille production, but her parents insisted. Her mother devoted twelve-hour days to what Veronica considered more of a societal party for her mother than a celebration of the joining of two lives. Michael threatened to pull a *The Graduate* and bolt out of the place. She thought he was joking. He was not.

"Certainly not right away" came eighteen months later and surprised both of them. It was a girl. A girl who, thanks to her mother's wealth and a stolen painting, would be immortal beyond words. Whose name would be a beacon of hope and comfort to those whose eyes were learning to beg.

PART II

FOUR WOMEN

CHAPTER 20

The light from inside Repose Gallery spread onto the desolate street, resembling an Edward Hopper painting. I passed the single-story building and turned right into the parking lot, finding a space that had a storm drain in it. The left front of the truck sank as I pulled to a stop.

Kathleen and I strolled around the side and in the front door. A short, plump woman with electric eyes offered us hors d'oeuvres. I plucked enough to earn an approving smile. Next on the agenda was locating the bar. I placed a fifty on the counter and instructed the bartender, a man in a starched white shirt and oily skin, to pocket ten, keep the whiskey flowing, and let me know when I hit my limit.

Food and drink. Let's rock.

The gallery had numerous rooms, and each artist had their own geographical turf. One artist favored Parisian streets in the rain. Another's heart was a prisoner to seashores and sunsets, the ho-hum classics. Others were more offbeat. A door with the image of Jim Morrison on it. (Cool.) A urinal with a beach scene painted inside it. (Not so cool.) A few others were abstracts—color and shapes with no apparent relationship or form. They reinforced that common quip that art is anything you can get away with. A melodyless song dropped from ceiling speakers. That ceiling also held a collection of cameras.

I scanned the room, looking for a woman who preferred her hair over her right shoulder—or was it her left?—when a woman stepped in front of Kathleen and me.

"Hi, I'm Charley," she said in a resonant voice. "I don't believe we've met." She extended her hand to Kathleen and then to me. We introduced ourselves. She addressed Kathleen. "Have you attended one of our functions before?"

"We have not. Charley with an *e-y* or an *i-e*?"

Kathleen is a stickler for spelling.

"*E-y*. The artists are tagged, like birds. Please engage them. They love chatting and sharing their creative process with others. They love it even more if you purchase something."

"Do you own the gallery?" Kathleen said.

"I do not. I represent the owner."

"Is that Demos?" I asked, throwing out the name Bentley had dropped. I was also betting that Karl worked for Demos.

Charley's dark, liquid eyes rested on mine. She was a large woman who radiated both commonality and lust, as if she operated a cupcake shop by day and a saucy bordello by night. She wore a pinstripe suit and had thick, short hair.

"You know Demos?" she asked me.

"I do not. I heard about Repose from a friend of Carrie Crowlings. Is she or Demos here tonight?"

"I'm afraid neither could make it this evening. Tell me, Mr. Travis," she said with an undertone of intimacy, "why the rush to meet people you do not know?"

"I seek unique paintings. I believe these people may be able to assist me."

"What type of paintings?"

"I'm drawn to the early work of the surrealists."

"Anyone in particular?"

"Dali has always aroused my interest."

"For yourself?"

"I represent a buyer."

"My. Imagine that. A Dali floating around."

"I didn't say a Dali was floating around."

"No," she demurred. "You did not. But if so, whom might your buyer be?"

"Mr. Deep Pockets. I was also hoping to meet Carrie's friend, Nick Harris."

"I don't believe I know him."

"Nor will you. He was found dead in an alley."

"That's terrible. You don't think his death is related to your Dali, do you?"

"I don't know. Did you know Nick?"

"I said I did not."

"I'm giving you a second chance."

"And I'm giving you the same answer."

I reached out and brushed her hair over her shoulder, exposing her smooth neck. She did not flinch. Her eyes never dropped from mine. A small hearing device was in her ear. I touched it lightly with my finger.

"Who's in your head?"

"I like listening to NPR."

"That's the best you can do."

"It is, all things considered."

"Is Karl around?"

"My. You certainly drop the names."

"Excuse me for my discourteous pace. I don't have anyone in my ear telling me what to do."

She gave me a cold look.

"Excuse *me*," she huffed. "I need to circulate among the other guests." She swirled away, speaking to two men whom she addressed by name.

"I don't recall you irritating people so effortlessly," Kathleen said. "Shall we stalk her?"

"Her curiosity will win. She won't let us leave without coming back to us."

Kathleen and I completed a leisurely lap around the studio. We struck up a conversation with a woman eager to expose her superior knowledge of art and another couple who, for $4,500, earned the honor of taking home the image of Jim Morrison on a weathered door. The bartender informed me at 9:35 that I'd hit my tab. Time to pony up or end the relationship.

Charley moved with fluidity in and out of conversational circles. We both tried to pretend we weren't tracking each other. She intercepted us as we approached the front door.

"Did you enjoy your evening?" she said.

"We did," Kathleen said, "But I need to cart him home. He gets cranky this time of the evening."

"That makes for short nights. Tell me, Kathleen, what is it that you do?"

"I'm raising two daughters."

That surprised me. Kathleen had always answered similar questions by referring to her professional life. She had a PhD in English literature and was a professor. I wondered if, in her mind, she had crossed some invisible line, and, if so, shouldn't an observant husband be aware of that?

"Charming," Charley said with dullness dripping from her voice. But then, as if reversing course, she reached out and squeezed Kathleen's arm. "I envy you," she said with uncensored honesty. "That sounds like such a worthy thing to do."

"I would like to meet Demos," I interjected, feeling a tad left out. "I told his Rottweiler, Karl, that my buyer is interested, but he suffers from a short attention span. He also believes that faster deals are cleaner deals."

Charley gave me a closed-mouth smile. "Demos. Karl. Carrie. Dead Nick. You seem more interested in people than in the art."

"People are the greatest form of art."

She shot Kathleen a look. "You live with that?"

"He's a good cook."

Charley cocked her head. "It's been nice chatting with you. Adventuresome, in a manner of speaking. A stolen painting not seen in fifty years? My, what an imagination."

Kathleen looked at me. "Did you say it was stolen, honey?"

I kept my eyes on Charley. "I did not."

"I don't recall fifty years either," Kathleen said, shifting her attention to Charley.

Charley waited as a loud group of four squeezed past us.

She said to me, "Are you a cop?"

"I am not."

She dipped her head at Kathleen. "How about you, Mom? Are you Cagney? Lacey? Kate Beckett?"

"None of the above."

"Can you arrange a meeting?" I said.

"Demos is throwing a party tomorrow," she said. "I'll see if I can snatch you an invitation."

She asked for my card. I gave it to her.

"A bit of advice?" she said, pocketing my card. "Slow down. Your speed is"—she paused—"intimidating."

I was down to five days.

The good news? My new rate card was two mill a day.

CHAPTER 21

Charley called the next morning.

I'd just finished exploding on my hundred-pound punching bag that was strung to the rafters in my garage, pummeling my hands to pulp. Before I attacked with my fists, I'd done a series of both left and right roundhouse kicks, reverse spin kicks, and straight kicks. The bag was unimpressed with both fists and feet. A girlfriend from a different life had used lipstick to paint a smiling face on the bag. Like that life, that lipstick was fading, the smiling face only there to those who knew where to look, and even then, it took effort.

"Love's a concrete pillow," Charley said.

"Come again?"

"You okay? You sound out of breath."

"I had a disagreement with my punching bag."

"Sounds like it won."

"It was a draw."

"If you insist. That's the password for the party I told you about. Tonight, at ten." She gave me an address west of down-town Saint Petersburg.

"Back up a second," I said. "It *starts* at ten?"

"Is that an issue?"

"Only for the sane."

"Said the man who had a disagreement with a punching bag." She hung up.

Ten o'clock?

And ends when—at stupid o'clock? What creatures come out at ten p.m.? That would foul up the next morning. I'm on the beach every day at five-thirty, sprinting to catch answers that, no matter how fast I run, run a little faster. But you just wait. One day, I'll catch those bastards. I used to answer the bell at six, but as I had the morning shift with the girls, my mania now started deeper in the night.

It got worse.

"We are *not* getting there at ten," Kathleen informed me when I told her of our evening's plans. "We'd be the first in the door. Eleven at the earliest."

"People are vertical at eleven?" I said.

She didn't answer. Every once in a while, I sense that I come up a smidgen short of her expectations.

I went outside and took a shower. I always shower outside —that's the side of "side" I prefer. I'd set up a towel stand and a wood table to hold shampoo. Problem was, I was out of shampoo. I'd squeezed the last drop out days ago but always forgot about it when I walked away. I vowed to remember to pick some up.

I DROPPED BY WETZEL'S office. I wanted to know how Veronica took the news of the death of her husband. I was hoping a meeting with Mr. Tightlips might be more fruitful than a phone call.

"She was saddened, as was I," he said in a voice that didn't sound sad at all. "Whatever his crimes were, he in no manner deserved such treatment."

I asked if Veronica would be returning early.

"She will not be cutting short her vacation, if that is what you're asking. Nor is she required to."

"All busted up, isn't she?"

"It is not for us to judge others' emotions. Find the Dali, Mr. Travis."

I departed in a huff. I wasn't sure of my next move but didn't want to go to Harbor House. I couldn't go there. Didn't feel like I deserved it. I drove three blocks to the Dali Museum. I'd been numerous times before with Kathleen and Morgan when we did museum days downtown. Maybe Dali's tortured world, his desire to paint the trackless waste of his mind, might help me make sense of mine.

"ART WORLD DILLY DALLIES OVER DALI" ran the headline of a *Wall Street Journal* article on January 18, 1980.

The largest Dali collection in the world was up for grabs.

Mr. and Mrs. A. Reynolds Morse, from Cleveland, Ohio, had been collectors of Dali's work from when they first met the artist in the early 1930s. When it came time to pass on their impressive collection, they insisted that it stay together. They did not want their life's pursuit piecemealed to museums and collectors throughout the world. The *Journal* feature with the catchy alliterative headline caught the attention of James Martin, a Saint Petersburg attorney. Why not Dali in the Sunshine City? The state chipped in three million, and the Morses' Dali collection trucked south to its new permanent home. The first museum was completed in 1982, the current impressive building with its winding three-story staircase in 2011. Over four hundred thousand people a year tramp through the halls, studying the paintings of a man who dared to see the world differently than his contemporaries.

Dali was born and spent most of his years in Spain. But he

and his wife, Gala, fled the war and lived in the U.S. from 1940 to 1948. It was during his years in the U.S. that Dali rose to fame. They were frequent visitors thereafter.

His full name was Salvador Domingo Felipe Jacinto Dali i Domènech, Marquess of Dali of Pubol. Probably the last kid in second grade to be able to spell his name. He was named after his deceased older brother, who died at age two. Dali started his career as an impressionist but soon veered off course to surrealism. Born from the chaos of World War I, surrealism, according to one of its leaders, Andre Breton, strove to "resolve the previously contradictory conditions of dreams and reality." Dali stuffed his paintings with the demons and angels that roamed his mind. That tortured his dreams. His father appeared in nearly every painting. And ants. The man loved ants. They represented death.

With the help of the indefatigable Gala, who championed his work with her every breath as well as modeling for many of his paintings (nice buns, Gala), Dali became one of the world's most famous and recognizable painters. All art needs to be authenticated, even more so if it's a Dali. A prolific artist who also did numbered prints, his voluminous output made his work susceptible to fraud.

The museum was also hosting a special Picasso exhibit. I wandered for two hours and finally grabbed a pressed Serranito sandwich and Cycle Brewing beer at the museum's café, Café Gala. By the time I left, I was weary of cubism, father figures, and ubiquitous ants and was pretty sure that neither Dali nor Picasso ever found what they were searching for and that their blank canvasses weren't that different from my punching bag and mad morning runs.

Veronica Stafford's neighbor was still not home.

CHAPTER 22

"How do I look?"

Kathleen popped up from her vanity and pirouetted. It was ten forty-five that evening, and we'd yet to leave the house. *Ten forty-five.* She wore a deep-blue floor-length dress slit open nearly to her thighs. It had a high collar in the front and an open back. I'd never seen the dress before.

I stifled a yawn. "Beautiful. How long have you had that dress?"

"You don't like it?"

I knew that was coming.

"I do."

"Does the back go too low?"

"Did you hear that?"

"Hear what?"

"Shh."

"Shh, what?"

"Our bed. It's calling my name."

"Does it? Go too low?"

"No. But you'll be cold."

"No, I won't."

"You're always cold."

She pecked me on my cheek. "Tonight, hell can't even hold me. And you better wake up, buster."

Ever since we adopted our second daughter, Sophia, Kathleen had been on a tear, buying new clothes, extending her daily walk, adding extra office hours on campus. It wasn't that she denied herself time and energy with the girls. To the contrary, it was as if she'd doubled herself, assuming that time did as well. I worried about her pace. She was never one to limit herself to a measly eight hours of sleep. Nine suited her just fine. But I doubted she'd clocked seven any night the previous month.

She gave Bonita final instructions. Bonita didn't need final instructions or, for that matter, any instructions. She told Kathleen to come back with a better man than me. Honestly, that woman bats me around like a toy mouse.

"Mr. Jake, you be good to Ms. Kathleen," Bonita said, adjusting my tie, which Kathleen had selected. "Let her walk ahead of you, you understand? My father never took the spotlight from my mother."

"Yes, ma'am."

"But don't let no man steal her. Her babies need her. You listening to me?"

"Yes, ma'am."

"No, you not. Don't be in no hurry to come home. I'm going to watch movies and talk to my sisters. No one listens better than sisters. No one listens worse than a man. Maybe a snail, but that's it."

WE ARRIVED AT 11:05. Which was about six hours before I was due at the beach, passing the same people at the same spots every day, which told me I'm not the only nut in the jar.

"Love's a concrete pillow," I said to a Black man with oak tree arms standing by a metal construction door.

"Ain't that the truth, brother." His silky voice, two octaves below middle C, rumbled the ground. He stepped aside. "No wonder we get headaches. Enjoy your evening, folks. That's a mighty fine dress, ma'am."

"Thank you," Kathleen said with an acknowledging dip of her head.

As we entered a cavernous room, Kathleen, in a husky voice, said, "I had an orgasm just *listen*ing to that man."

I stifled another yawn.

The warehouse district, west of downtown Saint Petersburg, was bulging with mixed construction. They call it gentrification. I call it a neighborhood where you still need to pack. And I was. Our ground-floor space was drywalled but had no separate rooms. A five-man, make that four men and a woman, combo played on a makeshift stage. Artwork was arranged on easels and on the walls.

Every *Dark Shadows* creature in the state of Florida was in the room. And every one was dressed to be seen. A woman in jeans with holes so large she could bypass her waist and wiggle in and out without taking them off. Men in tight T-shirts, their tattooed arms the main attraction. The run-of-the-mill high heels, illegally short skirts, and plunging necklines. A bearded man decked out in a naked woman costume. Another man in a Thomas Wolfe three-piece suit. Many in what can only be described as rags, as if by exhibiting how little they cared, they showed how cool they were. First place? A Black woman with long, thick, ironed pink hair, melon lips, and a snug cream dress hugging a mind-blowing curvaceous figure. Mother of God.

"It's chilly in here," Kathleen said.

"You're too hot for hell, remember?"

"I hope Joy's cough doesn't get worse."

"If we'd come at ten, we could be leaving now."

"What do they do, hang meat in this place?"

I ordered drinks from the bartender. Kathleen swatted me when I inquired if he had hot chocolate. We spent the next thirty minutes browsing art. Sculptures. Oils. Jewelry. Glass. Ceramics. 2D mixed media. 3D mixed media. 4D, anybody? But after my stint at the Dali earlier that day, my appetite for the visual arts was exhausted. Incredibly, the place got more crowded. As we approached midnight, it became difficult to maneuver through the crowd, which had little interest in the art but great interest in each other.

It was 12:15, and I was getting antsy. No one seemed in charge. There had been no sign of Charley. No Demos. I'd resorted to asking random people if they'd seen or knew Carrie Crowlings.

The lights dimmed. The band stopped. The crowd hushed. The bandleader, a dead ringer for Desi Arnaz, took the microphone.

"Ladies and gentlemen." Pause. "Your host . . . Deeeemooooooos."

He burst through a back door, a god made flesh. A motion of man draped in black. A bomber escort of women, all redheads in white dresses of various cuts, fanned out on either side of him. Four to a side. A moving, pulsating piece of radioactive art. The formation swept into the room on cue as the band struck up a snazzy piece. Each woman held a gold leash and walked a dog. A Great Dane. A Giant Schnauzer. A magnificent white poodle from the court of the Sun King. A brown labradoodle with an Aspen coat of fluffy fur. The overhead lights drummed and flashed. The women beamed smiles. Quaked the room with the sway of their hips. The gleam of their glossy breasts. The dogs were jazzed. Tongues flapping. Tails whipping. The frenzied crowd pawed at the dogs. Applauded. Whistled. The man fanned out his arms to allow the common people to feel him. To touch him. He never broke pace. His motion made him more elusive. Surreal. It was beautiful. Exhilarating, in a boring sort of way.

Two men stood at the door he'd entered through, their hands folded neatly in front of them. Their steroid muscles looked like popcorn on toothpicks. They wore earpieces. I'd noticed several others earlier in the evening with similar headgear.

"Demos," Charley said from behind. I hadn't been aware of her presence.

"Where did you drop in from?"

"He knows art, so don't bullshit him. You're no different from hunters who want to hang the head of a great kudu. You're here for the love of the hunt, as is he. You are as much an adversary as you are working together. Got it? Kathleen, that dress is exquisite."

"Thank you. Aren't you cold?"

"Demos likes nipples at attention."

"Does he know I'm hunting kudu tonight?" I asked her.

"He does."

"Are other predators here tonight?"

"You're the main course."

"Anything you wish to say regarding the death of Nick Harris?"

"Can't think of anything."

"Is Carrie Crowlings here? I'd like to meet her as well."

"Got a thing for her, don't you?" She kissed me on the cheek. "I just identified you for Demos."

"Go collect your thirty coins."

"Gethsemane awaits you."

Charley disappeared in the crowd. Kathleen struck up a conversation with two women viewing a painting. The painting was of two women standing in a museum, viewing a painting of two women looking at them. It was titled *Four Women*. Art either grabs me or it doesn't. It strangled me.

I had enough of the circus and wandered out to a small patio where the sound was two dozen decibels lower. On the way out, I passed a painting that looked like a tricycle in a field of hay. When I stepped back, the whole painting transformed into a portrait of Marylin Monroe. It reminded me of Dali's *Gala Contemplating the Mediterranean Sea*, which I'd seen earlier that day. Close up, Dali's painting is the nude back of his wife, Gala. From a distance, it's a portrait of Abraham Lincoln. Because Gala's ass and Abraham Lincoln have so much in common, right? Like clowns, surrealists don't fool me. They're pill-popping acid riders with a paintbrush.

Demos came out five minutes later. Karl and Flat Top trailed him. Karl approached a couple seeking refuge on the patio. He said something to them. They scuttled back inside. Flat Top posted himself by the closed door.

Demos gazed into the dark parking lot when he spoke.

"I own this building, but I'm not sure what I'll do with it. Perhaps I'll construct apartments but keep the ground floor for a bar. I've had modest success with downtown properties, and liquor has attractive profit margins. What do you think?"

His voice, teased with femininity, conveyed the false modesty that people employ to front titanic egos.

I said, "They must not be too choosy who they grant liquor license to these days."

That earned a cursory glance, but he returned his attention to the parking lot.

"Housing is a slow boat to a great fortune, but that boat is not for everyone. I understand you are a man pushed by time."

"I am interested in acquiring a certain painting," I said. "I've invested time and money in pursuing it."

He returned his attention to me. "Money?"

"I bought Karl and his mute friend a charcuterie board. Two, actually."

Demos laughed. It was a choppy, guttural noise with no trace of authenticity as if it was something he'd read about but did not comprehend. His face, large and void of angularity, resembled a topography map of worn foothills. He wore makeup. His cheekbones were accented, his flawless stenciled eyebrows a tad darker than his hair. A whiff of aftershave accompanied him. Sweet, like cosmetic-counter perfume. Despite his fanfare entry and *Cosmopolitan* face, his soulless eyes were dull and lifeless.

"My apologies," he said. "My men should be better mannered. I am Demos. And you are Mr. Jake Travis. Tell me, Mr. Jake Travis, how do you know about the death of Nick Harris?"

His question told me that he had talked with Charley. Or maybe he was behind the murder of Nick Harris.

"How do *you* know of Nick Harris?" I said.

"You must answer a question before you ask one."

"I have a contact in the police department."

"And he told you of Mr. Harris's death?"

I remained silent.

"Why were you searching for him?" Demos asked.

"My client indicated that Mr. Harris might have a particular piece of art worth pursuing."

"Tell me about your client."

"He insists on his privacy."

"Charley says you mentioned a Carrie Crowlings. Did your mysterious and omniscient client provide her name as well?"

"She's an amateur," I said, blowing through his question. "You shouldn't be asking me how I know of Carrie Crowlings and Nick Harris. You should be worried about how many other people know of them."

"I met with Carrie," Demos said. "She is, how to best put it?

Exuberant in her pursuit. But I like her brashness. Her flair for vernacular language is entertaining. Cheeky."

I said, "It will save us time if we agree we are talking about the same picture."

"Salvador Dali's *The Lost Body*." He reached into his pocket and brought out a slim cigarette holder. "Would you like one?"

I told him I'd pass.

He withdrew a cigarette. Karl stepped in with a lighter. I wondered if Karl put toothpaste on his brush at night. Demos inhaled, curved his neck back, and exhaled smoke into the air.

"The surrealists hold little interest for me," he said. "I like art that speaks to me. That arouses me. The silent scream of pleasure on a woman's face is something I never tire of. But a man exorcising his childhood demons? I think not. Although I understand this particular painting is not as insect-ridden as his later works. I've been told it has a haunting woman's face and that its composition is more traditional than his clock piece."

"*The Persistence of Time*."

"Yes. Tell me, does your buyer pursue surrealists?"

"My client pursues exclusivity. What is difficult to procure is more important than what is procured."

"And has he done this in the past, acquired exclusive art?"

"He has."

"How does he know of its availability?"

"I'm not in those conversations."

He took a leisurely draw from his cigarette and then flung it to the floor. Karl stepped forward and ground it under his heel.

Demos spoke to the night air. "I like the ritual, the first few puffs, but that's it. Someone once said cigarettes are a classy way to commit suicide."

"Kurt Vonnegut. He also said a cigarette is a stick with fire on one end of it and a fool on the other."

"You have"—he fluttered his hand in the air—"an effortless way of insulting people."

That's a compliment, right?

"Someone wanted information from Harris," I said. "I'm guessing he gave it."

"Are you insinuating I had something to do with the death of Mr. Harris?"

"Did you?"

"I abhor violence."

"But you don't deny its usefulness," I said.

"History has shown it to be an effective tool when judiciously deployed."

"That depends on who is writing the history."

"I will not contend your point. Karl informed me that you are intent on pursuing the Dali. Perhaps we can work together. Table our selfish pursuit."

"Do you have the painting?" I asked.

"I do not. Like you, I wish to view it to establish its authenticity. Fake Dalis are as common as drag queens in Key West."

I steadied my gaze on him. "With Nick gone, we're down to Carrie Crowlings. If she meets the same fate as Harris, game's up. You might wish to keep that in mind."

"You insinuate with the same flawless rhythm with which you insult. Why do you persist in thinking I had anything to do with his death?"

"Because you're not asking me about it."

"Due to the absurdity of the accusation." Demos studied me for a moment. "It is not necessary we work together. But if not, one of us will be sorely disappointed."

"I agree," I said, not wanting to sever communications with him.

He gave another flutter of his hand. "We'll be in touch. Enjoy your evening, Mr. Travis."

He turned and pranced away, Karl and Flat Top trailing him.

Before I hunted down Kathleen, I swung by for another look at *Four Women*. It was close to one-fifteen when Kathleen and I slipped out. I was tired. Kathleen was cold. Cold and tired.

I had four days left. Two point five million a day. If I succeeded. And I refused to believe that I would not, although I could not deny that the possibility had taken seed.

CHAPTER 23

Melinda Varker texted me at 7:53 the following morning. I had a spatula in one hand. My other hand was in my pocket where it held a squirming gecko so as not to harm the little guy.

First, the gecko.

Bonita had just returned from walking Sophia in the stroller. Sophia had been whining all morning, sharing with the world the irritability of having a tooth come in. Kathleen, scrambling to gather papers for her class, had admonished Joy for bringing a gecko in the house. Joy, with a sly smile that was a tad unsettling for her age, had slipped the gecko in my pocket. As she did, she winked at me.

Great Zeus. When did she learn to do that?

I placed the spatula down and checked my phone. The gecko squirmed.

Carrie is here. Cleaning out his desk. I'll try to keep her.

I replied using one finger.

Comkng.

Then again.

Coming.

I shouted to Kathleen that her egg was ready, instructed Bonita to read *Hamlet* to my girls in English, and dashed out the door, Bonita's torrent of Spanish trailing after me. Before I got in the truck, I gently placed the gecko in the Augustine grass, still damp from the irrigation sprinklers. As I did, I glanced up to the house. Joy stood by the window watching me. She gave me a thumbs up. Does that tyke have my number or what?

Turn around and she's three, turn around and she's four. Turn around and she's a big girl walking out of the door.

I SWUNG MY TRUCK into the small parking lot in front of Nick Harris's office. The same Kia that was there during my first visit was parked by the door. A carelessly angled red convertible sat next to it. A bird had used the passenger side of the windshield for target practice.

I swung the office door open just as a woman burst out. She held a box with both hands. A few picture frames jutted out of the top. Her hair was over her right shoulder. She had cupid's-bow lips and wore sprayed-on black pants. Her white blouse was a size too small.

"Carrie Crowlings?"

She shot me a nervous look and nearly lost her grip on the box. "Who the hell are you?"

"May I help you with that?"

"Sure. You can start by getting out of my way."

"I'd like to talk to you about Nick Harris."

"He's dead."

"I know."

"What about him?"

"I think he had something I'm looking for."

"Like what?"

"A painting."

She double blinked. "I've no clue what you're referring to. Step aside, or I'll call the police."

"For what?"

"You're harassing me."

"Are you always this pleasant?"

She wrapped an arm clumsily around the box and stuck her free hand in her purse.

"Ask for Detective Rambler. He's the man investigating the murder of Nick Harris."

She withdrew her empty hand from her purse. Carrie radiated nervousness, as if certain she was supposed to be doing something but equally uncertain as to what that something was. I recalled Melinda telling me that Carrie was always in a mad dash to get somewhere.

"What do you want from me?" she demanded.

I needed to tap her brakes a little and slow her down. "Can we go someplace and talk? I think we may be able to help each other."

"News flash, Tarzan: I don't need your help."

"Do you really believe Nick's death was a random act of violence?"

"If you know something I don't, let's hear it."

"Carson City is the capital of Nevada," I said.

"What?"

"Did you—?"

"I don't have time for this shit."

"I suggest you make the time for this shit, Carrie. The people who killed Nick Harris will kill again." She gave that a moment. I pressed a little harder. "Just a few minutes. A cup of coffee. I think we can help each other."

She shrugged her shoulders. "Like I said, I've no clue what you're referring to, but I could use a strong coffee. But in a public place. And separate cars. I'm not driving with some shitweasel I don't even know. Deal?"

"What happened to Tarzan?"

"Deal?"

"Deal."

CHAPTER 24

I, Tarzan the Shitweasel, followed Carrie a few blocks to the Central Coffee Shoppe. It was across the street from a gift shop Katheen had hauled me into several weeks ago when we were downtown for the Saturday Morning Market. I'd suffered a half hour in the store pretending to like the place, cooing in intimate agreement over decorative household knickknacks. We rarely get credit for the hardest things we do.

We settled at a window table. Two young women and a man walked toward us on the sidewalk. The man looked like John Lennon. His T-shirt read "Retire People." He might be onto something. He was on the end closest to the street, which is the proper place for a man when walking with a woman. He and the woman on the other end each held a hand of the woman in the middle, and I knew that it would not end well.

I asked Carrie how she landed in the art business in Saint Petersburg. She'd just finished shoveling sugar into her coffee. The Arabica beans never stood a chance.

"I ran a small gallery in East Lansing, Michigan," she said. "One miserable March day, we're talking no frickin' sun for three weeks, I decided to chuck it all. First Michigan, then the couch-potato boyfriend. Loser wanted to go to glitzy LA or gritty New York. Not me. You don't extend daylight going east or west. Besides, this country's always been about north and south. We packed the car. No destination. South of Toledo on I-75—it's flatter than a whore's purse around there—was a sign. Tampa, one thousand miles. Sounded good to us. When we got here, I dumped the stoner. He was just gas money. It was time to run my life on my terms. Doing what I want. Being who I want and where I want."

"How's that working out?"

"Superfantastic. I used Sunshine to meet people, and"—she flipped open her hands—"people are beating a path to my door."

I asked her how she learned of Nick's death.

"Let's back it up. Who are you?"

As "Linger" played over the speakers, I explained that Veronica Stafford hired me to find a missing Dali. That she was convinced her husband stole it. That I had reason to believe Carrie and Nick were an item and she knew of the Dali. I impressed upon her that I would buy the Dali from her and keep her name out of it. I told her I had the pleasure of meeting Demos and his troop of baboons. That Demos likely tortured Nick Harris before killing him. He was a man she should not play games with. Or trust.

Her comment to all that?

"Melinda, right? That little snitch tell you about Nick and me?"

"Really miss him, don't you?"

"Don't get preachy on me."

"You're a heartbeat from death, Carrie. You cast your lot with bad people."

"And you're good?"

"Your decision."

That paused her. I imagined she was still stoking her

dreams. Maybe she'd already mentally spent the money. Bought a gulf-front condo. A new wardrobe. Dreams never die. They hide. Smolder. Linger.

"I think I can take care of myself," she said. But she sounded as if she were lying to me as well as to herself, and we both knew that.

"I'm sure Nick Harris felt the same. How did you learn of Nick's death?"

"Melinda called me after the police crashed the office. They were looking for Veronica. Apparently, she's on some sort of sabbatical and doesn't plan to return for a few days. Can you believe that? Your husband gets killed, and you can't be bothered? What kind of wife is she?"

"What kind of husband was he?"

"Don't start with that crap. How do you know Ms. Perfect?"

I told her I was searching for Nick. Naturally, I started at his office.

Carrie twirled her hair with her finger, and then, as if being aware of the habit, abruptly stopped, only to start again.

"You're not a cop?"

"I am not."

"Private investigator hired by an insurance company?"

"No."

"Am I supposed to believe Veronica picked you out of a phone book? That woman plans every move in everyone's life."

"I don't know how she got my name."

"Nick said she craved secrecy. Got high on it."

"End it here and now. We agree on a price. I wire the money. We exchange the painting."

"I never said I had some missing Dali."

"Let's pretend you do."

"Okay. I can play that game. Hypothetically speaking, right?"

"Right."

"If I had this painting, *The Lost Body*, you'd discreetly pay me for it, and I'd never hear from you again. Is that right?"

I had never mentioned the name of the painting to her.

"Correct."

"How, hypothetically, of course, would we settle on a price?"

"What would you suggest?"

"Seeing what other paintings go for?"

"There are no comps," I pointed out.

"What an auction house might suggest?"

"Hot art doesn't get auction pricing."

"All right, know-it-all. What do you propose? Hypothetically, of course."

"Five million."

She snorted. "Five mill doesn't buy a used easel in the art world. It's easily worth twice that. Four times that."

"Ten million."

"Still no cigar."

"Ten million dollars. Do you even hear yourself?"

"Hey, I'm not dissing you. But I think—hypothetically, of course—that I can get a lot more."

"You've got to start focusing on the only thing that matters."

"Oh, the suspense."

"Never underestimate staying alive. Why do you think someone killed Nick?"

"It was a robbery."

"Were you born lying to yourself?"

"Piss off."

I leaned back to allow a little air between us. A barista ground a bag of coffee for a customer. I waited until the whining sound stopped.

"I'm not your enemy, Carrie. You need to clear your head. Dead people don't need money. What do you think Demos wanted from Nick?"

"Demos? I can handle that tick-turd."

"Tick-turd?"

"Don't get me wrong. I appreciate your concern."

"Tick-turd?"

She huffed out her breath. "I picked it up from *Smokey and the Bandit*. My mom got wet over Burt Reynolds. She played that movie nearly every week when I was growing up. Kept the *Playboy* with his interview on our coffee table. Burt in his baby-blue bunny ears."

"This isn't a movie where people crash cars at a hundred miles an hour, laugh about it, and walk away. Demos is a dangerous man."

But she wasn't done with her formulative years.

"I always wanted to be Sally Field. Duh—who doesn't, right? To stand on the side of the road in my wedding dress and have Burt Reynolds cruise into my life. I thought that was how it was supposed to work out. Frickin' A, no wonder I'm such a hot mess." Her eyes wandered out the window then darted back to me. "Let *me* tell you a couple things *you* don't know. There's no star over Bethlehem, and there sure as shit ain't no Burt Reynolds."

"I can help—"

"Her character's name was Carrie."

"Pardon?"

"Sally Field's character. My mom named me after her, like that was gonna bless me with good luck or something."

"It's a pretty name. Bentley—"

"Frickin' horror movie name's all it is. Mom didn't get that memo."

"Bentley told me you'd go by Mary Ann Simpson and Matty Walker. What's with the *Body Heat* lineup?"

"You talked with Bentley? How'd you . . .? Forget it. I don't care. The loser and I used to act out *Body Heat*."

"How do you act out—?"

"We're not going there. Nick's death was accidental. You know, a robbery gone bad."

"Let me know when we can move on from that."

She pursed her lips and glanced away. I wondered what burden it was to be named after a parent's delusion. Maybe she and Dali could do therapy together. She took a sip of sweet coffee, keeping the mug against her mouth as if to ward off a world that was reshaping itself faster than she could process. I didn't know whether the version of Carrie I was getting was her true self or her made-up image. But you can probably ponder that about everyone you meet.

"None of this is worth your life," I pointed out. "Worth doing business with a man like Demos."

"He seems nice enough to me. Enchanting, really."

"He has two bodyguards. Minimum."

She shrugged off my comment. "Who wouldn't want that these days? Nick said he had a quick buyer. That we wouldn't get as much as if we held on to it and shopped it around. But that it was fast and safe."

"Who?"

"He didn't tell me."

"You certainly asked."

"Certainly did. But he was mum. I urged him to slow down. Take our time and do it right."

I asked her if Nick had consummated the sale.

"I don't think so."

"Is the painting where you left it or not?"

"Hypothetically?"

"Hypothetically."

"I'm checking today or tomorrow. It's not ... always accessible."

"Did you mention to Demos the conversation you had with Nick? About a quick buyer?"

She squinched her face. "I told Demos that Nick might

already have a buyer lined up. But I wanted to take my time. You know, get the best price."

Exposing that disagreement to Demos, Carrie's willingness to forgo a quick sale in order to allow other buyers in, had likely resulted in the murder of Nick Harris. Demos could now work with just one person and not worry about being cut out of the deal. I asked her what else Nick told her about his hot lead.

"Not much. He indicated this person knew about the Dali. Its history. I got the impression it was someone close to Veronica. Maybe a family member on her side, not his. I don't know. He was pretty vague." She bought her hand up and rubbed her eye. "It's so sad. God, I'll miss him."

"Don't," I said.

She dropped her hand and puffed her breath out one side of her mouth. "Demos can't touch me. No Carrie, no Dali. See how that works?"

"He can make you talk."

"I told Demos he has the inside track. You know, leave me alone, and the Dali's yours—hypothetically."

"Have you considered, on some bizarre chance, doing the right thing and returning it to its rightful owner?" She looked at me as if I'd switched to a foreign language. "Do you know who the original owner is?"

"Some college in Orlando."

"Rollins."

"Whatever."

"Two wrongs don't make a right. Return it to them."

"Not gonna happen."

"You think Burt Reynolds would sell his soul for money?"

"You listening, airhead? I already told you, there ain't no Burt Reynolds."

"Ten million. Here and now. I might not be top dollar, but I'm a safe dollar."

She leaned in to the table. "Listen, I appreciate your offer. And I totally get what you're saying."

"Ten million, Carrie. You're set for life."

"Maybe I'm planning a big life."

I decided to stop butting my head against the wall. I asked her what Demos was pitching to her.

"He says he can fence it for me. Says he has contacts all over the art world."

"And you're buying that?"

"*That* is how these things work. I know what counts, and it's not the capital of Arizona."

"Nevada."

"Same difference. He gets twenty-five percent of the selling price. If I come up with a buyer on my own, he's out. But he has connections. My seventy-five percent of whatever he gets will likely be far greater than what I could do on my own. He thinks it can go for close to thirty million."

"He'll cut you out."

Maybe limb by limb, but I kept that to myself.

"I think not."

"Ten million dollars," I said, squeezing every drop of earnestness out of me. "Today. Show me the painting. The money will be in your account by five. You can be on an island this time tomorrow. A pina colada with a rum floater in your hands. You can *buy* a Burt Reynolds, Carrie. A baker's dozen."

"I'll take it under consideration."

"You're a fool to walk away from my offer."

"I'm not doing that," she said coolly. "I just want to see what else is out there before I commit. That's what smart girls do."

Well, not really. A smart girl would adhere to Woody Allen. Take the money and run. But Carrie's mother never got wet over Woody Allen. Can't blame her, but that was too bad for Carrie.

The fish was on the hook. I just needed to bring it in. Carrie was blinded by greed. She needed to open her eyes. Just a crack. Maybe a little time to let my words sink in would help. Striking out for neutral ground and giving her time to reconsider my offer, I backtracked and asked her how she met Charley and Demos.

"I worked at Repose. Charley would occasionally drop by. Said she had connections."

"To the fraudulent art world?"

"I didn't say anything about fraud. She told me once if I ever found a valuable piece of art, she could put me in touch with that crowd."

"What does she get out of it?"

"Charley?" She shrugged. "I assume she works for Demos. She brought him in."

I asked her why she wasn't at either Repose or the warehouse party the previous nights. She said she was tired of Repose. "I've moved on from there." She indicated she had a migraine the night of the warehouse party. "I got them all the time in Michigan. I thought moving to Florida would take care of that."

What were people thinking when they came to Florida— that the state line was drawn with a magic marker? That all preexisting conditions were forbidden from crossing that line? I don't blame them. We've all been conned by the airline industry into thinking luggage can be lost. Here's something right up there with knowing the capital of Nevada: you never lose your luggage. To the contrary, not only is it impossible to lose, but we pick up things we never wanted, never ordered, don't know what to do with, and can't get rid of.

"People like Demos don't settle for twenty-five percent," I said, corralling my thoughts. "He'll find a buyer and cut you out. You'll be lucky if you just end up in prison."

"I came to Florida for a reason. I'm planting my flag here.

Making my life here. It's a free state, and I'm a free woman. Everyone knows the dice are loaded, but I like my chances."

There it was again. Florida. And then I fully understood Carrie. Knew what I was up against. Why she was immune to reason. I'll explain later.

I decided to revisit something she'd said earlier.

"You indicated Nick said something about selling it to someone who knew its history. Maybe even a family member. What can you add to that?"

"He barfed up something about it going home. Like whoever he was dealing with was family or something like that. Nick was always too sentimental. I don't have that bug."

"Ten million," I said. "I'll wire it today."

"Let's keep in touch."

"Ten. Million. Dollars."

"I said . . . let's keep in touch."

I gave up.

We exchanged numbers. We left the coffee shop, although it was painful to do so. I was so close. She only had to say yes, and Harbor House would get the money. I just couldn't get her to commit. I wondered if that failure rested on me. What I said. How I said it.

Despite her boisterous attitude, I felt an obligation to protect Carrie. For, like the gecko in my pocket, she knew nothing of the world she had entered. She was alive only because Demos didn't know where the painting was, and his first brutal attempt to learn its location had, for some unknown reason, backfired.

I was navigating downtown traffic when Rambler called and presented me with that unknown reason.

CHAPTER 25

"The body was moved," Rambler said.

"Harris?"

"Unless you got another stiff for me, and if you do, I don't want to know. Harris frequented the bar in that area. A few people recall seeing him there that night, but alone. It gets better."

"Oh?"

"The bullet wasn't necessary. Nick Harris died of a heart attack."

I swung into a medical building parking lot in order to concentrate on the phone call.

"You sure?"

"Coroner says a ruptured artery took your boy out of the game. His heart was a time bomb. The bullet was postmortem. They scared the life out of him."

That made sense. Harris would have coughed up the Dali. He wouldn't risk his life for it. But Demos didn't know where it was. Harris must have died before he told Demos.

"Why the bullet?" I asked Rambler.

"Your pick. To scare whoever has the painting. Or someone

wanted it to look like a random robbery gone bad. Or maybe it was junior's first assignment, and he'd been dreaming for years of that moment. We've had this conversation. Thugs, remember? Brainless mutations of the race. Who the hell is Demos?"

I told him about meeting Demos at the warehouse party.

"Bottom dollar says Demos is behind Nick's death," I said.

"Any proof?"

"I can smell it on him."

He grunted. "I get it. Too bad noses are inadmissible in court."

"And you?"

"No weapon. No original crime scene. Died of a heart attack. Case is all but forgotten. The head shot, though, is a little disturbing."

"A professional job?"

"Can't be ruled out."

"Got a name for you," I said.

"What am I, your secretary?"

"Carrie Crowlings."

"*Crow* or *cow*?"

"The bird."

"What about her?"

I explained who Carrie was, gave him her phone number, and explained that she was romantically involved with Nick Harris. Well, as romantic as a person like Carrie could be.

"She knows where the Dali is," I said. "She's too stupid to be afraid. Maybe you can talk some sense into her."

"Right. I'll slot her in between last night's homicide where a mother took a random bullet in the shoulder while breast-feeding her baby in a Walmart parking lot."

"That's a homicide?"

"Don't screw with Mama. When a piece of trash approached her and demanded her purse, she pulled a Glock 43X out of the glove compartment—my mistake, the gun compartment—and put a hole in his heart. Problem is, that was her second squeeze. Her first attempt took out an old geezer returning his cart."

"If you got time, I'd—"

"A baby on her tit and a gun in her hand. Welcome to the Sunshine State."

"I'd appreciate whatever you could do."

Rambler blew his breath out and said, "Got something else for you. Ever hear of a firm called Shearson Consulting?"

I told him I had not and asked what they were engaged in.

"They're a private security and investigative firm. Low profile. Underground low. They called and wanted to know if we had anything on Harris's death."

"Why the interest?"

"Didn't say. Just said they represent a client. Gave us confidentiality stuff. Watch yourself. The room is getting crowded."

I asked him to keep me in the loop if he heard from Shearson again. I couldn't see why a private firm would be investigating the death of Nick Harris. Maybe a few of his annuities went south.

I googled Shearson Consulting. While plenty of firms bore that name, none appeared to be the type of business to be inquisitive about a murder. I did find one with a glossy website that boasted of international reach. It even mentioned recovering "lost art," but nothing specific. That was not surprising. By nature, investigative firms are discreet—that is why one engages them in the first place.

Wayne Gibson called just as I merged onto I-275 South. He had confronted his secretary, Shona. She confessed that a man had approached her seeking information on a missing Dali. She told him she knew of no such thing. But when I had called to set up my appointment, she had called the man back and told him I was meeting with Gibson.

I asked him if he'd gotten a description of the man from Shona.

"She said he was short and thick, like a wrestler. He paid her five thousand dollars. I told her that in exchange for keeping her job, she could donate the money to the homeless shelter and keep me informed if they contact her again. And you? Anything?"

I didn't feel like rehashing the past few days.

"Not yet."

"Keep me posted, going forward."

Painful.

We disconnected. I tried to clear the Babel in my head, reboot my mind, and hope that when it all filled back in, everything would be clear. It's never worked before, but like Carrie, I, too, can dream.

CHAPTER 26

S peaking of Carrie...
   I couldn't shake her. My inability to close the deal had been marinating in my thoughts ever since I left her. We were so close. I could feel it. But was that really on me? Who walks away from ten million? *Tax free.* Carrie does, and I'll tell you why. What made her so immune to common sense. So obstinate.

To understand Carrie, you have to understand Florida.

It was named by Juan Ponce de Leon after a Spanish Easter celebration, the feast of flowers. *La Pascua de las Flores.* The twenty-seventh state trailed Michigan by eight years. It edged out Texas by nine months, joining the soon-to-split nation in 1845. It lay dormant and forgotten for the next century. In 1940, it was the least-populated southern state, themselves sparsely populated compared to their Yankee cousins. It found its stride only after they obliterated mosquitoes and introduced air conditioning. The north discovered its golden beaches when men who had convalesced in its hotels-turned-hospitals during the Second World War piled their new families into station wagons for a two-week vacation.

Land of sunshine. State of dreams. Zip codes of illusions. Its biggest import is restless, searching souls. It hustles them from their northern cloud-soaked homes to its promise of sun. Sand. Eternal green. At its best, it delivers. For who cannot prosper under such inspiring mornings and seductive nights? Who does not feel at peace strolling white sand beaches (1,350 miles of shoreline!)? But at its worst, its position in the southeast corner of the United States serves as a clogged drain. A cesspool of uprooted people, unmatched in any American state, swirling down the bowl, clinging and clawing to their dreams.

It peddles its sex, immune to all protocol, all sense of responsibility. Developers urged newspapers not to cover hurricanes. Weathermen were instructed to say partly sunny instead of mostly cloudy. And never let reality muck things up: an early postcard of beautiful downtown Orlando was actually a picture of Halifax, Nova Scotia. They advertised in magazines. Fort Lauderdale: "Indispensable luxuries. A hot bath. A good meal. And no letdown at sundown." When Hollywood Hills, flatter than an iron skillet, was being marketed, the bus driver was instructed to downshift. Give those Northern dreamers a sense of arrival. *We're actually here! Hollywood Hills, Florida, baby! We did it!*

They sold land at ten bucks a month. Dreams on an installment plan. And they came and they came and they just kept coming. A wardrobe of lost souls, of fervent postulants seeking travel-poster lives. Dig the names they dazzled and bagged them with: Silver Springs. Weeki Watchee. Cypress Gardens. Sunken Gardens. Tiki Gardens. Parrot Jungle. Monkey Jungle. Jungle Larry's Safari Caribbean Garden. Live Baby Gators!

Then the one that shattered every record. Blew a hole in the ozone layer.

The Magic Kingdom.

When, for the first time in his life, Walt Disney flew over

central Florida, gazing upon the flat, characterless land beneath him, nothing in the universe could lasso his imagination. Disney was an inexorable dreamer, an unstoppable body of motion. And on the date of Disney's flight, November 22, 1963, while the Arthurian dreams of a nation died, the fantasia dreams of a man took root. Disney would not live to see his dream any more than JFK would be one of the 650 million people who watched man walk on the moon. But over 100 million people would walk in Disney's dream. He created a state within a state. A dream within a dream within a dream.

Florida. It'll bust your balls. Suck your titties dry. Tell you that all you need to do is apply sunscreen and your worries are gone. Carrie was a product of that hustle. She came down from Michigan, and nothing in the world would block her pipe dream. Her migraine-bent version of reality. Her Burt Reynolds quest.

I couldn't blame Carrie. She'd been bitten by Florida.

Those dissonant thoughts reverberated in my head as the sailboat *Magic* drifted past the end of the dock, its mainsail luffing in the aimless wind. Morgan brought over grouper filets he'd caught at five-thirty that morning when the tide was running. We decided to grill them outside, for the evening begged to be enjoyed. The eastern horizon, which is the first to welcome both dawn and dusk, was turning a communion-cup purple. The low tide emitted the reek smell of life and death rolled into one, for like the eastern horizon, the oceans are alpha and omega.

While Kathleen bathed Sophia, I was in charge of Joy, who scampered barefoot through the grass, startling the birds that stalked the shallow water. I'd recently installed a fence to keep the girls from going kerplunk off the seawall. It was Kathleen's suggestion and then her insistence. I'd originally fought the idea, not wanting to mar my unobstructed view. As I sat there enjoying my wine and not worrying about Joy cracking her head, I wondered what other boneheaded miscalculations I clung to. Scary.

Hadley III slunk through the cat door. She looked at me like she always looked at me—as if she'd never seen me before in her life. I'd had her for twelve years. I knew she liked me. A week before, she'd deposited a dead palm rat in my left running shoe. It was not the first time.

"How was the hunt today?" I asked the cat.

"Naow."

"Tell me more."

She eyed me and swaggered away, searching for less conversation. My type of cat.

"Twenty minutes?" Morgan said.

"Closer to thirty."

I snatched a towel and went outside. Joy scampered by. I swooped her up in one arm and marched her, giggling, to the outdoor shower. I flipped on the handle, took off her clothes, and stuck her under the warm water. Still no shampoo so I lathered her with soap, rinsed her, wrapped her in the towel, and carried her under one arm into the house. She put on her PJs. Smiling dolphins, pelicans, and turtles.

"I'm not tired," she said as I settled her on my lap to read.

"I know. But they missed you."

"Who?"

"Your stuffies. Brown Monkey. Blue baby dolphin. Edwin the turtle. The starfish twins. They've been waiting all day for you to come back to them."

"What do they do when I'm not here?"

"They talk. Laugh. And wait for you, peanuts. Although I did see Brown Monkey in a tree today."

"You did not."

"I'm surprised you missed him. He was looking for coconuts."

"I think you're a coconut."

"I know I'm a coconut."

"Eskimo kiss."

I leaned over and we rubbed noses. I read to her and then kissed her goodnight on her cheek. I used to fear that when I kissed her, my demons would cross over. I don't think that now. I don't know why that fear left me.

BOTH GIRLS WERE ASLEEP. Dinner was over. It was no longer the drawn-out experience of wine, food, and music thoughtfully paired as it had been before children. That page had turned. Across the bay, the streetlights of the Tierre Verde bridge arched into eternity while the violet lights underneath the bridge glowed the water. The moon fought for attention from behind a cloud, and a boat idled by, trailing a wake of soft music.

"Do you want me to take the morning shift?" Kathleen said.

Kathleen wasn't even on speaking terms with mornings.

"The morning shift," I said flatly.

"Mm-hmm."

"Why do you even ask?"

"It makes me feel good."

"And if I said yes?"

"Man, oh man, would we be in trouble."

"Got something for you," I said, standing up.

"Oh goody. A present?"

"Yes. For both of us, really. Something different."

"Hot dog! Tell me you bought me October in Tennessee."

"Hold tight."

I went out to the truck and got the painting. I'd swung by earlier that day and picked it up. I'd paid for it the night we met Demos but told the artist I'd collect it later. I brought it out and leaned it against the glass table, facing her.

"You bought it," she exclaimed, her eyes darting between *Four Women* and me. "When? That night?"

"I did. I just picked it up today."

"Thank you." She landed a quick kiss on my cheek. "Look, Morgan."

Morgan walked around to view the picture of two women in a painting hung on a wall, looking down at two women in a museum looking up at them. He patted me on the back. "Good job," he said. I swelled with pride. Affirmation from Morgan is beyond praise. It's damn near anointment.

I left Kathleen and Morgan discussing the painting and went to the kitchen to do the dishes. Dirty dishes have a short lifespan in my house. I filled the coffee maker with water but would wait until morning to grind the beans. I rinsed the sink. I folded the dish towel and placed it in its spot. Straightened the counter stools. Locked the doors. I like the rhythm and rhyme of everyday tasks, the poetic elements of our lives. They seem inconsequential, but like seconds to minutes, particles to matter, nothing exists without them. If you've been close to death, you know their sweetness. They are heaven on earth.

When I returned to the screened porch, Morgan was reviewing his day at Harbor House. Domingo, a man who had lived there previously and managed the property, had died over a year ago. We were looking for someone new but had yet to find that elusive person, and money was tight. Morgan explained that the AC had been serviced that day. It was recommended that we get two new units. Because of code changes, they would need to be elevated. Morgan noted that the quote was twenty percent greater than when we had looked into it a little over a year ago. It was also suggested that each unit be fitted with a pair of UV lights to help prevent mold. Each bulb was a little over four hundred dollars—we needed four. Their lifespan was two years. Tops.

"Ten million would make a big difference," I said.

"If we had the ten," Morgan said, "and someone promised another ten, that, too, would make a great difference. The money will not give us more hours in a day."

"We're just getting by," I said, eager to defend my actions. "It will put the endowment on firmer ground."

"True," Kathleen said. "But the rubber hits the road when one person touches another. Not when the bank account adds a few zeros."

The hell? Am I the only one who sees that money buys good deeds? Shelter? Food? Beds? UV lights?

A few minutes later, Morgan crossed the dark, shadowless lawn to his house next door. The solitary candle Kathleen lit every night flickered against the impenetrable darkness. Kathleen kicked off her shoes and rested her feet on the table. She reached behind her and untied her hair, fluffing it around both shoulders.

"I'm not sure Morgan buys into the 'bigger is better' notion," she said.

"Food and shelter have a unique appeal to those who are hungry and roofless."

"Without a doubt. What did you and Joy talk about when you put her to bed? I heard her giggling."

"I told her the dolphins and turtles wait for her all day. That Brown Monkey was climbing a palm tree today."

"When I went in to kiss her goodnight, she asked if dolphins got lonely. I said no, they had friends. What does she know of lonely? Is she lonely?"

"Our house is a zoo."

"You can be with people and still be lonely," she said.

"The soul that seeks beauty sometimes walks alone."

"She's a little young for Goethe. I'm not arguing that money wouldn't make a difference, but you need to talk to Morgan.

You boys need to be on the same boat. This whole Dali thing is not for him."

"You just said . . ."

"I know what I said."

LATER, WE MADE LOVE. It was slow and easy and quiet, our bodies consumed by something we did not understand. Afterwards, silence roared our crumbled world. Kathleen's pulse throbbed against my chest.

"What if she is lonely?" Kathleen said.

Here we go. Kathleen knows I'm not capable of serious conversation in bed. That has never deterred her from following her own agenda.

"I'm sleeping," I said.

"Do you think she is?"

"No."

"But what if she is?"

"She's not."

"You're saying that just so you can go to sleep."

I faked a snore. She nudged me in the ribs. Not subtly.

"I'm worried," she said. "It's one thing to teach a child to read, but to know their emotions is different. I don't know if I can be that tuned in if I'm not with them more."

I pretended not to hear her. An old trick that we all know doesn't work.

She lifted her face in front of mine.

"Hear me?"

"Breathe," I said, for we'd not done it for a long time, and I was suddenly fearful that we would never do it again.

With our mouths inches apart, she exhaled. I took her stale breath in for mine, knowing that every day a few more cells die. The temporariness of it all took hold of me, and as we breathed our recycled breaths, I didn't care what they thought. Ten million could help a lot of lives, and I could be the one to make that happen, and maybe it was Florida talking, but I wasn't ready to give up on that dream.

I had three days.

CHAPTER 27

A dolphin, when it echolocates, can see your bones. Your organs. Your heart. So it is with Morgan. He senses a person's being. I can't help but think that, in some manner, he is more evolved. That he jumped a million years ahead of the rest of the pack.

He sat cross-legged at the end of his dock. Like Elijah going into a cave to hear God, Morgan goes to the end of his dock every morning to greet the sun. A band of orange ran across the base of the horizon beneath the bluing sky. The sun, trumpeting its magisterial arrival, burned through the morning fog like a neon pumpkin. The last of the ancient gods would soon release its fury, scorching us with a brilliance so great, we are forbidden to look at it.

I took a seat on the bench behind him and pulled my baseball cap over my eyes. A dolphin surfaced and then another next to it. Morgan kept his back erect, his shoulders square. After a few minutes—I'd tried to time my arrival to when he would be completing his meditation—he stood and took a seat beside me. His moon talisman hung around his neck. It never left his body. Morgan is a selenophile and the lunar cycle guides his life.

"Do you think Claire will get a fresh start?" I asked.

Claire was the one-earring woman from Harbor House whom Morgan had taken in. She'd departed yesterday.

"We talked before she left," he said. "On the commitment that requires. She knows she can't keep living how she has been. Knowing what you don't want is often more instrumental than knowing what you do want." He looked at me. "How is your search coming?"

I filled him in. Upon hearing my own words, I realized I'd made alarmingly little progress.

"Ten million dollars," I said, as much to me as to him. "It can make a difference."

He kept his gaze over the sun-speckled water. A fishing boat anchored on the sandbar. The fisherman tossed his bait net high and wide into the water. After it sank, he pulled hard on the line, his back bent, hauling it into his boat.

"My father's greatest pleasure," Morgan said, "was seeing the joy on the faces of those he took sailing. The feel of a line running through his hand. He turned down all offers to expand his business."

Morgan was raised on a sailboat. His father and mother conducted weekly charters. He and his sister served as the crew.

"A roof helps."

Morgan nodded. "An African proverb says the beginning of wisdom is to get a roof. You are a builder, not I. That is not the line that runs through my hands. Money does not help me. I cannot build roofs, but I can touch hands."

"Let me handle it."

He nodded. "I will."

"If I don't find the Dali, it's a moot point."

He paused before speaking.

"There were many ports my father would not enter. I asked him why. The ports were popular and appeared to pose no more danger than any other port. He replied that dirty money hid in those ports. Anchored in her waters. And while such money was ubiquitous on the seas, that was no reason to accept it. To moor next to it."

"If my search makes you uncomfortable, give me the word. I'll stop today."

"I can't do that. You're right. The money will make a huge difference." He looked at me, for his eyes had been locked on the fisherman. "I've always been wary of money. The compromises. The uncertainties that accompany it. The seductive logic people employ to acquire it." He placed his hand on my shoulder. "Search. It is the rope running through your hands."

I nodded as if I understood. And maybe I did, for I suspect we hide from those things we know to be most true.

I left Morgan on his dock and took another shampooless outdoor shower. A great white egret approached me. It hung around the end of the dock when I fished. Did it realize it'd been some time? I dried off, wrapped a towel around my waist, and rounded the corner to the back of the house. The bird, unafraid, took a minor step back.

"Sorry, buddy. Been a little busy."

Unlike Hadley III, the bird didn't answer.

As I opened the door to the screen porch, my phone, which I'd left on the table, rang. I picked it up and punched it.

"It's gone," Carrie Crowlings said before I could say hello, her voice cracking with hysteria.

"What's gone?"

"Don't give me that shit. You know what I'm talking about."

"The Dali?"

"Did you steal it?"

"I don't have a clue where it is. Or was. Where are you?"

"Nick's office."

"Stay there. I'm on my way. And Carrie? Lock the door."

CHAPTER 28

Twelve minutes later, I swung into the parking lot outside Nick Harris's office. Carrie flew through the door before my feet hit the ground.

"Tell me if you know who has it," she demanded. "And don't fuckin lie to me."

"I'm clueless."

"You're lying."

"I am not."

She paced in front of me, slapping her thighs with her hands. Her hair was splayed over both shoulders. "Okay. Thank you. I think. But who took it? No one knows where we kept it."

I asked her to tell me what happened.

She stopped her directionless movement and blew her breath out. "I wanted to check on it—you know, like we talked about. Make sure Nick didn't sell it from under me. But it's not here."

"Where did you and Nick hide the painting?"

"The closet."

"You stuck Dali in the closet?"

"From what I know, that's where the corn-nut belonged. It

was locked. Only Nick and I had a key. His new girl, Ms. Effing Perfect, wasn't given access."

I recalled Melinda telling me the closet door was locked and that only Nick and Carrie had keys. Melinda's car wasn't in the small lot. I assumed she didn't start work for at least another hour. Then this bomb: I could have kicked in the closet door the day I'd met Melinda and game over. Best not to dwell on that.

"When was the last time you saw it?"

"I don't know. A week ago? No. Six days. The migraine knocked me out for over a day and a half. I planned to see if it was still there when I came to clean out my stuff. But Melinda was there, so I couldn't." She punched out her breath. "I've swung by several times, and that little twit was always here. The hell she burning both ends of the candle for? Nick and I checked on it last Monday night. You know, to make sure it was fine. It was wrapped just as we'd left it."

"And you're sure Melinda doesn't have a key? Or a cleaning service? Landlord?"

"Fucking shit. I can't believe it's gone."

"Are you certain—?"

"I heard you. Positive. We planned it in advance. Had a lock installed on the door. Two keys. One for him. One for me."

I told her I wanted to look at the closet. We went inside, and I examined the door. It showed no signs of a forcible entry or being tampered with.

"I already did that," she said curtly. "Someone had the key. Do you think they got it from Nick?"

I thought of the time sequence. It was not good.

"You told me Nick had a quick buyer. Someone possibly even related to Veronica. Perhaps he consummated the deal and died a day later. Or relocated it and never got a chance to tell you."

She brushed her hand through her hair. A choreography of

frustration and anger. "Terrific. Then we'll never know where it is. But I don't think he would do that without telling me. I mean, like, right away."

"He never got the chance."

"I bet Demos got the key from Nick. That little fuckturd."

"You called him enchanting yesterday."

"Changed my mind."

"Think. Did you or Nick tell anyone else?"

"No. Would he do that? Kill Nick? Steal the painting?"

"I've been trying to tell you, Carrie. He's a mobster."

"I'm going to call Charley," she said. "Tell her I want to meet him."

"Are you going to tell him the painting is gone?"

She looked at me as if noticing me for the first time that morning.

"Should I?"

"If you don't and he has it, he'll know you're lying. The best we can hope for is that if he has it, he might still cut us in."

"Think he'd do that?"

"Not how you think."

"What does *that* mean?"

"He'd pay us for our cooperation. To be quiet. At best, I could still buy the Dali, and you can get a fee. That's *if* he has it. Tell me more about this quick buyer Nick mentioned."

"I told you all I know," she said in frustration. "He was pretty vague. You know she—Veronica—is going nuts, right? Early Alzheimer's or something. He said he'd tell me more, but then he got himself killed."

"Heart attack."

"What?"

I explained that the autopsy report said he died of a heart attack.

Carrie planted her hands on her hips. "Really? Huh. He'd been having minor chest pains, even thought of going to a doctor. I told him it was probably indigestion. Heart attack at his age? Imagine that. Wonder if he carried life insurance? His wife's probably still the beneficiary."

"Really loved him, didn't you?"

"Here's what I know about love: the guy who wrote "Annie's Song" took a chainsaw to his lover's bed. Hey, betcha you didn't know that, didja?"

"John Denver."

"Who the hell is he?"

"He's the guy who—"

"I don't care. Find the Dali. Hear me?"

CHAPTER 29

"Demos would like to meet with you," Charley said. "Not Carrie. Just you."

It was an hour after I left Carrie. I'd called Charley as soon as I was in the truck. I explained that Carrie no longer had the painting and that I was pretty sure Demos knew that, but that did not dampen my interest in acquiring it. I lobbied her to arrange a meeting.

Privately, I thought that if Demos was now working only for himself, it might increase my chances of acquiring the Dali at a reasonable price. Demos no longer had to split the proceeds. Or I could just steal it from him. That would be more fun. Would I cut Carrie out? Absolutely. After our last meeting— going forward—I needed to start taking Carrie Crowlings at face value. Carrie was easy to look at, her language amusing. Fun. But she was a dozen time zones west of reality.

"When and where?" I said to Charley.

"Tonight. Eight. On his boat. Vinoy Marina. He has a house in the historic district, but he likes conducting business on his boat."

"Name?"

"Name, what?"

"Of the boat."

"*Sex-Sea.*"

"I'll be there."

"One more thing."

"Yes?"

"Demos is . . . complicated. A maximalist. The boat seems to bring all that out in him."

"Meaning?"

"You'll see."

She disconnected.

Eight p.m. The other end of the day. Hours I could not afford to lose, for time and tide wait for no man.

I didn't feel like doing odd jobs at Harbor House. I found it increasingly hard to do anything other than search for the Dali, no matter how trivial my actions might seem. I'd bought into the game. My time had become a financial statement. Every hour now six figures. Every minute accompanied by a dollar sign.

I needed to temper my laser focus on Demos and investigate other scenarios. Although I did not share it with Carrie, I was warming to my theory that Nick had unloaded the Dali on someone he or Veronica knew. Carrie had indicated that Nick might have struck a deal with someone on Veronica's side of the family. She didn't have much family but had been married long ago.

Wetzel had given me the name of Veronica's first husband, Michael Fredericks. A little research revealed that a Michael Fredericks, Rollins class of '71, had remarried and then gotten a divorce years later. He'd retired from teaching at the University of South Florida, and the trail went cold after that. While at Rollins, he majored in art. Interesting. I couldn't find a phone number for him. I did find an address for a Michael A. Fredericks, a name that fit the retired USF professor. His modest unit well off Beach Drive had been listed, then taken off the market. No one answered the bell when I rang the unit. I pestered people at USF but found no one who knew of him or was willing to help me.

I changed tack. Perhaps talking to Fredericks's second ex-wife might be a good backdoor tactic. Maybe she could shed light on the man. Introduce new players. Maybe not. In his *Institute of Oratory*, Marcus Quintilian of La Rioja, a Roman scholar, said it's easier to stumble across accidental innovation than to write the thing you are after. Modify that just a bit, and you have the PI's golden rule: you are more apt to stumble upon the truth than if you intentionally set out to find it. Just ask Rambler. That's why cops knock on dozens of doors. Interview hundreds of people.

At least playing detective would keep me occupied until my meeting with Demos.

As hard as it was to find Michael Fredericks, it was a breeze locating his second ex-wife. Dr. Sally Herrington lived forty-five minutes south in Lakewood Ranch. She had a PhD in European history and had chaired the department at the University of Central Florida until her retirement eight years ago. I jumped in my truck without bothering to call and was soon cresting the Sunshine Skyway Bridge. I didn't have time to play phone tag and would rather meet her in person. Either she was home or she wasn't.

SALLY HERRINGTON'S RED FRONT door belonged more in Stars Hollow than in a mazed neighborhood of Mediterranean ranches in Florida. The homes, in an attempt to look unique, all looked the same.

I punched the doorbell. The door swung open.

"Doctor Herrington?"

"Yes?"

Like a rancher's face showed signs of years on the range, Doctor Herrington's weary yet finely focused eyes told of a life of academic scrutiny. Those laser eyes drilled into me as I stood on the sidewalk, a step down from the red front door.

Before I could launch into my spiel, she said, "You don't look like some kid from the south side of Chicago selling magazines." Her vespers voice was soft yet firm.

I introduced myself and explained that I had questions about her former husband, Michael Fredericks, and a missing painting that I had been retained to find. That I would greatly appreciate a moment of her time. As I talked, an insect tickled the back of my neck. I resisted the urge to swat at it.

"You think Michael stole a painting?" she said. "Michael?"

"I have no reason to believe that your ex-husband knew anything of the painting, but the more I know, the better my chances."

"We've been divorced for close to ten years. Or is it fifteen?"

"I realize that."

"What? That I don't even know how long I've been divorced?"

"That you're divorced."

"He left me for her."

"Veronica?"

"Who else?"

"They never remarried."

"I know."

"She's married to Nick Harris."

"If you say."

"Are you saying they're not married?"

She shook her head in disappointment. "I was referring to matters of the heart, not legality."

I didn't chase that. After our staccato exchange, I was beginning to regret the drive. I mustered all my sincerity. "A few minutes would mean a lot."

She hesitated. "I'm just relieved you're not pushing magazines. Those people don't shut up. Follow me."

She didn't wait for a response but turned and strolled through her house and out the rear door. I followed, scratching the back of my neck, but whatever had feasted on me was long gone. Orchids of different colors surrounded a shaded courtyard. Water gurgled from the green mouth of a concrete frog. I was thirsty and hoped she'd offer me something to drink. I regretted not taking a swig of water before getting out of the truck.

"Michael and I had some good years," she said after we settled into cushioned chairs with oriental designs. Mine had small dried leaves on the seat. I thought of brushing them off but thought it might offend her.

I asked her if she spoke to her ex-husband much.

"Not really."

"Was the divorce amicable?"

"Michael is the gentlest man to stroll the face of the earth. He's a painter. A poet. A renaissance man of the arts. How does one get mad at such a man? His idea of meanness, of payback, was not unloading the dishwasher in the morning. Even that aggressive act challenged him. If I waited a few hours, he'd get around to it."

"What do you know about his time at Rollins College?"

"Is that where the painting is missing from?"

"I'm not at liberty to discuss that, Dr. Herrington."

"No. I suppose you're not. Not much, really. And it's Sally. Michael and I met close to thirty years ago at a symposium at UCF. We dated, fell in love, or fell into convenience. I'm not sure if I know the difference. He told me he'd been married briefly right out of college but that it didn't last."

"To Veronica Stafford?"

"Yes."

Her patio backed up to a pond with a walking path adjacent

to it. A man and woman hiked by at a brisk pace, the woman chatting away, her right hand flaying in the air as if conducting her words. The man took a drink from a water bottle. Lucky guy.

Sally said, "Tell me again why you think Michael has anything to do with a stolen painting. What kind of painting?"

"A Dali."

She arched her fine eyebrows. "As in Salvador?"

"The one and only."

"Actually, there were two. He was named after his deceased older brother. Hardly, one would think, a good parenting decision."

"Did you and Michael ever have children?"

"Are you always this direct, Mr. Travis?"

"Yes, and it's Jake."

"Good to know. We decided not to have children. Something I only regret because I refuse to think about it. We were happy in a mindless, non-introspective sort of way. Him teaching, doing his paintings, dabbling in poetry, and me wrapped up in the battles of Waterloo. Talavera. All things fourteenth-century Europe. Then, one day, we each looked up from our obsessions and saw a total stranger. Like that Simon and Garfunkel song. Bookmarks marking what we lost.

"He told me he wanted a divorce. Before responding, I finished the paragraph I was reading about feudal wars in southern France. That told me some of the blame was mine. It was for the best. All we ever did was inhabit our separate studies. I'm less lonely living by myself. At least now I'm not expecting companionship."

"What was his reason for the divorce?"

"He didn't need one. I read his poems. I knew his passion wasn't for me."

"Was it for Veronica or another woman?"

"Michael was only capable of falling in love once."

"Why did they divorce?"

"Do you think that's right?"

"What's right?"

"That you can only fall in love once."

"If you say so."

"I'm asking you."

"I think it depends on the person."

"That's a listless response. Have you talked to him? Asked him why he and Veronica divorced?"

"I can't get in contact with him."

"Do you have his cell?"

"I do not. Could you share that with me?"

She said she would. I asked her Michael's version of the dissolution of his marriage to Veronica.

"He told me they just drifted away," she said.

"Did you believe him?"

She pursed her thin lips. "Michael, gifted as he was with words, was more gifted in silence."

"Did they ever get back together?"

"Not that I know."

"But you said—"

"Not legally is what I meant."

"Veronica remarried not long ago," I said. "Did he ever say anything about that?"

She shrugged. "We don't talk. Apparently, she moved on, and he didn't."

"Veronica's husband, Nick Harris, was murdered a few days ago."

"Oh, that's horrible. Did his death have anything to do with your missing Dali?"

"I don't know. Did Michael ever mention a missing painting?"

"No."

I asked her if Michael collected work by other artists.

"We're academia, Mr. . . . Jake. We have no money."

"Did he ever associate with people who might buy and sell art?"

"You're barking up the wrong tree. Michael was a beatnik, not an art hustler."

Frustrated, I said, "What question am I not asking?"

"You never asked me if *they* had a child."

I recalled Faye Wilkinson mentioning that Veronica had gotten pregnant. It was a comment I'd let slip by, and I now realized I should have questioned her further.

"Did they?"

Her gaze wandered over the walking path. A breeze tingled red chimes hanging from a jacaranda tree. Sally Herrington was petite, wispy, like a wind chime, and I wondered where her mind went when the wind touched her.

"It was he who didn't want children," she said, staring away from me. "Strange, for I thought he'd make a wonderful father. He said they would interfere with his work. But I never fell for that." She turned her face to me. "They have a daughter. Something my loving husband felt compelled to keep from me throughout our entire marriage. And apparently, they are as close now as they have ever been."

CHAPTER 30

I leaned forward in my chair as if I was physically closer to finding the Dali. I was beginning to believe the painting knew I was in pursuit, and the closer I got, the further it receded, like those vexing answers I chase on the beach every morning. I cleared my throat. Is there any water in this county? I asked Sally if she knew where their daughter was.

"I do not."

"You said they were close."

"With a preface. 'Apparently.'"

I leaned back, scratched my neck, and asked how she learned of Veronica and Michael's daughter.

"I discovered letters Michael had written to Veronica. After the divorce, Michael boxed up his stuff and moved out. A year or so later, I realized I was missing some papers. Research articles. Although they are online, I wanted the original work to be at UCF. I've gifted my work to the department where it sits on dusty shelves. That grants me a serene, albeit false sense of immortality.

"I keep my work in an air-conditioned storage unit. I was rummaging through boxes and found one with Michael's name on it. The box must have gotten misplaced. I opened it. I found the letters—unsent—stuffed in with books about Thomas Eakins. Michael went through an Eakins phase. He said all artists did."

"Unsent?"

"You heard correctly. The letters were from Michael to Veronica, reminiscing about their daughter. How old she is now. The trip to Paris they took. Her school. Some cabin in New York they went to each year. Michael has a daughter. He was seeing her while he was married to me. Like a double life. Who doesn't tell his wife he has a child? Why would he keep that from me?"

"You certainly asked him."

"He said he couldn't talk about her. But that it wasn't what it seemed. Recall, we were divorced by this time. While we were married, he traveled a lot. Trips to universities, art exhibits. Looking back, I think he was hooking up with her then, but I had little interest in hounding him or reconstructing a past in which I played the fool."

"You said the letters were never mailed."

"I called him out on that. He failed at any plausible explanation."

I couldn't fathom why Veronica hadn't told me about her daughter, but there was no reason for her to do so. Maybe she was trying to hide her shame for having a stolen painting. Afraid her daughter would see someone other than who Veronica thought she was. There were too many possibilities to examine.

"Your painting was mentioned," Sally said, breaking me from my musings.

"Excuse me?"

"In the letters. Just one mentioned it. Said it had considerable value, and they should return it in some manner so as not to incriminate themselves."

I asked her if the letter mentioned the painting's title.

"No."

"The artist?"

"Dali."

"Why didn't you tell me this earlier?"

"Tell a stranger that I married a man I never knew? Who didn't have the decency to tell me he had a daughter? Who bared his soul in love letters never to be sent? It's not an attractive narrative for me. Apparently, I've spent a good portion of my life in ignorance. Maybe that's what I get for spending half my conscious hours on the other side of the world six hundred years ago. Are we to assume that the painting mentioned in the letter is the painting you're searching for?"

"Apparently."

That brought a smile. Sally's lips were thin and delicate, as if meticulously etched onto her face.

"That's the best you can do after I bare my soul?" she said. "Mimic me?"

"No offense intended."

"None taken." She stood, and I did likewise. "Now, if you'll excuse me. I've had enough golden memories for one day."

I asked her for Michael's phone number. She gave it to me. I thanked her for her time and started for the door. Then I turned and faced her, for I had one more question.

"Do you know his daughter's name?"

"Jamie. Much like yours. Good luck with your search, Jake."

CHAPTER 31
VERONICA

1974

Not every road is on a map

They were in a café having coffee and splitting a doughnut with vanilla icing that went down so effortlessly that Michael popped up to get another one. While he was gone, Veronica took a deep breath. Then another. She'd been putting it off for a week. It was killing her. Shredding her insides.

Michael approached the table.

Now. Get it over with.

He reclaimed his seat. He said, "The girl behind the counter—"

"I'm pregnant."

"What?"

"I'm pregnant. You know. Knocked up. A bun in the oven."

"You?"

"Yes. Me."

"Wow. Who's the lucky guy?"

She reached across the table and punched him in the arm.

"How?" Michael asked, his face now masked with serious-ness. "I don't mean *how* how, but we took precautions."

"A diaphragm is not one hundred percent. One of those little swimmers must have gotten through."

"Way to go, little guy."

"What are we going to do?"

"What do you mean?"

"It's legal now, if we don't want it."

"This isn't really about what's legal or not, is it?" he said.

Veronica took a nibble of a doughnut that had icing on it. A morning shower pelted sporadic drops of rain against the window. The paint on the windowsill was chipped, and she thought the loose paint looked like icing. It momentarily took her back to when she and her mother made a gingerbread house. The roof of frosting. She'd always been closer to her father, but there were just enough good memories of her mother that, if not to make her excited about being a mother, prevented her from being a total skeptic on the subject.

"Vee?" he said.

"No," she blurted out, confused as to why at such a moment her mind would wander. "It's not. What do you want to do?"

"What do *you* want to do?"

"Not play this game."

"Let's buy diapers," Michael said confidently. He stuffed a piece of doughnut in his mouth.

"If we do that, there's no going back."

"We wannato whait, but whatz a wheare or woo?"

"What?"

He finished chewing.

"We wanted to wait, but what's a year or two?"

"We have no money," Veronica pointed out.

"They don't eat much."

"Then why do they poop so much?"

"'Tis a mystery."

"What do we know about raising a kid?"

"We'll figure it out."

"I don't think I'm ready for this."

"I doubt anyone ever is," Michael said. "And you'll be ready."

"Are we past legal? I mean, I could take it or leave it. But that sounds so callous."

"Have an abortion because we missed the mark by a year or two? That hardly makes sense. When I paint, it never turns out the way I envisioned. Art seeks its own path. I think life is the same way."

Veronica tried to process that. She'd always been a little wary of Michael's creative side. She was a woman who had to consciously allow herself the freedom to feel. To express herself. She had never surrendered her passion to Faye as much as she had *planned* to surrender her passion to Faye.

"Not every road is on a map," Michael said, nudging her. "Pretty sure the best ones aren't."

Veronica stared at the droplets of rain on the windowpane.

THAT EVENING, THEY MADE love while "The Boxer" played on the stereo. She thought of the world waiting for her. For them. *No. That's not right. We're creating a new world. Our world.*

Michael took Veronica's face in his hands. "Penny for your thoughts," he said.

The moment drowned her. She couldn't articulate her thoughts or feelings. For the tidal passion between her legs was nothing compared to the calming softness of his hands. When those hands cradled her face, an Atlantic fog washed over her world. That which so dominated her mind ceased to exist.

Worries. Doubts. Regret. All of it. Gone. Her soul finally at peace in the autumn meadows of her mind.

Forty-eight years would pass before Veronica shared a penny's worth of her thoughts.

CHAPTER 32

I stepped aboard *Sex-Sea* a little after eight that evening. Flat Top searched me.

"You know, I never caught your name," I said.

"Follow me."

"That's the best your parents could do?"

He ignored my sophomoric remark and led me to the aft of the boat where he said, "Stay." He had a surprisingly high voice for such a large man. He slipped away, and I leaned against the rail, my back to downtown. Orion's Belt had recently become visible. A celestial sign of the shortening of days. The season of night was coming.

I had called Michael Fredericks driving away from Sally Herrington's house. The call went straight to voice mail. I'd left a message. I texted him. Nothing. I needed a break, and they just weren't coming. I was thinking how to force the action when a ridiculously slender woman approached me.

"Hi, I'm Harper," she said, as if she was in a business meeting. "May I offer you something to drink?"

"What are my options, Harper?"

She stuck her leg out of the slit of her dress.

"What's your pleasure?"

"Jameson on the rocks would be fine."

"Will Macallan twenty year suffice?"

"If I said no, what else could you offer?"

"Probably more than you can handle."

"I can handle a lot."

"Hey, that's my line," she batted at me.

"I didn't mean to steal anything from you."

She stuck out her other leg—the dress split on both sides. I hope she knew that when she bought it.

"Maybe I should steal something from *you*," she said.

"What could I possibly have that you want?"

"Hmm, something I take great joy in getting and won't give back."

"You're scaring me, Harper."

She took a step in to me. She traced her hand down my chest. "God, I'm thirsty."

She started to unbuckle my belt.

Jake's First Dictum. Jake's First Dictum.

She lowered herself to her knees. She fumbled with my belt.

Jake's First Dictum. Or was it dick first? Yeah, that's it. Dick first. No, not dick first, you dickhead. First Dictum.

I took two steps away from her, although part of me instantly registered displeasure with that decision.

"I'll take that twenty year now," I said, fastening my belt.

"You have something against pleasure?" she said in a tone of mock hurt, her eyes searching up to mine.

"I'm just a man who loves his single-malt whiskey."

She stood, oozing her body into mine. "Why don't we make the most of the moment?"

Smiling dolphins, pelicans, and turtles. Smiling dolphins, pelicans, and turtles. Smiling . . .

"I appreciate the offer, Harper."

"You appreciate the offer," she said flatly. "Pity."

She slunk away in her six-inch heels. She returned a few minutes later with my drink in a glass tumbler. She handed it to me.

"To a man who prefers single-malt whiskey to, well, you know."

"When will Demos be joining me?"

"Demos," she said, as if unfamiliar with the name.

"This is his boat, is it not?"

"It is," she said with an indiscernible smile. "He'll be by . . . shortly. Or not at all."

She slipped back into the main cabin, leaving me to wonder what other creatures were onboard and if I'd mistakenly wandered into the wrong universe. I strolled over to the rail. Tall condos, pillars of light wrapped in black, ascended into the sky. A jet stream of people coursed the sidewalks on Straub Park.

After I'd dialed Fredericks, I called Wetzel. He confirmed Veronica had a daughter but said, per Veronica's instructions, he was not permitted to discuss her at this time. When I pushed him on that, he reminded me the clock was ticking. Like I didn't know? Every time I talked to that man felt like a step backward. He didn't strike me as dishonest, but rather as a man with a thousand varieties of honesty. Each one neatly categorized on a shelf where they rested next to their first cousins: deception, mirage, disingenuousness, and the occasional straight-in-your-face lie.

From behind me, a woman's husky voice said, "My apologies for keeping you waiting, Mr. Travis."

I turned and faced—

Demos?

It looked like him, but he was a she and a damn good-looking one. Wrapped in a tight deep-blue dress with a high neckline that hugged her/his/their body. I could have passed Demos on the street and not known him. His pancaked face was a wild pantheon of colors. It was hard not to stare. Hard not to admire the sheer artistry. The gumption. The painted sex. For he'd become a woman. And women can shift trade winds with a puff of a breath. Stare the sun back into the sea. Smile away the thunder and figure out which remote control turns on the TV.

Karl stood behind her. Flat Top looked bored. They'd seen this show before.

"Demos?" I said.

"Denise, tonight," she said. Her voice was softer now. Lyrical. She flapped a hand in the air. "Sometimes, dear, I don't know in the morning who I will be in the evening. Tonight, I felt like being Denise. The water brings her out in me. Or does the land bring Demos out of Denise? Such *quest*ions."

"You have a beautiful boat, Denise."

"Thank you."

But I didn't like *Sex-Sea*. It was sleek and void of any classic lines. I wondered how hard it was for him to keep his voice different from that of Demos. Or was it hard for Demos not to sound like Denise? The windmills of their sexuality going round and round.

Denise said, "I see Harper got you a drink. It's unfortunate you didn't allow yourself to be raptured. Why do you deny pleasure?"

"I hardly think I offended her."

"She swallowed her, hmm, pride. Tell me, Mr. Travis, have you been to open water? Where there is nothing to see and no hope of spotting land?"

"I have."

"I find it clears my mind. Makes simple those things that have gotten complex. Would you agree?"

"If you say so."

"That is what I need to do now. Make things simple. For my mind is conflicted."

Well, there's an understatement.

She motioned with her arm. "Please."

We took opposing chairs. Denise crossed her smooth shaved legs. She held her hand out, and Karl handed her a flute of bubbling wine. She took it without looking at him.

Denise said, "I understand that Carrie Crowlings no longer has the painting."

His comment told me that Carrie had told either Charley or Demos.

"So she says."

She gave me a coconspirator smile. "And do you believe her, dear? By the way, that dress Kathleen wore the other night was exquisite. A woman's back is"—she shuddered her shoulders—"artistry beyond compare."

I wasn't going to engage her in a discussion of my wife's back. I said, "If I did believe Carrie, I'm not sure I'd confide in you."

She chuckled and pointed a shiny red fingernail at me. "I think we are the same person. No?"

"You did look in the mirror this evening, didn't you?"

She rolled her head back in laughter. "Oh, that's delicious. I did. And I swooned over what I saw. I'm not afraid of who I am. And you? Who's to say you don't have a *Jacqueline* in your closet? No? Not all of us are so gifted." She put down the flute. "But business beckons us. I do not believe Carrie misplaced the painting or that it is missing. I believe she, and perhaps you, are scheming to keep me out."

I thought of Charley's statement. *Demos is complicated. A maximalist.* She knew what I was in store for. Took pleasure in a veiled warning. I bet she got a kick out of that. What else did Charley know about Demos that she didn't confide in me? I couldn't figure Charley out. Where did she fit in? It was as if Charley was a puzzle piece from a different box and—

"Jake, dear?"

"Yes?"

"I asked if you and Carrie have formed a team. A pact."

"No. I think you got the key from Harris and have the Dali."

"Oh, darling. Such a misguided boy. And why would I invite you here?"

"To hear my high bid and cut Carrie out."

"I do not have it."

"We're just chewing fat."

She gave another fake shudder. "A most unpleasant expression. I think if you took it, you would show up tonight. To display your innocence and not draw attention to yourself."

"Carrie panicked when she told me it was missing," I said. "She was distraught. She kept it hidden. It's gone. Only she and Nick had a key to the closet where it was stashed. It would seem to me that whoever killed Nick Harris got the key and now has the Dali."

No way would I share my budding theory that Veronica and Michael's daughter had circled back into their lives and had possibly acquired the painting. That bit of knowledge gave me the inside rail, and I was not giving it up. I'd play along with Demos so as not to arouse suspicion that I knew anything more than he did.

Demos—Denise—said, "And you think that was me?"

"I do."

"And so, we chew fat."

"Do you have the painting or not?" I said.

"I do not. And you?"

"No clue where it is. But I don't trust you, and you don't trust me."

"I'd like to, dear. Trust you. But I am wary of a person who denies themselves pleasure."

I ignored her jab. "By the way, there's no need to pick up anchor and head for international waters. Harris died of a heart attack. Not a bullet. The only question is what his assailant got from him before he died."

"Stop it. I've told you, I had nothing to do with his death."

Her constant denial didn't fool me. What was the alternative, admit to murder?

Denise continued, "If you find the Dali, come to me first. Do we understand each other?"

"I don't work for you."

A smile spread over her face.

"Oh, but you will, dear. You will."

She flicked a finger. Karl stepped over to us. He punched his phone a few times and held it out to me. It was a picture of Kathleen walking out of a building at the college she taught at. My heart thumped in my chest.

Denise said, "So, you have connections with the police. Really, dear, do you think that scares me?"

My neck coiled with tension, and my insides churned. A battle cry arose within. No more smiling dolphins. I nailed my eyes to her/him. "If you value your life, you and your goons will never go near my family again."

"Oh, Jake. We were getting along so well. Where is the Dali?"

I stood. "I can see myself off. And Denise?"

"Yes?"

"I'm not afraid to hit a woman."

"And I'm not afraid to have a man hit on me," she husked out in a voice that would strip the chrome off a fender. She rolled her head back in laughter. But, as I pointed out earlier, Demos didn't know how to laugh, and Denise was equally ungifted in that area.

She stood and strolled up to me. She stuck her face within inches of mine: her breath liquored, her perfume a fresh-cut rose. She kissed me on the cheek, her tongue flicking out. She pulled away. My body stiffened. I fought the urge to strangle her to death. Him. Someone. Anyone.

"Do be careful getting off the boat, dear," she moaned in a Frank N. Furter voice. "We had a little rain, and things are . . . hmm, so slippery."

I CALLED GARRETT DEMARCUS as soon as I was out of range of *Sex-Sea.*

"Talk to me," he said.

Garrett's version of "Good to hear from you, buddy."

"I'm searching for a missing Dali painting."

"Interesting."

"I seem to have irritated an art dealer. He has a violent streak."

"How violent?"

"Suspected murder. Murders. She just flashed me a picture of Kathleen."

"She?"

"The art dealer. I met them twice. He was a man the first time, a woman the second."

"You fall off the wagon?"

"Bone dry."

There was a pause.

Garrett said, "Next flight lands at eight-forty a.m. Need me earlier?"

Garrett often flew private jets.

"No. That'll work."

He disconnected. Garrett had yet to utter a parting valediction in his life. He was a true friend, and I believe if you have a couple of those in your life—as I do—you are a blessed person, and if you have more, you're fooling yourself.

I was angry with myself. I should have called him earlier.

Those children's books were tainting my vision of the world. Here's something not in children's books: Dolphins don't really smile. They can't even move their facial muscles. That ridiculous Joker grin on their faces is there even when they engage, albeit rarely, in infanticide. I was glad Garrett was coming. His presence would keep me focused, for he tolerated no delusions. He lived his life as if he were in Anne Frank's hideaway, a machine gun in his hand, the Nazis at the door, and, oh God, please, let them in.

Here's something else not in those children's books: the Nazis are always at the door.

CHAPTER 33

Garrett was standing outside my house at 6:10 the next morning when I sprinted down the street ending my run. A full moon had been setting over the Gulf, casting a pale glow on the water. It's a special treat to see the moon rise over the bay, as it had the previous night, and witness it slide into the Gulf the following morning. It would have been more special if I'd gotten more than four hours of sleep. Morgan and I had split the night keeping watch on the house.

"What happened to the commercial flight?" I asked Garrett, still fighting for my breath. A man on a bike zipped past us, his lights pulsating in the dark.

"Tell me about the creature who has the picture of Kathleen."

"Give me ten minutes."

After a quick shower, still no shampoo, Garrett and I hit the Starbucks at Dolphin Village.. I'd left a note for Kathleen in the event one of the girls popped an eye open before I returned. Should that be the case, they'd climb into bed with her, a storybook way to start a morning, even for a non-morning person.

We settled at a corner table by the front window. A trash

truck rumbled down Gulf Boulevard, its yellow lights blinking. Palm trees offered vertical adornment to an otherwise unattractive strip of jumbled signage and mismatched buildings. Developers had long ago sacked the land, making no effort to honor the original aesthetics. They'd uprooted the jungle of green and replaced it with cinder block motels and strip centers. Little remained of the native beauty.

"How far will he go?" Garrett asked after I dumped everything. My last comment had circled back to my meeting with Demos/Denise on his/her boat. The picture of Kathleen. For clarity, we decided to call Demos *Demos*. If he wanted to be Denise, fine by us. But we had to pick. The limitations of the English language were not our fault, nor would we allow the words at our disposal to confine our views of the words.

I took a sip of stiff coffee. "Demos recognizes no boundaries. Acknowledges no rules."

"Do we need more muscle?" Garrett said.

Muscle. Garrett kept in contact with some of the old outfit who were now private contractors. They represented a life I was trying to leave behind. I was finding that hard to do and didn't know whether I wasn't trying hard enough, or, like Demos, I was split. Ambivalent as to where my true path lay. I also have a PhD. Mine is in saving big issues for another day.

"No," I said to his question. "At least, not yet. Demos was just spreading his feathers. We can always play that game. Flash him a few pictures."

Garrett grunted. I deserved it. Flashing a few pictures doesn't stop the Third Reich. I gotta get my head in the game.

Eager to atone for my pacifism, I told him that I was working on getting more information. "He has a house in the historic district. It's not under his name. Once we have the address, we can turn the tables on him."

Charley had told me Demos lived in the historic district, which was just north of downtown. That was the same neighborhood where Veronica lived. But there was no property under his name. I'd called Charley looking for an address. She had not returned my call.

We hashed out a few plans, but the best plans are born of opportunity, and you can't order opportunity.

WHEN WE RETURNED TO my house, Garrett went to Morgan's, where he bunked when he was in town. Morgan and Garrett were, on the surface, polar opposites. But they had grown close over their passion for kite surfing. Morgan belonged to a club, and when the wind blew off Fort De Soto, he could be found skimming the waves at thirty knots and reaching over forty feet into the air. Garrett had quickly mastered the sport.

I called Carrie Crowlings, but she didn't answer her phone. Or respond to a text. I called Melinda Varker to see if she'd heard from Carrie. She had not.

I threw together a quick breakfast. Kathleen was always good for two eggs over easy. "Just one," she'd say, when I asked if she wanted any. I'd fix her two and she'd eat them both without comment. I cleaned the kitchen, taking pride, as I said earlier, in the simple yet rewarding job. Bonita was running late as she had dropped by a drugstore on the way to our house to get an ointment to rub on Sophia's gums. Kathleen handed Sophia to me, kissed me on the same spot Demos had, and told me to stay out of trouble. She dashed out the door. She had a class starting in ten minutes. No way.

I took Sophia outside and settled in a shaded spot in the yard. I called for Joy to join us, but she just giggled and kept her hot pursuit of geckos. I took Sophia's tiny fingers and pointed at dolphins, whales, and starfish in a cloth book. A book that would have you believe there is no evil in the world, and all creatures live in harmony. But I knew that big fish eat smaller fish, and smaller fish eat even smaller fish, and everything eats shrimp. At least we're not shrimp. That's not much to take away from four decades, but it's solid.

"You going to stare at that one page all day?" Bonita said. I'd not heard her approach.

"I like starfish."

"Your mind is not here. Give my little girl to me before you infect her."

I gathered *my little girl* in my arms, stood, and handed her to Bonita, who, as far as I could tell, was becoming the big fish of the household.

I called Detective Rambler and gave him a heads-up that Carrie Crowlings was not answering my calls. I also told him that Demos had a picture of Kathleen. He asked if I'd like him to drop in on Demos and "rattle" him a bit. Before I could respond, he continued.

"We did some digging on your new playmate. He has a string of bars, restaurants, and parking garages up and down the coast. He also owns several art galleries. All legitimate, but everything's under a labyrinth of titles. Like you, I can smell him. How much time you got on your painting?"

"A few days."

"Someone's yanking your chain. You know that, right?"

"Beginning to suspect it."

"I suggest you get over that beginning part."

He hung up.

He called back.

"Do you?" he said.

"Do I what?"

"Want me to rattle him."

"I appreciate the offer. But not yet."

"Did you call in your friend—what's his name?"

"Garrett."

"Well?"

"I did."

The line was quiet for a beat.

"I'm not scraping more bodies off the pavement, scum or not. Understand?"

"I do."

"No, you don't."

He hung up again before I could answer.

Charley finally returned my call.

"You rang?" she said.

"Do you know Demos's address?"

"Why?"

"Do you know it or not?"

"Someone got out on the wrong side of the bed."

"I can't get hold of Carrie."

"Neither can I. You know The Tavern at Bayboro?"

"I do."

"Meet me there in an hour."

"Anything you can just tell me now?"

"One hour."

"I'll be there. By the way, I met Denise. It would have been —Charley? Hello?"

The line was dead.

Michael Fredericks's phone again went straight to voice mail. At least he enlisted a machine to hang up on me.

CHAPTER 34

The Tavern at Bayboro is tucked away on the downtown campus of the University of South Florida. I parked my truck in a nearly deserted lot that required a student sticker. Towing enforced. I'd never had an issue with there and hoped today wouldn't be the exception.

I placed an order at the counter, grabbed a beer, and selected a weathered wood table outside. I prominently displayed my kitchen flag on the edge of the table. Order 84. The clientele was a brew of college students and locals. Some with laptops, others slaved to their phones. And dogs. Always dogs. Everyone's worried about AI taking over the world. It's the dogs we've got to keep an eye on. Any creature that persuades a human to love it, feed it, groom it, shelter it, attend to its medical needs, and walk behind it at a respectful distance and pick up its shit is a lot smarter than we give it credit for.

Charley strode out of the restaurant ten minutes later on the balls of her feet. She wore a wide scoop-neck sweater that fell off one shoulder and nearly draped to her knees.

She scraped back a chair, took a seat, and planted her flag next to mine. Order 88.

"How long have you worked with Demos?" I asked her.

"There's this new word. It's called hello."

"Hello. How long have you worked for Demos?"

"How long have you've been drinking before noon?"

"Ever since your sexually ambivalent friend flashed me a picture of my wife walking out of a building. Have you met Denise?"

"I have. I told you Demos was a maximalist."

"The breadth of the definition escaped me. You had fun with it, didn't you?"

"Don't be a fool. I didn't know he had pictures of Kathleen."

"Why not just tell me?"

"Would it have been nearly the experience?"

Good point.

She continued. "Demos has an off-the-charts IQ. He bores easily. Likes games. Denise is a game he plays with himself."

"Or is Demos a game for Denise?"

"I doubt she, or he, knows."

"I think your friend's capable of great violence."

"Oh, I know he is. And he's not my friend."

"Looks like it from where I sit."

"You need to change chairs."

I asked her for a little backstory on her and Demos. How she started working for him. She explained that she met him at an art show in LA a little over two years ago. That they bumped into each other a few times since then.

"He's been linked to several violent acts," she continued, "and possibly one murder but never charged. And I don't work for him. I'm a freelance consultant. I help establish authenticity, or lack thereof, and help evaluate buyers. I've worked on a few pieces with him. He's moved other paintings but nothing the value of the Dali."

"You said you knew he was capable of violence."

"He sliced off the ear of a person who was competing with

him for a piece of art. The van Gogh message was back off, and you can keep your remaining ear."

"And the murder?"

She paused. She cast her eyes down and then up at me. "A woman. She did some business with Demos. Thought he was legitimate. When she found out he wasn't, she did the right thing and tried to expose him. She's not been seen since."

"No body, no crime."

"Bullshit. He did it," Charley punched out with anger, and I wondered what was behind it.

"He or Karl?'

"Does it matter? The woman who tried to expose him? There were others. The end is always the same. It's the method that changes. A drowning. A car accident. A drive-by shooting attributed to a turf war, but there was no turf war. Nick Harris is but one in a long list of those who drew a bad card and crossed paths with Demos. Denise. Karl. The rest of the freak show."

A waitress stopped by. Her T-shirt read "Surrender Dorothy." I checked the sky for flying monkeys—they're nearly as creepy as clowns. She dropped a black bean salad in front of Charley and took her flag. Since when did 88 come before 84? Surrender Dorothy returned a moment later with my grouper sandwich. I asked for ketchup for my fries.

"No problem."

Well, I hope not.

"Who's the chicken and the egg here?" I asked Charley.

She waited until she was done chewing. "I don't follow."

"Who first learned of the Dali?"

"That would be me."

"Through Carrie?" I said but wished I hadn't led her.

"Yes. At Repose Gallery. I keep tabs on a lot of galleries. Repose has a reputation. Nothing major, so this was a bit of a surprise. When my contact called and said Carrie showed up with her wild tale about an early Dali, I reached out to Demos. He has a big appetite and bigger connections."

"Your contact?"

"My contact."

Something in her wording seemed off, but it slipped away. I asked her what was in it for her.

"I'm strictly a finder's fee girl. Easy money. Nominal risk."

"Good business model."

"And I bloody well know it. I don't steal. I don't harm. I facilitate the movement of rare pieces of art. You'd be shocked how much of what you've seen has a checkered past. But I've never intentionally represented a piece I believed was fraudulent or recently stolen."

"You rely on the statute of limitations to absolve you of guilt?"

"If it was lifted two generations ago, it's fair play."

"What's it like surfing the world for your finder's fees? Beholden to your little lies that, because of the passage of time, no one's hurt by your efforts."

"You think that white picket fence is who you are? Look at you. Blindly pursuing money. Searching for a missing painting that to date has left one person dead."

"It's for a good cause. And that death isn't on me."

"Good to know."

Surrender Dorothy arrived with ketchup, pausing our verbal fencing. I positioned my plate between us. I'm a huge proponent of fry diplomacy. Charley considered the offering. She snatched a fry. Then another. Her eyes raised to mine. Cicero, this was before Mark Antony beheaded him, said the eyes are the interpreters of the soul or something like that. Charley's dark, liquid eyes reminded me of the choral music I used to hear in church before my family disintegrated. The sense of belonging, of wholesomeness that it bestowed. There was something unadulterated about her. Like Stacey

Remington ordering spaghetti. I sensed she wanted to keep that part hidden, tucked away for reasons unknown. I perceived similar overtones in myself, but we're not going there.

"Why did you want to meet me?" I said, breaking my reverie.

"He'll cut your throat without hesitation."

"Thanks for the hot tip."

She picked up her fork and stabbed a piece of lettuce. "Don't be an ass. I'm not against you."

"If he's so violent, why hang with him? I'm sure the rip-off art world is big enough for the both of you without having to work together."

"Better yet, be an ass. You're good at it. I got my reasons."

We were silent for a beat, each retreating to our corner.

"I appreciate your concerns," I said, offering an olive branch.

"I'm acting in your interest, despite your pigheaded inability to see that."

Her words struck a chord. Was I acting toward Charley as Carrie was acting toward me? I reached for my beer but only nudged it, repositioning it on the table by a few meaningless inches.

"There's a rumor out there," she said.

"Oh?"

"Last time I talked with Carrie, she told me Nick was approached by some sort of family member. Perhaps someone who knew of the Dali and wanted to keep it in the family. She's afraid he facilitated a quick sale."

"She told me the same," I admitted. "But she was vague, claiming that Nick died before he revealed anything specific."

"You believe her?"

"I do."

Her breath escaped her. "Unfortunately, the possibility that the Dali is long gone will not temper Demos's enthusiasm for it."

I flirted with telling her about Veronica's daughter but, as with Demos, decided to keep that tidbit to myself. I didn't fully trust Charley and her Swiss-cheese history. I asked her why Demos was so desperate. Who or what was chasing him?

"He owes money. To people who, like him, will use a person's ear to convey a message. He sees you as both a threat to outbid him and to steal it out from under him. Yet he wants you around in the event you find it before he does."

"He's undecided."

That earned a sly smile.

I said, "And if I find it first, he'll swipe it from me."

"Deploying any necessary means."

We pretended to pay attention to our food, knowing we were each contemplating what to say next. I didn't totally buy Charley's earlier explanation of how she'd learned about the Dali. I tried to rewind my mind to her previous comment that had sounded off-key, but it wasn't there. But that wasn't the source of my next question. Not by a long shot. Demos made a mistake flashing the picture of Kathleen at me. Transgressions must be punished. That's in those children's books, right?

"Can you set up another meeting with Demos?" I asked her.

"Why? So you can cause trouble?"

"Can you?"

"I'll try," she said, her eyes welded to mine. "What do I tell him?"

"Tell him I want to work with him. Bang out the details."

"Why *do* you want to meet him again?"

"I got my reasons."

She gave that a few seconds.

"Want some advice? Go back to your picket fence. None of this is worth it."

"I can't locate Carrie."

"Did you hear me?"

"Did you hear me?"

"Neither can I."

"If she shows up floating in Tampa Bay, is that covered by your finder's fee?"

She abruptly stood. "Would it justify your blood-nose for money? I've said what I came here to say."

She huffed away, leaving me staring at beer I no longer wanted and never really wanted, so why did I order it?

My updated rate card: five million dollars a day. But for some reason, that thought only depressed me. Would any of it really matter in the end? David Hume said the life of man is of no greater importance to the universe than that of an oyster. So why the struggle? The worry? Because this oyster refused to believe he was just another oyster. Wanted to believe that ten million dollars could help a lot of other oysters. In the dignity of a roof over a person's head.

Here's a break: my truck was still there.

CHAPTER 35

I sequestered myself in the study with a bag of Goldfish crackers and opened my laptop.

Birth records in Florida are confidential for one hundred years from the date of birth. They are only available to parents, legal guardians, and those who have been granted access by a court order. I could find no information on a Jamie Stafford, Jamie Fredericks, or any Jamie that might be related to Veronica and Michael. Yet Sally Herrington was positive that Veronica and Michael had a child. Faye Wilkinson had also indicated as much. Carrie confessed to both Charley and me that Nick was approached by some sort of family member about acquiring the Dali.

I called Wetzel and demanded that I be permitted to talk with Veronica before she returned—batty or not. He refused. I told him I was no longer interested in his game. He replied that that had always been my prerogative, and "Is there anything else I can do for you?" The more I talked to that man, the less I liked him. The less I liked him, the more I begrudgingly respected him.

I buzzed Sally Herrington and inquired if she had recalled

anything after I left that might help. She did add that Michael, while unwilling to offer a greater explanation concerning his relationship with his daughter, had been adamant that it "isn't what you think." Sally said that at one time, she'd considered that Veronica and Michael had adopted a girl or maybe financially supported a young woman. Upon my questioning, she said she knew of no one who could help corroborate the story or add insight. I didn't believe that last part but had no choice.

A little more research revealed that the art world was as fraudulent as it was legitimate. It was not unusual for even museums to be victims of fraud. The FBI had, just a few years before, raided the Orlando Museum of Art, seizing twenty-five works that had been part of a Jean-Michel Basquiat exhibit called *Heroes and Monsters*. The paintings were said to have been discovered in 2012 in a Los Angeles storage unit. But one of the paintings was done on the back of a FedEx shipping box. The label on the box was not used by the company until after Basquiat's death. More recently, a Vermeer, *Girl with a Flute*, which hangs at the National Gallery of Art, was deemed to have been painted by one of Vermeer's students. While I had no reason to believe that *The Missing Body* was fraudulent, what if it was? What if I was pursuing a worthless piece of canvas? What's that line from a Bee Gees song? If I'd only seen that the joke was on me.

I even investigated Wayne Gibson, the comptroller at Rollins College. If you were the steward of a missing multimillion-dollar painting, would you sit idly by when someone not in your employ searched for it? Rambler's warning rang in my head. *Someone's yanking your chain. You know that, right?* But Gibson seemed clean.

Charley called as I was pushing away from my computer. My eyes were weary, my back complaining about lack of movement.

"Demos agreed to meet you," she said. "Arnie's Steakhouse on Thirty-Fourth. Nine tonight."

"Demos or Denise?"

"I haven't a clue."

"I appreciate you doing this."

"Then you didn't hear a word I said when we met."

I called Garrett and told him we were on for that evening. That we'd created opportunity. I can't be certain, but I think he grunted in anticipation. We disconnected, and I reached into the bag of Goldfish crackers for something that was no longer there.

CHAPTER 36
VERONICA

1974

Mobil, Eastern U.S.

They decided on a road trip. One final blast of glory on America's pulsating asphalt artery. Where the day's sole destination would be a motel that you check into in name only. For the uncountable miles have made you a different person, a traveler-empty version of yourself. Part of you was shaved off with each numbing mile, until you are a vacant vessel, waiting to be filled by new experience. Your senses amplified, your current life suspended.

They'd been discussing where to go, the lack of money constraining their imaginations. Veronica mentioned her family had a cabin.

"It's in Ellicottville, New York," she said. "My grandfather bought it eons ago. Some of my first memories are there. But it's not an easy place to reach. We can drive forever or fly to Buffalo, Cleveland, or Pittsburg and rent a car.

"It's nothing fancy," she added. "My grandfather liked to ski, both downhill and cross country. A ski resort, Holiday Valley, is there and some other one I can never remember. Holly something. The cabin's five minutes from Ellicottville, which is a nice town. I want to take our child there. She'll be the fourth generation of Staffords to set foot on the property."

"Or he."

"Or he."

"Is it really called Holiday Valley?"

"It is."

"Far out."

Michael went to his car, which was parked on the street. He came back a moment later and spread a map, Mobil, Eastern U.S., on the kitchen table. One-third of the United States laid out next to the metal napkin holder and salt and pepper shakers that needed cleaning.

"Here." Veronica pointed at a place on the map a little south of Buffalo and off the eastern reach of Lake Erie.

Michael studied the map. The roads looked like the artwork of a demented spider. No symmetry. No pattern. He found small-print Ellicottville surrounded by equally insignificant crossroad towns. Ashford. Sugartown. Maples. Little Valley. Great Valley, which certainly was not.

"It's in the middle of frickin' nowhere," he exclaimed.

"It's free. I'm at four months. Let's go before we talk ourselves out of it. Before I can't sit for over twenty minutes. Besides, there's a lot to do in the middle of frickin' nowhere."

Veronica thought her last comment sounded like something Michael would say. She wondered if, after decades together, they would absorb each other's patterns of thoughts and mannerisms. Hadn't she read that somewhere?

They left two days later. Four a.m. Michael tossing in a book he'd just bought by an author he'd not read before.

Michael had installed an under-the-dash eight-track player in his 1968 two-door Bonneville. It was Veronica's job to feed the machine. During the Hollies' "He Ain't Heavy, He's My Brother," the eight-track would change right before "brother," creating, "He ain't heavy, he's my"—*ker-chunk*—"brother." They played it over and over, singing along with the song, timing the *ker-chunk* perfectly. They made up a brother for Michael—he had no siblings—and christened him Ker-Chunk. Decided that Ker-Chunk had a great sense of humor and was currently a junior at Stanford studying physics. And then Veronica thought this: If Ker-Chunk was humorous, would he really be studying physics at Stanford?

They rolled into the driveway a little after eleven, the crunch of tires on gravel telling them that asphalt roads only take you so far. They were too tired to do anything other than collapse into bed.

The next morning, Michael fixed a stoic cup of coffee and stepped out to the back deck. It fronted a small lake ringed with colored leaves that told of the coming nakedness of winter. It was worth every mindless-mile minute. Every *ker-chunk*, every hairpin curve, every filthy restroom. The air was fresh. Cool. While each mile was inconsequential, collectively, they had repositioned him on the globe.

Veronica came up behind him, wrapped in a checkered blanket. In her youth, her mother had called any patterned blanket an Indian blanket, but in this case, it was. It had been purchased at a nearby shop from a Seneca woman. The Seneca were one of six tribes of the Iroquois Confederacy who believed they had the right to live and hunt on the land before being informed, by men with gunpowder, that their world was finished.

They stood side by side, their faces to the lake, their youthful, buoyant hearts beating life.

"What do you think?" she asked nervously. It had been a long haul.

"I love it."

"Are you just saying that?"

He turned and faced her. "You, we, can use it anytime?"

"My father spent the summers of his youth here. He'll never sell it. He pays a local man to look after it. He begs me to use it, but it's not convenient. Inconvenient as hell, actually."

"Our kids will love it here."

"You think?" Veronica said, the future rising in her voice.

"Absolutely. You get something like this, you don't let it go. No matter the effort to get here. Hike in the summer and fall and ski in the winter."

"But you don't ski."

"Don't hike either. But it's time for both."

"Like buying a hammer?"

"Like buying a hammer."

They spent the afternoon ducking in and out of local shops in Ellicottville. They loitered in front of one store, its display window arranged with children's clothing and books. Veronica entered it as if drawn in by a magnet. They emerged twenty minutes later with a blue monkey stuffy and a cloth book they would misplace and never see again. Having exhausted the small town's offerings, they decided to see a matinee before seeking dinner.

The old theater in the town no longer played first-run movies. At best, it snatched something from the past ten years. That month, on Thursdays, Fridays, and Saturdays, it was showing *The Thomas Crowne Affair* with Steve McQueen and Faye Dunaway. Veronica and Michael watched it with twelve other people. He ate popcorn. She was unapologetically selfish with her box of Junior Mints.

"I don't get it," Veronica said as they strolled out of the theater, hand in hand.

He dropped his popcorn cup in a lidless trash can. He held out his free hand to her. She gave him the empty box of Junior Mints. He tossed it in the can. He missed. They decoupled as he bent down, picked up the box, and plopped it in the can. They eagerly joined hands again as if the brief reprise had stretched them to intolerable endurance.

"Get what?" he said.

"I can't believe I ate that whole box. The song. 'The Windmills of Your Mind.' It plays when he's hang gliding, but what does it mean?"

"Nothing."

"Nothing?"

Michael said, "He can't decide whether to go ahead with the plan or not. You know, the big heist. Stealing the painting. He's trying to clear his mind by flying. Getting above it all. But nothing comes to him. It's just as confusing above the clouds as it is underneath them. They put the song in to show that."

"How did you get that from the movie?"

"Didn't. I read about it."

"Cheater."

"But it makes sense, don't you see? Searching for answers doesn't mean you'll find them. The windmills just go round and round. Like the number eight. No beginning. No end."

"Uh-huh. What else did the article say?"

"About the movie? Not much. It was mostly about Faye Dunaway."

Faye.

"It's a pretty song," she said, trying to keep her mind in the present. "But I don't know if I like it. It's too haunting."

"That's why it sticks with you."

"Maybe I don't like things to stick to me."

Michael said nothing. But his silence, his willingness to drop a subject, and by dropping it, leaving it open, often frustrated Veronica. It agitated her that he seemed so comfortable, so accepting of matters she struggled to understand.

They found a tavern and ordered a pair of burgers and a Molson's. They shared the beer and then ordered a second. The back counter of the bar was stuffed with knickknacks. A small plastic Elvis. Big Bird. Jesus. GI Joe. GI Jane. Someone had painted her tits pink. Beer signs: Genesee. Iron City. Frankenmuth. ("If you like your beer hearty . . . you're in for the heartiest treat of your life.") Black-and-white pictures of smiling people on the slopes. Their clothing thick and puffy. Their skis long and skinny.

"Let's come every year," Veronica said as they walked back to the Bonneville. It was slippery and Michael had a firm grasp on her arm. "I'd forgotten how brilliant the colors are. Florida's nice, but there's more to the world than green."

They assured each other they would. Come every year. But a tissue has a better chance against a bonfire than the fervent promises of the young ever have of coming true when ambushed by advancing years.

The temperature had fallen rapidly while they were in the bar. The Bonneville was a ghost-mobile crusted in a white layer of frost. Michael opened the door for her. She sat down. The vinyl seat was cold, and she put her hands under her. The trip back to the cabin was too short for the Bonneville's heater to even make a statement. Veronica felt as if she'd be cold forever. She thought of how hot it was when she and Faye showered together. She tried to get it out of her mind, but she couldn't. She wished Michael had never mentioned her name, but she knew it wasn't his fault.

They left two days later. South of Pittsburg, as Michael jostled with semitrailers, Veronica blurted out they'd left the blue monkey on the shelf.

"He'll be waiting for us next year," Michael promised. "It will come soon enough."

CHAPTER 37

Arnie's Steakhouse was a single-story, nearly windowless cinder block building. Two tiresome streetlights ambered the wide asphalt parking lot. A dull, dusty-pink neon sign stood by the edge of the road. It was missing a few letters. It looked like this:

A NIE'S TEA HOUSE

We stepped through the front door—a battleship-gray piece of metal more suited for a bank vault—into a large dining room with dark-paneled walls. The two front windows had heavy curtains rendering them meaningless. A bar ran across the back, its dozen stools vacant. But the restaurant was clean, which gave it a comfortable, even cozy feel.

"We close at nine," a woman said, irritated that we were there. She was wrapping silverware in napkins. She didn't bother with more than a quick glance at us. "If you want food, you need to order right away, but I don't think the kitchen is gonna be very happy."

"We're just here to grab a drink," I assured her. I wondered why Demos had chosen the place if it closed soon.

"Suit yourself."

Garrett and I took a table facing the front door. I went to the bar and ordered a whiskey and a water for Garrett.

Karl came through the door at 8:55, followed by Demos and Flat Top behind him. Karl went to the only table that had customers. He said a few words. They nodded. Thanked him. They stood and hastened out the door. Karl dropped a bill on the table. The waitress locked the door behind them. She never acknowledged Demos and his entourage. She exited the room through the swinging door to the kitchen. She did not return, and I knew why Demos had selected Arnie's.

Karl grabbed a chair and scraped it over to our table. Demos sat down on it across from me. He was black on black tonight. But the cosmetic-counter perfume was still there, as were the rouged cheeks. And the soulless eyes, reminding me that despite what someone wears, their colors stay the same.

"Where's Denise?" I said.

"She won't be joining us. It's getting too intense for her taste." Demos kept his eyes on me but jutted his chin at Garrett. "Who's your friend?"

I ignored his question. "Do you know where Carrie is?"

"Like Denise, she won't be joining us tonight."

"Did you ever consider what happens if you kill all your sources, or are you too stupid for that?"

"I'm not interested in harming anyone, despite your nagging accusations. I merely want the Dali. I can get top price for it. Make it worthwhile for all of us."

I nudged my chair back. I told him that my buyer thought we'd hit a dead end. That Demos couldn't deliver. That he might back out.

He nodded at Garrett. "I don't think you'd bring in muscle if you're contemplating retreating."

"He's a local chef. We're just scouting the competition."

"I did not come here to chew fat."

"Why are you here?" As I spoke, I planted my feet evenly

apart. Neither Karl nor Flat Top moved. I wasn't worried about Garrett. He slept with three eyes open.

Demos eyed me warily. "I believe you are the one who initiated the meeting."

That's right, Demos-head. And my reason had nothing to do with Dali. But I might as well see what I could get out of this basket case before the main event.

I said, "Carrie told me someone had been in contact with Nick prior to his death. She claims not to know who."

Demos nodded. "She told me that as well. That it's possible Harris moved the painting without telling her. Even if he moved it, I believe the painting to be worth far more to my contacts than he likely would have sold it for."

"Let her go. She's told you everything she knows."

"I will be the one who determines that. If I had her, of course." He leaned in across the table. "It would be most unfortunate if someone has already purchased it, and you came into possession of such information and chose not to share it with me. I know people. Can pay you well."

"I know a few people myself."

"We both know my contacts are far more cultivated than yours." He downshifted the tempo of his speech. "You need to appreciate the risk created by your stubborn insistence on uncooperating."

"And you need to appreciate the risk that accompanies threatening people."

Demos eyed Garrett. Garrett's hands were on the table, spaced evenly apart. I'm pretty sure he wasn't breathing.

"Don't," I said.

"Excuse me?"

"Start something that will end badly for you."

Demos hesitated and then broke into his signature non-laugh. "I like you, Mr. Jake Travis. You're a little . . . unfinished.

Like a painting where the artist has lost interest and walked away. But I like you. Your wife. Your chil—"

Garrett vaulted out of his chair. He wrapped his arm around Demos's head. He drew a knife and pressed it against Demos's throat. I sprang to my feet just as Karl grabbed his gun. I gave him a swift kick. He went down but held on to the gun. Flat Top took a wild swing at me. I hit him in his solar plexus. He doubled over. I twisted my foot on Karl's hand, snatched his gun, and took a step back. Karl sprang to his feet, eyes raging.

"I was just commenting," Demos said, "that I do not understand why a family man like you is in this business." His voice smooth despite the presence of the stainless-steel knife against his throat. "I assure you, I am no threat to your family. I am not that type of man."

I stuck my face in his.

"You won't see us coming next time. Understand?"

"I apologize for my insensitivity."

"Do you understand?"

Garrett's knife drew blood.

"Yes. But again, I am not that type of man."

"No, but you're that type of woman."

"She is more interested in baking shows," Demos moaned. "You've made your point."

Garrett withdrew his knife. Demos hesitated, as if he didn't want to show weakness, but then rubbed his neck. I handed Karl's gun to Garrett. He kept it aimed at Karl. Flat Top was still bent over, gasping for air.

"Carrie Crowlings is a dreamer," I said. "Let her go. She can't help you."

"If you care so much for her, bring me the Dali."

"I don't have it, and I'm not your Dorothy."

"Oh, but you'd make such a good one. You and your friend. We both know the painting was in the possession of Veronica

Stafford. We cannot locate her. Not that it matters. Her husband, Nick Harris, took it. It is possible he unloaded it faster than anyone thought. Do you know of any family members of Veronica?"

"No," I lied, still unwilling to share what I knew with this sleazeball. Then, to see if he would reveal his source, not that I would believe him, I added, "Why do you ask?"

He shrugged. "Carrie said the picture might have stayed in the family. She said Harris told her he made a mistake. She thinks he realized the foolishness of not attempting to get the highest price."

"Any names?"

"No."

"Why pay yourself for something you already possess?"

"It does stump me."

"Let her go," I repeated.

"I will not harm her. I assured her that she will be compensated when I find the Dali. I tell you this to impress upon you that we can work together. If you find it first, bring it to me. We will both walk away happy."

Flat Top straightened out. He took up position a few paces on the other side of Demos, away from Karl. For the record, I had no doubt that Demos intended to cut me and Carrie out once he had the Dali. "Cut out" covers a broad and expansive spectrum of silencing people. Sort of like Charley referring to Demos as a "maximalist."

Demos was not denying that he had Carrie. Yet he kept insisting that he had nothing to do with the death of Nick Harris. Well, murder was a tad more serious offense, but kidnapping was not child's play. Yet, for a man fond of games, he refused to be drawn into one concerning the last day of Nick Harris. But if Demos had not killed Nick Harris, or attempted to as Harris died of a heart attack, who had? Was it possible—?

"Mr. Travis?"

"Yes?"

"I said I will honor my words. We can work together or apart. But work against me and you will not be so lucky."

"You think luck has anything to do with this?"

"You won't see us coming next time." He cocked his head at me. "I did get that right, didn't I?"

He turned and swaggered toward the door. Karl pointed a fat finger at me, squeezed an invisible trigger, and followed his lord and master.

Veronica Stafford was due back in thirty-six hours.

CHAPTER 38

VERONICA

1975

A riddle from the pharaohs

It was two months before her due date. Before two became three.

They secured a used crib. Diapers. A small dresser for baby clothes that Michael picked up at a flea market for ten bucks. Veronica didn't like it because the top drawer got stuck. Michael switched it with the bottom drawer. He hung pictures. Used the hammer. Veronica bought seven books on raising children. She read them all, the yellow highlighted passages a testament to her scholastic approach in her forthcoming role.

Jamie was born under the Aquarian full moon. The first three months were organized hell. Michael had gotten a full-time teaching job, and Veronica, for the life of her, could not fathom any joy in having a baby. The highlight of her day was when Michael burst through the door. He took over for her, walking Jamie in his arms. Singing her to sleep every night. She resented his natural ability to calm their child. The same love he gave her, he now showered upon their daughter. While that heavenly trait endeared him to her, it also irritated her. Made her jealous. And then she was ashamed of being jealous. Around and around swirled her cocktails of emotions. She'd underlined that as well—in her seven books. She'd belatedly admitted that underlining a passage did not necessarily translate into understanding it.

Then Jamie smiled.

Timid at first. Infrequent. Then broader. At every smile, Veronica became more relaxed. More natural. More Michael.

At nine months, on a Sunday morning, Michael rose from bed and returned with their infant daughter. He placed her under his raised legs. They read the *Times*. Listened to Crosby, Stills, and Nash. Linda Ronstadt tugging their hearts in "Long Long Time." Veronica: "It's still too syrupy for my taste." The Stones' "She's a Rainbow." The coffee grew cold. Unnoticed, the hour hand slipped past noon.

They packed up Jamie and ventured into the world. Now, instead of being surprised that the world existed beyond them, they were eager to surprise the world. *Look what we did. Just look!*

Sometime during that non-September start of a new year, Michael noticed that the snow globe was Sahara dry. He picked it up to throw it away. But he couldn't, foolish sentimentality often tripping his steps. He placed it back on the shelf. Without the water, the flakes looked frail and brittle. The trees desolate. Yet he saw beauty in it, like his painting that Veronica had admired when they first met. That painting was wrapped in a closet. He still hadn't told her what it was of. That he would one day paint another one, even more lifelike than his first attempt, was something he realized only at the end. He would never see his opus. That would be for another man.

A riddle from the pharaohs: How can an artist with perfect eyesight finish a painting but never see it?

CHAPTER 39

The girls were asleep when I got home from Arnie's. Kathleen and I settled on the screened porch, the moon taking a peek over the horizon as if it were actually contemplating whether or not to appear. I filled Kathleen in on my day. She seemed distracted, more focused on the candle then my words. Knucklehead that I am, I plowed through. After I finished and while thinking of how Veronica's daughter might have circled back into her life, I realized I'd done all the talking.

I asked Kathleen about her day.

"I told the school I'll do one class a semester. Starting now."

"Did I hear you right?"

"Did you hear that I'm cutting back?"

"I did."

"Then you heard me right."

Kathleen lived to teach. To discuss with others the literary themes that frame our lives. I recalled her comment the first night we'd met Charley. *I'm raising two daughters.* I thought at the time that it was a statement that an observant husband should pay attention to. But in my quest to find the Dali, this nonobservant husband had not taken the time or made the effort to follow through. We're never the rock stars we think we are.

I said, "You can do that on such short notice?"

"Not really. They weren't too happy. But I banked on a piece of advice you gave me years ago."

"Drink like you give a damn?"

"No. But that's a dandy. Better to beg forgiveness than ask permission."

"Talk to me."

"It's easy," she said with an uncharacteristic shrug. "My time with our daughters is far more rewarding, important, than whatever I do away from them."

"And balance?"

When we'd adopted Sophia, we discussed the need for balance. But it's a tricky word. Its definition more a work of art than a signed constitution.

"Even when I'm in the classroom, I'm not there," Kathleen said. "I stare out the window. Words on pages no longer hold meaning, let alone any magic. I wonder what the girls are doing. We've outsourced our daughters to Bonita and there's not a finer person for the job. But I want that job. Not job. That life. To enjoy the impermanence of the days. One course a semester will keep me in the game."

"How far will you cut Bonita's hours?"

"None. I'm also enrolling in an art class."

Kathleen was a gifted sketch artist with a talent I always thought worth nurturing. But that is the opinion of one who struggles with stick figures. Still, I was a little taken back by her sudden coming about.

I said, "You're on a roll. Am I safe?"

"You survived the first round."

"It's because I cook, right?"

"Doesn't hurt."

"And your condo?" I said, sensing a gentle earthquake in

our lives. Mr. Tuned-in here.

Kathleen, before we married, lived in a downtown condo. Going back to when we first met, she lived on the island across from me. That was when she lied to me about almost everything, had a different name than she does now, and died.

You should probably know about this.

Her first husband had been murdered over his knowledge of mob finance in Chicago—her hometown. Afraid that she knew enough to incarcerate them, they went gunning for her. Garrett and I left four dead on the beaches of Fort De Soto. As insurance that they wouldn't try that stunt again—and so she wouldn't spend the remainder of her life fearing a knock on the door—we staged her death and granted her a new last name. Colonel Janssen was instrumental in securing her a new identity as well as a Jane Doe corpse. As I said earlier, I later broke off the relationship with Janssen, but it doesn't escape me that he was the right man at the right time.

North of Chicago, where summer occasionally fails to make an arrival, rests a grave marker with the name Kathleen Cunningham etched in it. We don't discuss it much. I often wonder if that's a mistake, but it seems such a serious issue, and who's ever up for that?

The condo.

Kathleen sold her island home and embraced city living. Within a fifteen-minute stroll of her front door were over fifty restaurants, bars, and coffee shops. Six museums. Concert halls and spacious waterfront parks that held a continuous rotation of art shows and markets. After we married, we kept her condo as a weekend getaway. This arrangement infused our lives with the best of both worlds: laid-back beach living and the stimulating lifestyle of the city. Over the past two years, we'd used it less, the hassle of moving the family there for forty-eight hours not worth the effort. We'd discussed selling it but had never reached a decision, which was totally hers to make.

Kathleen said, "I'm listing it. With Stacey."

"My strawberry girlfriend?

"You said she needed a listing to get her career going. Why not help her?"

I asked her what she planned to do with her books. She had converted one of the bedrooms into a Trinity College library.

"You're building an addition so I can replicate it here."

"*That's* why you're keeping me on the payroll."

"You're a fast one."

"How long has this been percolating?"

"Long."

"Well, I'm glad I was able to be a sounding board and help you navigate these important decisions in your life."

She stood, stepped over to me, and plopped on my lap. She's always been a lap sitter. It's one of those junior-high moves, reason 3, that dynamites my heart. She positioned herself and tilted back her head.

"Knowing you support me is more important than being involved. I needed to decide. Place old me next to who I am today. Examine my life. What is relevant. What demands change. What to keep. What to let go."

"You know this is legions over my head."

"The art classes will take less than half the time I'm dropping from teaching. I'll pick up twice as much time as I spend with the girls now."

"And that's advanced math for you."

"And don't I know it, buddy. I told Bonita."

"Before me?"

"Naturally."

"Of course. Is she on board?"

"Thrilled. She said she hated to see me leave in the mornings. That she knew it was hard for me."

"Do I need to ask about Morgan?"

She rubbed her chin. "I might have bounced it off him as

well." She spoke with a tinge of—allow me the liberty of adding my apparently meaningless, and certainly unsought, opinion—deserved guilt.

"You're just me," she said, as if I were broadcasting my thoughts.

I clawed my hand through her hair. But sometimes touching only reminds us that we are separate. That no matter how hard we try, all we do is feel the thin outer layer. The inside forever beyond our reach.

Kathleen said, "Bonita's worried about you."

"Bonita knows my name?"

"I didn't say that," Kathleen said with a guileful smile. "She thinks you're energy without direction. That you and Morgan are drifting away from each other, and that's not good for you."

"Bonita said this?"

"Yes, sir."

"It's not you talking?"

"Absolutely not, sir."

"Insightful person, that Bonita is."

"Yes. Lucky to have her, we are."

"Tell me, Yoda, why the Bonita angle?"

She twiddled some hair behind my ear. "It's fun. And, in your preoccupation with the Dali, you haven't been listening. I told you Morgan was less enthralled than you with your quest."

"I spoke to him the next morning."

"Oh babe, we're talking listening, not talking."

"What am I supposed to do? Turn my back on ten million dollars?"

She pecked me on the cheek. "I would. But you'd be nuts to. You need to do this, and I'm your number-one cheerleader."

"One way or the other, it's over in two days," I said, eager to end the conversation that was spinning nowhere.

"What's your plan when you're done searching?"

I had no answer for her. That was why she asked the question. Kathleen was the conductor of our lives. The baton bearer who kept the disparate parts graceful, fluid, and in harmony. And I? I was a rover, the third-chair Wrecking Crew trumpet player who, in one note, could blare out the entire ensemble. Everyone knows when the trumpet player screws up.

AT 4:29, AFTER BEING taunted by sleep for hours, I got out of bed. I couldn't shake Kathleen's sudden coming about. Her sacred grasp of the present, her innate ability to capture the days while I lost the years.

I went to the study where Kathleen had me hang the picture of the four women. I stared at it for a long time. New picture: a man looking at four women. I glanced outside to the street. All was quiet, but Garrett was up and watching. He, Morgan, and I had worked out a schedule. I hadn't shared that with Kathleen as I didn't want to worry her. Rambler also said he'd have a marked car cruise the neighborhood several times during the night.

I left the study and went to the girls' room. The wall was decorated with pelicans and egrets. Turtles and gulls. I sat in the cushioned rocking chair, the whole world in the room. The whole world still. I recalled from my school days the last two stanzas of Longfellow's poem "The Children's Hour":

I have you fast in my fortress,
And will not let you depart,
But put you down into the dungeon
In the round-tower of my heart.
And there I will keep you forever,
Yes, forever and a day,
Till the walls shall crumble to ruin,
And moulder in the dust away!

CHAPTER 40

The following morning found me at low tide. The clock was ticking. The rebel minutes stepping out of time and accelerating their pace. All my efforts in finding the Dali had amounted to nothing. Less than nothing.

After my morning run, and another shampooless shower, I hit Seabreeze for breakfast. I grabbed a backless stool at the counter. The open windows gathered in the scent of water and the growl of outboard engines as boats churned Pass-a-Grille Channel. I ordered two over easy, dry wheat, crisp bacon, hash browns drowned in onions, and coffee from a waitress I didn't recognize. It came piled on a plastic plate that had suffered years of utensil abuse. It is my experience that all good breakfasts come on plastic plates, and the more scratched, the more chipped and faded, the better the breakfast. A man next to me tried to start a conversation. My lack of participation did not defuse his yammering. I took a gulp of good cheap coffee, and the world seemed a better place.

I left a twenty on the shellacked counter, slipped off the stool, and drove to Harbor House. I labored there for hours. I prepped the back porch that needed a new layer of paint. I installed a new garbage disposal. Reattached a gutter and downspout I had repaired less than two years ago. My previous attempt had failed because the wood was rotting. We needed new siding. Preferably a composite material that would withstand the harsh elements of the west coast of Florida. Trouble was, it was bank-breaking expensive.

A few days ago, I didn't feel as if I could go to Harbor House. Now, I didn't feel like I deserved to go home, and Harbor House was the only place where I had value. But that reeks of self-pity, and I don't tolerate that feeling.

After I checked in with Morgan, I headed over to the pink palace less than a mile from my house to try and get away from it all. Sometimes we travel great distances and go nowhere. Other times, we barely move yet cover great distance. I was aiming for the latter.

The hotel was built in the 1920s by an Irishman from Virginia, was named after a character in a play by a French dramatist that was turned into an English opera, and is set in a town named for its Russian counterpart. I keep thinking there's a lesson there, but if so, like those answers on the beach, it remains beyond my grasp.

Here's ironic trivia. In 1940, the Irishman who built the hotel suffered a fatal heart attack in the lobby of his dreams. We lifted his last name, Rowe, for Kathleen's new last name after we staged her death. Credit for suggesting the surname goes to Morgan.

The missing Dali slipped from my mind as I took a seat at the outdoor bar with a swimming pool on either side. Muted TVs in the corner of the ceiling showed replays from football games. A water Pilates class was in session in the shallow end of the north pool, and the air was teased with food and sunscreen and the squeaky voices of young children. Guests at Rowe Bar idled in their outdoor chairs, stretching time beyond reason.

I pretended to think. Who knows? It might actually work one day. First up: Charley. Some of her comments kept coming back to me. *I keep tabs on a lot of galleries. I contacted Demos.* But like a name you can't recall, I couldn't resolve the source of my puzzlement. I tabled her. Next up was Demos. His continual insistence that he had nothing to do with—

My phone rang. It was Wayne Gibson. I'd just taken the first bite from a cheeseburger.

"Mr.Gibson."

"Any progress in finding our friend?" he asked.

I quickly swallowed. "Nothing hard."

"Certainly, something."

I took a sip of iced tea.

"Mr. Travis? Am I interrupting you?"

"There's a cast of misfit toys each professing not to have the Dali," I said. "It's possible that Nick Harris sold it before he died. It's also possible that whoever tried to kill him didn't get the information they were looking for."

"What makes you suggest that?"

"The cause of death was a heart attack, not a bullet."

"I see," Gibson said. "Might it have slipped through our grasp?"

"It was never in our grasp. Does the name Jamie Stafford, or Jamie Fredericks, mean anything to you?"

"No. Should they?"

I told him there was noise about keeping the Dali in the family. That Jamie was Veronica's and Michael Fredericks' daughter and that I couldn't locate her.

Gibson said, "Do you think Ms. Stafford is using us? Pretending that she wants to return the Dali to clear her conscience when in reality she has no intention of doing so?"

I'd considered that, but that thought didn't reconcile with the Veronica Stafford I'd met. Unless she totally snowed me, which is always a possibility.

"I don't see it that way," I confessed.

"Nor do I. But I'm not afraid to follow the evidence. Going forward, keep me posted."

And the day had been progressing so well.

I assured him I would, and we disconnected. Chase, the bartender, slowed down enough on the other side of the counter to ask how my lunch was. I told him it was the finest lunch on the west coast of Florida.

Back to playing PI. Earlier that morning, I'd done a little research.

Arnie's Steakhouse was owned by Parrot Cove, LLC. That LLC was owned by West Branch Industries, LLC. The only address was a post office box. West Branch owned a smattering of restaurants and bars. I had no reason to believe I'd found all the businesses owned by the two LLCs, just the easy ones. Arnie's, while a legitimate business, was likely used to launder money. The way the waitress didn't mind when Karl shooed the customers out the door. The door she immediately locked after those customers left. How she never returned.

I called Rambler. He confirmed that many of the small businesses he tied to Demos were the ones under the LLCs.

Garrett and I had discussed our plan earlier, deciding to wait until the afternoon to make sure someone was at Arnie's. They were open for dinner only. We wanted to put pressure on Demos. First, to keep him away from my family. Second, to convince him that finding the Dali was not worth the risk, and finally, to possibly save Carrie, although she should probably be moved into the number two slot. Or dropped altogether.

I'm kidding.

I couldn't look Kathleen or Morgan in the eye if the only thing that came out of my searching for the Dali was a pair of deaths, no matter how little involvement I had. Morgan, after all, had warned me that some ports should not be entered.

. . .

235

AS THE CAR IN front of me fumbled with the self-service exit gate in the hotel parking lot, I mused whether Veronica, facing that long night, was using me to find her daughter. If mother and daughter had a falling out years ago and, in some manner, the Dali was being used as emotional currency. Something about the feeling didn't fit, but some part of it seemed eminently correct.

I left another message, it would be my last, on Michael Fredericks's phone. I didn't want to tell him I was searching for a Dali. That might threaten him. Didn't want to tell him I was working with Veronica. He might put two and two together. Nor did I want him to know I was hunting his daughter. As in my previous messages, I stated that I was interested in his work at USF and to please give me a call, but by now, I knew that was not going to happen, and by the time my turn came and I inserted the card to raise the gate, only Kathleen and the girls remained in the fortress of my mind.

CHAPTER 41

A security camera hung over the back door of Arnie's Steakhouse. Garrett hugged the wall, reached up, and ripped it loose. I tried the back door. It was locked. We both went around to the front door. When we entered, a woman with battle-gear makeup said, "Honeys, we don't open till four." She was not the napkin-folding personality-starved woman of the previous night.

"We heard the head chef here is great," I said. "What's his name? Dominque?"

She crinkled her face. "You mean Lalo?"

"That's it," I said, slapping my thigh. "I knew it was something like that. We'll find a bar and come back when you're open. Mind if I hit the head first? I've been on the road."

"Bars have bathrooms."

"Ma'am, I gotta pee like a racehorse."

She tilted her head toward the rear. "Go ahead."

As Garrett sauntered out the front door, I thanked her and marched through the dimly lit dining room. The woman went about placing silverware, which had been wrapped in napkins the night before, on the tables. The restrooms were at the end of a hall, out of her sight.

I tried the door next to the restroom. It was locked. I knocked.

From inside: "Who is it?"

"Lalo."

The door cracked open. I rushed inside, closing it behind me.

"Who the hell are you?" a man demanded.

His untucked shirt ballooned over baggy pants. He had just enough hair that he should have combed it, but he didn't. None of that mattered. This did: a cluttered desk piled with paper held a pair of Goliath monitors, and I knew we'd hit pay dirt because you sure as heck don't need those twin beasts to operate A nie's tea House.

I unlocked the back door. Garrett slipped in.

"What's your name?" I asked the man.

"I said, who are you?" he demanded.

"I'm the knock on the door you knew was coming one day."

His eyes danced with nervousness.

"Parker," he said.

"What do you do for Demos, Parker?"

"I . . . I don't know who you are talking about."

"Don't lie to me, Parker."

"What do you want? Who *are* you?"

"Maybe your friend. Maybe not. That's up to you."

"Listen, I don't really know anything. I run the books, you know?"

I told him we were looking for a woman named Carrie Crowlings.

"I never heard of her."

"Tall. Likes her hair over her right shoulder. Maybe left. But all on one side. Packs an attitude. Language to shame a sailor. Have you seen her? Heard her?"

His jaw quivered. His eyes held mine with fear.

"I don't . . ."

Garrett stepped forward, towering over him. "Tell us the truth, you get back to work. If not, you're taking a ride."

"Yeah. Yeah, Okay. Sure. I might have seen her."

"When and where?" Garrett said.

"Let me check my calendar."

He took a brisk step to his desk. He sat down behind it. He started to reach under his desk. Garrett seized him by the collar and yanked him off his chair.

"Hey, what are you doing?"

I kneeled down and looked under the desk. A black button was mounted on the right side.

"Did you hit it?" I said.

"You got to understand. They'll hurt me."

"Did you hit it?" I repeated, although I didn't think he had.

"No."

"They'll never know we were here," Garrett said. "We disabled the camera. Tell us about Carrie. The woman with the hair."

"They were in two nights ago for dinner and we reviewed some stuff. I overheard that they're planning to take some woman on his boat. That if she knew, she wouldn't take it to her watery grave. I don't even know if it's your gal they were talking about."

"They discuss any other woman?" I asked.

"No."

"When's the boat ride?"

"Tonight."

"How did you get roped into this?"

"I don't know—"

"Answer the question," Garrett said.

"Okay. Easy, man. They came in here a couple years ago. Said they liked the steaks. Returned a few times. They asked me to move a little money for them. You know, add it to my deposits. Keep a slice for myself. It was that or close the door. I couldn't get any help. Worse yet, I'd hire someone, and they'd never show up after the first night. I raise my prices, and my customers bolt. Oh, and my daughter was just going to college. I needed the money."

I asked Parker if he'd picked up any chatter about a missing painting.

He shook his head. "No. I was back and forth between their table and the office. I didn't get complete sentences. Bits and pieces, you know?"

"Your best bet is to jump sides now," I advised him. "You keep slaving for Demos, you'll end up buried in concrete or behind bars. What would your daughter think of that? With a little luck, you can keep the restaurant and get him out of your life. I have a contact in the police. He can run it up the chain. Bring in the feds. Think of your family, Parker."

He pondered that, but not for long.

"Okay. But only if my family is protected."

"I can make that call. Tell me about Demos. I've got him tied to Parrot Cove and West Branch LLCs."

Parker hesitated before coming in. "They're insignificant ones. His big ones are 1854 Properties and Delilah Enterprises."

"Word is he's squeezed for cash. What do you know about that?"

"Nothing."

"Bullshit," Garrett said. "You run the money. Do you do wire transfers?"

Parker hesitated. Wiring untraceable money over state and international lines was a serious offense.

"Make your call," he said in a suddenly defiant tone. "I'm done."

Garrett said, "Ever hear of a man named Nick Harris?"

"Make your call."

I asked for his cell number and told him Detective Rambler would call him within fifteen minutes. That he could trust him.

I called Rambler as we raced downtown to the marina where *Sex-Sea* was docked. I explained who I believed I had just left. A fashion-challenged accountant working in the rear office of a throwback steakhouse who funneled cash for Demos. I asked if he'd looked further into Demos's holdings. He had not and was unfamiliar with either of the new LLCs that Parker had mentioned.

He was, though, familiar with Arnie's.

"A cop hangout in the eighties," he said. "The old guard still croons about it. I'll pay your boy a visit. Any of this make you closer to your missing Dali?"

"Not yet," I admitted.

"Keep at it. I've always been more successful at accidentally finding something than setting out to discover it."

Told you. Whether they heard of him or not, cops love Marcus Quintilian of La Rioja.

AS WE SPED DOWNTOWN, I felt both calm and charged. Relaxed, on edge.

Maybe I couldn't draw a stick figure worth a hoot. Maybe I peaked at installing garbage disposals, scrapping rotted wood, and playing multiple chess matches blind. The army was pretty stoked about that, but what's the point? But I wasn't without another attribute that had served me well. That would never show up on standardized testing. That had kept me vertical over the years. It stemmed from a piece of advice I'd gotten when I first joined the army. A comment in which I recognized myself. The older man who gave it to me said he'd first heard it from his father, who was part of the bomber squads that raided Japan in WWII under Curtis "Bombs Away" Lemay. He felt it his responsibility to pass it down.

We were sitting on the tall wooden stools at the bar at the Platzl Hotel in Munich having a pilsner. "I'll give you a clue how to fight a war," he told me. He picked his teeth with a fingernail. He was always picking his teeth. "Make believe you're already dead. The rest comes easy."

There's a strong suit for you.

CHAPTER 42

S*ex-Sea* had already pulled up anchor by the time we got downtown. I reversed course and bolted to my house. If Parker was right, Carrie was on a one-way cruise. Demos would head offshore. He would need to clear the Sunshine Skyway and get out of the main channel as it was busy and not at all conducive to dumping a body.

I called Morgan and told him to have *Impulse*, my thirty-foot Grady-White ready.

"And Morgan?"

"Yes?"

"Check the red spinnaker bag."

I pulled into my driveway and slammed the truck into park. Garrett and I sprinted around the side of the house and out to the dock. Morgan had *Impulse* idling in the water, her twin Yamaha 300s emitting a foaming, anticipatory purr. We jumped in. While it was still light, it was the time of year when the remnants of the day quickly gave way to the dark.

"Where to?" Morgan said.

I told him to head to the Sunshine Skyway. That with luck, we would intercept *Sex-Sea*. Morgan cut hard to the port and glanced to make sure Garrett and I were secure. I'd taken a seat and Garrett had a grip on the aluminum rail. Morgan thrust the twin throttles down.

We spotted *Sex-Sea* idling under the bridge. Morgan kept his distance so as not to be detected. We were in luck. It was a calm evening, and other boats were out, although most were racing in from a day of fishing on the Gulf.

I reached into the port-side cubby and pulled out Morgan's old red spinnaker bag. I opened it. It held passports. Currencies. An assortment of guns and knives that I kept oiled and operational. A first aid kit. Two satellite phones. It looked like the artifacts of a former life. A life roaring back to me.

Okay. So I missed it. Just a bit.

Yes, Virginia, someone has to fight the bad guys.

"Keep a safe distance," I reminded Morgan, putting down the remnants of my life. Morgan was experienced on the water at night. He didn't need me telling him what to do any more than Bonita did. But, as with Bonita, I felt good saying it.

The last of the sun's rays, reflecting on cumulus clouds, faded to deep blue. *Sex-Sea's* wake rolled behind her like liquid corn, her azure aft lights creating an effervescent glow. We shadowed her for three miles. She stopped and appeared to be adrift. The dark had command of the sky, wrapping us in thick black.

"Anything?" I said to Garrett. He had a TRYBE monocular night goggle pressed to his eye.

Before he could answer, Morgan, staring at *Sex-Sea*, said, "She's got people on the aft deck."

"Copy that," Garrett said.

I said, "What are—?"

"Someone, or something, just got tossed overboard," Morgan said, his eyes intent. Morgan's vision would shame an osprey.

"Copy that," Garrett repeated.

Sex-Sea started to turn back toward the channel.

"She's coming about," Morgan said as he gently pushed both throttles forward. "I'll stay slow and dark. I got the spot."

"Can you make out anything else?" I said to Garrett.

"Negative."

"Dead or alive?"

"Can't tell."

"We don't want him to know we're here," I said, stating what we all knew. But what none of us said, and what we all knew, was that if Carrie was in the water with a cinder block or two tied around her ankles there was nothing we could do.

While Garrett peered through the night vision goggle, Morgan lifted his eyes to the star-dotted sky. He rarely looked at the water or the mass of keyhole black that enveloped us. Ten minutes later, when *Sex-Sea* was far behind us and headed back under the Sunshine Skyway, Morgan announced, "This is the spot."

The three of us strained our eyes in the black. Morgan cut the engines, letting the silence roar. *Impulse* rolled in the water.

"Searchlight?" Morgan said.

I handed him a Fenix searchlight I'd recently purchased. He swept the water with a narrow road of white.

"Did you hear that?" Morgan said.

Morgan has dog ears. My left ear, thanks to an explosion in Sandland, is largely for decorative purposes.

"Hear what?"

"There. Again."

"I heard it," Garrett said.

Morgan turned the key. He took a quarter turn to the port, putted for less than a minute, and then cut the engines.

Even I heard it this time. Off the starboard side.

"Over here, you idiots."

"Carrie," I yelled.

"Jake? Is that you?"

"Stay put. We'll come to you."

"I'm going to kill those shitballs. Both of them."

"Both?" I shouted.

"Demos and his fairy friend, Denise."

"You met her?"

"Jumpin' Jesus, do we really have time for this? Get me out of this saltwater tub."

CHAPTER 43

VERONICA

1975

The Dali

S he found the painting when Jamie was fourteen months old, on a day she'd planned to clean the kitchen floor. She'd been meaning to do it for over a week, and with Jamie asleep, she'd run out of excuses. Michael had kept the floor presentable by putting damp Bounty paper towels—"the quicker picker-upper"—under his feet and skating to ABBA's "Waterloo."

She was rummaging around in the disordered utility closet in their two-floor apartment, the bedrooms were upstairs, looking for floor detergent. She was about ready to give up when she saw it. A narrow, thick cardboard tube snuggled in the corner. She pulled it out. There was no writing on it. Each end had a plastic cap. One end was still stapled to the tube. The other was not.

She placed it on the fieldstone flooring. She'd been

meaning to buy a rug to soften the entry and bottom of the stairs but had never gotten around to it. She popped the art tube open.

Inside was a rolled canvas. Some sort of paper. She pulled it out and unfolded it. It was a painting. One of Michael's? She held it up. It did not look like something Michael would do. Certainly not the Michael she knew.

Around two feet square, it was of a woman's nude body, her head too large. In the background, a solitary leafless tree stood by a characterless sea. The woman's body was not proportioned. The curve of her neck unnatural. Her face was shrouded so that only one eye was visible. *Sorta like the picture Faye took of me.* Her lips were a redemption shade of red for which Veronica had no reference. She also had no reference point for the picture. It wasn't erotic. Certainly not a portrait. Surreal, maybe? A name was scrawled on the bottom. Salvador Dali. She trolled her finger over the surface. Rough. It was not a print.

The name sounded familiar. She rolled it up and slid it back into the tube.

She brought it up that evening after they were done watching M*A*S*H. Fed up with eleven straight days of liver or fish, Hawkeye ordered ribs from a Chicago restaurant. He managed to get them delivered to South Korea under the guise of medical supplies. As he sat down to finally enjoy them, a fresh batch of wounded soldiers arrived by helicopter. Instead of eating ribs, he rushed to the operating tent, his hands soon dripping blood. They talked about the episode but failed to clarify any meaning from it. Michael insisted that *was* the meaning of it. The whole goddamn war.

"Korea?" she asked.

"Korea. Nam. It doesn't matter. Only the dead have seen the end of war," he said, quoting Santayana, although he didn't know the source of his words.

Veronica refused Michael's bait to again debate existentialism. To engage him in his quest for truth, his willingness to look beyond his years to find it. Faye had never shown any interest in philosophical mumble-jumble, opting instead to toke a joint. Veronica occasionally found herself missing that easy way out.

"I found a painting in the closet today," she said. "It was rolled up in some sort of tube."

"It is an art tube."

"Who is Salvador Dali?"

He'd been drying dishes. He tossed the towel over his shoulder.

"Dali is a Spanish artist known for surrealism. He spent his life searching for a form of art that expressed his world. His stuff is pretty wild."

"Why do you have it? *How* do you have it?"

Michael folded the dish towel and placed it neatly on the counter. Veronica always tossed it next to the sink. You could tell who was the last to use the towel by looking at it. The majority of the time, the towel was neatly folded. Once, Veronica had gone into the tiny kitchen before Michael came home and messed up the towel to make it look like she'd been cleaning.

Michael said, "I was walking out of the administration building my sophomore year and saw an art tube leaning up against an exterior door. I opened it. Saw it was a Dali. I had no clue why it was there. It should not have been. I picked it up, intending to take it to the fine arts building, but I never did."

"Is it valuable?"

Michael hesitated.

"Michael?"

He scrunched up the left side of his face. "Maybe? Yes?"

"Which one?"

He bobbed his head. "It likely has some value. But it's small. Hard to say."

"What do you intend to do with it?"

"Give it back, obviously. When I took it, I was ticked that it was just sitting there by the door."

"I'm not mad, babe. But . . . when? How? And what do you say?"

He nodded, as if they'd arrived at the central thesis. "I'll tell them I forgot I had it. Thought it was one of mine and never got around to opening it. I need to figure that out."

"Or, I'm just suggesting, leave it in the fine arts building. Stick it in some deserted class. Someone will find it."

"What if that someone is like me and just carts it home?"

"That's not who you are."

"Apparently it is," he said.

She thought of the time she'd purposely messed with the dish towel. "You know better," she said, admonishing herself as much as him.

"I'll take it back tomorrow," he said with conviction. "I'll give it to Dr. Beck. We're close. I'll tell her I was looking through old art tubes. And, holy cow, one was a Dali. No clue how it got mixed in with my stuff, but I wanted to give it back right away. That's it. Easy peasy."

"Remember, you got Jamie in the morning. I've got a class till noon."

"I'll take it when you get back."

"And the light bulb at the top of the steps is out. It's so dark without it. I'm always afraid I'll trip in the night."

"Got it. Your mom still coming to babysit?"

"She is. Think Hawkeye ever does it with Hot Lips?"

He nodded. "God, I hope so. That woman needs a hard fuck, and that man needs a good woman."

His uncharacteristic comment surprised her. Michael was

not a vulgar man. Not a sexist. So why the remark? Was he upset with himself for harboring the Dali? Doing something that wasn't him and then worrying that maybe that *was* him?

If so, she knew exactly how he felt.

CHAPTER 44

I lowered the aft ladder and helped a wet, naked Carrie Crowlings climb out of the water. Morgan handed her a towel. She wrapped it around herself, appraising it as she did so.

"You got anything better than this?" she said to me. My boat is where old towels go to die.

"Let me check the closet."

She flipped her wet hair over her right shoulder. "What are you even doing out here?"

"Searching for mermaids. We—"

"That fartfucker Demos. He refused to believe that I didn't know where the Dali was. He stripped my clothes off, like he was going to allow his crew to have their way. Threatened to dump me in the water. Hell, he did dump me in the water. Said we were miles from shore, and I'd never make it. I told him I had no idea where it was, and if he wasn't such a shit brain and killed Nick, we'd know. Even then, he insisted he didn't do it. Karl picked me up and held me by my wrists over the side of the boat."

"Didn't they—?"

"Demos asked if I changed my mind. I played the crying girl part. You know, please don't drop me, blah, blah, blah. Little fuckturd. I told him I didn't have a clue where the damn painting is. Then shit-turtle Karl let go. What the hell, right? I thought they were bluffing. I knew I'd make it to shore just to get retribution."

Morgan shot me a look. As strong as her attitude was, the outgoing tide was stronger.

She knifed me a look. "Why are you here? And don't give me that mermaid line."

"We got a tip that you might be in trouble."

"And . . . so you came to rescue me?"

The three of us said nothing.

"I would have made it," she said, in a tone fashioned to convince herself.

Morgan shuffled his feet.

"Okay. Fine. Thanks. Whatever."

I said, "We followed—"

"No. I'm serious. I get it, guys. Really. Thank you. I appreciate it."

"You're wel—"

"I was worried about sharks, though. They got sharks here?"

"They do," Morgan said.

She nodded. She took in a deep breath and released it, puffing her cheeks out.

"What tip?" she asked.

I didn't want to tell her about Parker. "Someone we ran into who knows Demos."

"Charley?"

"No."

"'Cause there's something funny about that slinky ass."

"In what way?"

"Dunno, Captain Nemo. But I don't think she's who she says she is. Just a feeling. What's our plan to find the Dali?"

"Let's get to shore first. Maybe even find you some clothes." Then I added, "I take it you've met Denise?"

Her eyes brightened. "Wild, right? Want my two cents? That scalawag's the one you gotta watch."

Morgan ran north along the shore until we reached Pass-a-Grille Channel. We passed a coast guard cutter hauling ass south. Someone else was not having a good night on the water. I explained to Carrie that if Demos was willing to throw her overboard to find the Dali, chances were he didn't have it either. The Dali was gone. She had no retort to that, which surprised me. She asked again who tipped us off. I brushed it off with a vague answer about a contact within Demos's organization.

A hundred yards off my dock, Morgan cut the throttle back. I found another towel in the cuddy under the fire extinguisher. I handed it to Carrie and took a seat across from her.

"Where do you get these rags from?" she said, drawing the towel around her shoulders.

"Tell me what's funny about Charley," I said. Another question popped into my mind, but I couldn't hold it.

"She was on the boat. At first—"

"Just now?"

"That's what we're talking about, right? She seemed to defend me. You know, telling Demos to back off. But in the end, she just disappeared. Took off. Like she didn't want to be around for my ceremonial departure. But for a moment . . ."

"What?"

"I don't know," Carrie said in a rare display of uncertainty. "I caught a glimpse of her earlier. She didn't see me. She was sticking a gun in her purse. Who the eff is she anyway?"

"I thought she was a friend of yours."

"Me?" She snorted. "Hell, no. I mean, I ran into her at Repose Gallery. She's plenty nice enough. But nothing she ever says adds up. I mean, she heard a Dali was on the market, so she jetted in from who-knows-where?"

I searched my mind for what Charley had told me about herself. That she facilitated stolen art. Heard a Dali was available in Saint Petersburg, Florida. Worked with Demos in the past. Warned me to return to my white-picket-fence life.

I keep tabs on a lot of galleries.

I bet she did. I bet it was her job to do so.

"There's more," she said.

"Tell me."

She hugged her towel around her neck. "I overheard Charley on her phone before we left the dock. She told whoever she was talking to that she hadn't a clue. That it was still missing, and she wasn't having any luck finding the daughter. She—"

"Whose daughter?"

"Didn't say."

"Did this daughter have a name?"

"No. May I continue?"

"By all means."

"She listened for a little and then said, and I quote, 'Ten million or not, he's as clueless as when he started.'"

"She said that? Ten million?"

"Yeah. That mean anything to you?"

I shot a glance at Garrett. His eyes were waiting for mine.

"No," I lied. I asked her where she'd been the last day as I couldn't reach her.

"Demos's house. Downtown. Nice place. I spent most of the time hanging around his pool with imported eye candy. But shit-turtle Karl wouldn't let me leave or have my phone. That's where I met Denise. I mean, how screwed up is that?"

"I think he's just different people."

She tilted her head. "Really? What gives you the faintest clue?"

255

I asked if she knew his address.

"Remember, I do north and south. Nothing else."

I asked her to describe his house.

"Big front porch. Yellow siding with white shutters. Brick drive. Four or five blocks north of the Vinoy."

The question that had flashed in my mind came back to me. It wasn't a question but something Demos had said. That I couldn't shake. Like a crumb that kept washing around the sink, not wanting to go down the drain.

"Demos told me that you told him that Nick thought he'd made a mistake."

"What about it?" Carrie said.

"What was his mistake?"

"That he sold it for so frickin' cheap."

"Did he say that? Explicitly?"

"No. But what else could it have been?"

"Is it possible that he regretted swiping it from his wife in the first place?"

"No—I mean, I suppose, but I don't see that. He said he got a quick deal. I think that deal was so easy he regretted not trying for more."

I dropped my line of questioning, for it was taking me off my map. But what if my map went only so far?

After we docked, Kathleen found some clothes for Carrie, although she wanted to shower off the saltwater first. I called Jimmy Strauch, an old friend who worked with the coast guard. Strauch and I met when, after I left the army, I spent months working shrimp boats off Fort Myers Beach. I'd left the area before I drank myself away. I headed north two hours, found a house on the water that faced the morning sun, and planted *my* flag. Strauch and I kept in touch ever since, grabbing a beer every six months, using the summer and winter solstice as reminders. He said to give him a few minutes. He called back in five.

"We got a person overboard call. A woman called it in."

"Got a name?"

"Negative."

I thanked him and disconnected.

Charley tried to save Carrie. She was talking to someone who knew I was pursuing the Dali. Who knew the dollar amount involved. I had a good idea who she was talking to. And why. I couldn't blame him. I'd do the same thing in his shoes.

Garrett and I discussed a plan. One way or the other, the Dali gig was over tonight. We were getting ready to drive downtown and find Demos's house when Carrie stormed around the corner from the outdoor shower.

"Hey champ, how's a girl supposed to clean her hair with no shampoo?"

CHAPTER 45

VERONICA

1975

Cue the clown

Michael was in it for the fresh grapefruit juice. Veronica wanted another orchid. Maybe a pair of earrings from the vendor whose work she'd always admired.

They set off for the Saturday market a little after eleven. Michael pushed the stroller, and Veronica wore her wide-brimmed hat with the red ribbon she'd bought the last time at the festival. That had been three months ago. Jamie had blown through her diaper. Her clothes. A bee stung Michael. The young family had limped home, a little afraid of the big, bad world.

On this striking Saturday morning, there were no aggressive bees. Jamie giggled and laughed at the air. While still driven by primitive desires, at fifteen months, she was developing a sense of humor and play, a coyness that Veronica thought magical.

Veronica talked with the mother of the twins. They were just a few months older than Jamie and lived in the same apartment complex. They agreed to meet in the park across the street the following morning. In a rare mood to engage with strangers, Veronica struck up a conversation with nearly every vendor. Was it the presence of her daughter that made her, not necessarily a better person, but a person more engaged with other people? She'd changed. She knew this. Her feelings for Jamie had created a chandelier of emotions. A world beyond any world she had ever known.

Veronica found her dream orchid, white with pink spots. Michael secured a gallon of grapefruit juice. They settled on a park bench in the shade. The noon train to Palm Beach collected passengers.

"What did you get?" Veronica said. Michael had wandered off by himself while the two women in his life had fondled earrings. He opened a bag and took out a picture.

"Nice. What is it?" Veronica said.

"A restaurant in Paris. It's an original from a woman who has the tent by the fresh grapefruit stand. This is her first time here."

"It looks small. Quaint."

"Want to go there sometime?"

"Paris?"

"This restaurant. See this table?" He pointed at a four-top table on the sidewalk. "Let's eat there."

They had plotted and dreamed of travel ever since their road trip to New York—they both yearned for a European tour —but Jamie's arrival had sidetracked their dreams.

"Do you know where it is?"

"I do. She told me."

"Deal," Veronica said. "And London?"

"We'll do them together. Take two weeks and split time between the countries."

"I'll check some books out of the library," she said, her senses already exploding with the musty odor of books, for

Veronica loved libraries. The Alexandria knowledge housed under a single roof. Knowledge protected by gutters. Fire hydrants. Knowledge that had weight. Girth. The college library, Mills Memorial Library, boasted over 150,000 books. A strong selling point in attracting students and competing with those kingdom-endowed East Coast schools. Veronica had spent much of her pre-Jamie life there and looked forward to someday introducing her daughter to its hallowed halls. To infuse her with that which she so loved, which meant so much to her. She often found herself so bursting with the future she feared missing the present.

Veronica would never again set foot in that library. It would become a traitor, a symbol of the cold and indifferent world. Things you love that care nothing about you and what a damn fool you were to think it was ever a two-way relationship.

They stopped at a tent where a man was drawing caricatures. They discussed whether they wanted one or not. Veronica was yes. Michael was less than enthusiastic. While they wrangled the issue, a clown who had been circulating through the market approached them. Upon spotting Jamie, the creature bent down to her level and planted his paint-plastered face in front of hers. He popped a flower out of seemingly nowhere and sprang it in front of her face.

Jamie screamed in horror, her small arms flapping wildly in the air, her eyes wide with virgin fear. Michael quickly inserted himself between the clown and his daughter. He lifted her out of her stroller. She continued her unholy wailing. The clown tilted his head and made a goofy face. It only intensified Jamie's horrific discontent.

"Please," Veronica said. "If you don't mind."

The clown shrugged. It clown-footed away.

"I forgot to ask you," Veronica said after they'd finally calmed their daughter. "Did you return the Dali?"

"Dr. Beck was out. She's at some art show in Tampa. She'll be back on Monday. I'll take it then."

"And how about the light bulb on the steps?" Veronica said, as if suddenly aware of a list of things that needed attending to. "It's so dark without it, and I can't reach it."

"I'll get it when we get home."

On the way back to their apartment, they window-shopped menus on Park Avenue. Veronica's mother was in town and had offered to sit for them that night. They hadn't had dinner out since forever.

CHAPTER 46

Albert Einstein said, "The last thing to collapse is the surface."

Everything might look fine. But underneath it all, the stressed pillars of our lives break away until, like the walls of Jericho, it all comes crumbling down. Leaving us to marvel how the surface could disappear so quickly. And then, upon examining the ruins, the opposite: amazement over how it lasted as long as it did. How could we have not known? Not have seen?

While speeding downtown, I called Wayne Gibson. He was the only person other than Wetzel and Veronica who knew of my assignment. If I were him? No way would I trust someone not employed by Rollins College to find the Dali. I would hire my own insurance fraud investigator. What I lobbied for Veronica to do in the first place.

And that is exactly what Wayne Gibson had done.

"Mr. Travis," he said after the third ring.

"Did you hire Charley to find the Dali?" I said.

Silence.

"I don't know that name."

I corrected my mistake.

"Did you hire Shearson Consulting to find the Dali and tell them that I was pursuing it in return for a ten-million-dollar gift?"

Gibson skipped a beat and then confessed. "It makes no sense for us to know it's out there and to *not* make an effort to find it. Piggybacking on Veronica's efforts—and I mean no disrespect—is not a prudent course of action for the college. It is, after all, our painting. Veronica likely has knowledge of who took it and even where it might be. For us to sit back and use her man was never a viable option. I'm sure you understand."

"Tell me about Shearson."

"They're an international investigating firm that specializes in stolen and fraudulent art. Their efforts, they assured me, should in no manner interfere with your work."

"Did they give you the name of who they put on the case?"

"No. Is he your Charley fellow?"

"What else did you tell them about me?"

"Just that you're looking. And they wanted to know your incentive. I did nothing to hamper your own efforts. I merely want two horses in the race."

I asked him if he planned to pass on any progress I made to Shearson.

"I represent Rollins College and will act in the best interest of the institution. May I make a suggestion? Going forward, perhaps you and this Charley fellow can join forces. I hardly think that, at this stage, there is anything to lose. Shearson has indicated to me that our chances of finding the Dali are diminishing by the hour. I fear we are at the precipice."

I assured him that I would work with Charley. We disconnected on amicable terms, only because, as opposed to R. Wetzel Brookings, who was a hard man to like, Wayne Gibson was a hard man not to like.

Charley said she'd been working with Demos on and off for years. I wondered if she and her firm saw him as a stepping stone to other contacts in the fraudulent art world. Just as the police will use a small-time drug dealer to gain access to a bigger fish. Or maybe Demos was the big one. It seemed more personal to her than that. *I got my reasons*, she'd said over lunch. But I didn't know her well enough to determine whether she was speaking for the job or for herself.

While cruising the downtown neighborhood looking for a house that fit the description Carrie had given us, we passed Veronica's house. There appeared to be a single light on in the front room. I realized I'd never made contact with her one neighbor who was absent when I canvassed the neighborhood. That house next to hers was now aglow.

A house that matched Carrie's description of Demos's house was three blocks north of Veronica's, one block west.

I dropped Garrett off and parked two streets away. I fumbled around in the center console, found an ATM receipt, and scrawled a note on it. I marched to the house, skipped up to the front door, and punched the doorbell.

Karl opened it. Guess I got the right place.

"Mr. Travis. To what do I owe the pleasure?"

"I'm here to collect my money. You owe me for half a char-cuterie board."

"Let's settle the bill in the back alley."

"Perhaps later. I need to talk to the demented demagogue, Demos. Or Denise. I'm not picky."

He opened the door wide and motioned me in. He patted me down. I'd left my gun with Garrett.

"Go," he said, extending his arm.

I started down a small entry hall that led to a long living room with white bookcases at one end. I walked slowly, trying to get the lay of the house.

"Keep moving."

We entered a large room that had been added on to the 1920s home. A wall of windows looked over a spacious pool and patio. The pool's lights created dancing shadows in the trees. A dozen or so people were lounging around. A few were in the pool. Music played. Everyone held a drink. The men were young and the women younger.

"I must have misplaced my invitation," I said, keeping my eyes on the patio, trying to get a lay of the property.

"The door to your left," Karl said.

As I reached for the door handle it swung open. Flat Top stepped out.

"In," he squeaked at me. He jutted his head toward the room from which he had just come.

I stepped into a wood-paneled study. Demos sat behind a large desk. Charley, legs crossed, reclined deep in a sofa. Both Flat Top and Karl came in behind me. Demos was dressed in all black, except for a white scarf around his neck. I'm pretty sure it had pink glitter on it. I hope he knows that stuff clings to everything.

"Still looking for the Dali?" I said. "Or have you finally faced the truth that when you killed Nick Harris, you tanked everyone's chance of finding it?"

Demos stood and wandered over to a bar cart. He opened a jar, took out some nuts, and popped them in his mouth. He placed the lid back on the jar. He faced me. His topographical face dusted with makeup and mascara eyes made him resemble the Smoky Mountains in autumn.

"Mr. Harris's death was unfortunate," he said in a tone that indicated Harris's death wasn't any more unfortunate than a bug smacking a windshield. "It is equally disconcerting that you insist I had a hand in his demise. Neither of us profited from his death. How did you find this house?"

"I used my nose."

"Shame you haven't lost your gift of insult."

"Who are your pool buddies?"

"Visitors, like all of us. I like parties, Mr. Travis. Glamour.

Mystique. Sparkle. The world on its own is a dull and uninspiring place. Speaking of friends, where is yours? The tall, marbled Black man with the short fuse?"

"He had Bible study tonight."

"Is that so?" He popped a few more nuts in his mouth. Must have held some back the first time. "Perhaps he is studying the Book of Romans. 'Never take revenge, beloved, but leave room for the wrath of God.'"

"If the apostle Paul wanted to outsource the fun jobs, that was his prerogative. Why don't you give Carrie Crowlings a call? Bring her in, and let's hash this out. Either one of us knows where the Dali is, or we don't."

"I agree, dear. Unfortunately, we can't get hold of her. That leaves you and me."

Demos never used *dear* with me. That was Denise talking.

I said, baiting him, "If you can't reach her, wouldn't you be worried? Or do you have reason not to be concerned about her?"

He eyed me warily. "Tell me, Mr. Jake Travis, why are you here?"

"I had a lovely chat with your accountant," I said. "Parker won't be showing up for work anymore."

He bobbed his head slowly. "You are, if nothing else, a mildly resourceful man."

Well, I was shooting for a little higher than that.

I took a victory lap over to the bar cart. I opened the jar of nuts and tossed a few salted cashews into my mouth. Demos's world was about to crumble, and there was nothing he could do to stop the avalanche. Since the days of Al Capone, the most efficient way to put gangsters behind bars was to trace the money. With Parker in our pocket, Demos was toast. I might not find the Dali, but I was taking this nutcase out of circulation.

"The feds have him or soon will," I said, puffing my feathers. "Just imagine what's in that little mind of his."

"I might have underestimated you. You know, it is not necessary that you depart this house in the same manner in which you entered."

"Gentlemen." Charley sprang up. She marched over and positioned herself between Demos and me, facing Demos. "I'm sure Mr. Travis is just trying to raise your ire. We all want the same thing. If the two of you stop butting horns, we might give ourselves a fighting chance." She turned to me. With steel in her voice, she said, "Think you can manage that, Jake?"

Her eyes pleaded with mine. I stepped into her, reached into my pocket and took out the ATM receipt. I pressed my hand into her soft stomach. Without taking her eyes off mine, her hand wandered down and took the paper. On it, I'd written *Shearson Consulting. I know.*

"I'll do my best, sweetie," I said and took a step back.

"I want a trade," I said, turning to Demos. "Give me Carrie. And the Dali or, if you don't have it, cease your pursuit. In return, I'll forget I ever met Parker."

I knew, of course, that he didn't have Carrie, and I had no intention of forgetting Parker. If Demos was holding back, he wouldn't trade his kingdom for the Dali. If he was clueless as to its whereabouts, at least I could put him in a pinstripe suit. His nightclub act would sell well in prison.

I had Demos in checkmate. Game over.

He rolled his tongue in his mouth. "Funny. I have neither, but I do have someone else. Karl, would you please bring our guest in?"

Karl left and returned a moment with two men, both in jeans and black T-shirts. I recognized them from the night I'd first met Demos at the warehouse shindig.

Parker stood between them.

"Parker," Demos said, "is there anything you'd like to tell Mr. Travis?"

You ever been in the first car of a roller coaster that had just summitted its steepest incline? Ready to take the plunge? I didn't know how steep the drop was, but I was about to plummet face first and find out.

"Yes," Parker said, his pissy little eyes mocking me. "Mr. Travis seemed to think my steakhouse was some sort of front for illegal operations. I went along with his fantasies for my own amusement. Paying vendor bills can be excruciatingly dull. He correctly identified two of our LLCs—Parrot Cove and West Branch—but I blew them off. To deflect his interest, I made up two other ones: 1854 Properties and one I called Delilah Enterprises. You know, just to toy with him."

I recalled Parker hesitating before telling me about the LLCs. Conjuring up his lies while I stood there thinking I was a big shot. Is the room expanding, or am I shrinking?

Demos said, "1854?"

"Oscar Wilde was born that year."

Demos grinned. "Oh, Parker, I do love your style. And Delilah?"

"The song by Tom Jones."

"I do not know that song or that performer. Do you think I would enjoy them?"

"I do. His Welsh voice conveys great sense of raw sexuality. You'll also appreciate his signature song, 'What's New, Pussycat?'"

"How do I not know these things? So much of the world still awaits me. And the detective who dropped by?"

"I assured him I was just playing along with Mr. Travis's fantasies."

"And did he believe you?"

"He did not. But he knew that I knew there was nothing he could do. I did exactly what you trained me to do."

Demos kept his eye on me when he addressed Parker. "And you told them I was taking a woman out on the boat, is that correct, Parker?"

"Yes, sir. As I explained in my call to you right after they left, I thought it might help you keep tabs on them. Again, I apologize for that, sir. I used poor judgment."

"As I said earlier, not your best decision. But we are not here to cast stones." He faced Parker. "Enjoy the pool party, Parker. There are more than a few pussycats slinking around. Tomcats as well. If I recall, your taste runs skinny. Am I correct?"

"You are," Parker said. "I believe we are all endowed with the same amount of sexuality. The thinner you are, the more sex per square inch."

"Sign me up for your laboratory experiments. You did bring a suit, did you not? Not that such outerwear is necessary."

"I keep one upstairs. Oh, one more thing."

"Yes?"

"I remembered to tell him I had a daughter. You're right. That line softens people up. Mr. Travis totally bought it."

"Naturally. He has two daughters of his own, an arrangement that most certainly obfuscates his view of the world."

"By the way, I love your scarf."

"Thank you. There'll be a little something extra in your next paycheck."

Now, as promised, is Jake's Second Dictum of Life.

You are never as smart as you think you are.

CHAPTER 47

Parker winked at me and pranced out the door. The two men who accompanied him left as well, one landing a smirk as he turned around.

Demos took position on the corner of his desk. "You were saying, Mr. Travis?"

My self-esteem was lower than a snake's ass. At least I'd won one small battle. I had Carrie up my sleeve, whatever that was worth, although I was beginning to think it wasn't worth diddly-squat.

"It's just a matter of time," I said, tossing out a pathetic rejoinder. A real Hall of Famer.

"I pay my people well, Mr. Travis. Stupidly well. Silly that you think you could turn such loyalty."

"The Dali," I said, for I was overcome with the weariness of the chase. Of the company I was keeping.

"Do you still insist on pretending to represent a mysterious buyer?"

"Do you still pretend not to know where Carrie Crowlings is?"

"If I may," Charley said. "I think the time has come to

conclude our search and, sadly, our time together. Nick Harris obviously disposed of the Dali prior to his death." She shot Demos a look. "All the bullying in the world won't turn back the clock. The Dali could be five thousand miles from here by now. Our efforts are best suited for other endeavors."

Demos shifted his attention to me. "Mr. Travis?"

"I agree. The Dali disappeared with the last beat of Nick Harris's heart."

He stood, strolled behind Charley, and traced a finger down her back.

"You made a call tonight on the boat," he said. "To who?"

Charley hesitated. That was unfortunate. In such cases, a fast bad lie trumps a slow good one.

"A friend. Trying to make dinner arrangements."

"And your friend was interested in a description of where you were?"

"Are you spying on me?"

"Answer the question."

"She asked where I was. I told her I was on a boat. Do you have a problem with that?"

"What is your friend's name?"

"Beatrice."

"You have a friend named after Dante's muse? The inspiration for 'Divine Comedy'? How apropos. But I think not."

"I don't care what you think."

Demos walked over to the bar cart and helped himself to another fistful of nuts. He chewed them slowly as if to convey his dominance of the situation.

He said to Charley, "How long have you and I been associated?"

"Too long."

"It has not escaped me that in our previous transactions, those we dealt with often ended up in legal difficulties. The law, after you pass through, suddenly aware of their activities. Mine as well. Yet you seem to rise above it. May I see your phone, please?"

Charley remained silent.

"Your phone, Charley," Demos said.

"I'm not giving you my damn phone," Charley spit out.

Demos laughed. "No. I imagine you're not. And if there is a Beatrice in your contacts, you did not call her from the boat. How long have you been feeding information to whomever you're working for?"

"I work for myself."

"Please tell me you were well compensated or at least that you did it for sex. Otherwise, my impression of you will be forever shattered."

She squared herself in front of him. Her eyes hard. Her voice firm. "Francis Rampton."

"Who?"

"You know who I'm talking about."

"Oh yes. Ms. Rampton," Demos said in the same bored tone he used to dismiss Nick Harris. "She sold me some authentic prints. She then threatened to go to the authorities when she discovered that I'd made copies. She found them at an art gallery on Bond Street—Galerie Bartoux, was it not? Across from the Victoria's Secret store. What an unfortunate event for her. I had no choice. It would have set an unhealthy precedent."

"Her abused body was found in an alley. It's your calling card, like Nick Harris."

Demos flipped his scarf over his shoulder. "That is such a ... harsh accusation, dear. Must you talk like that?"

"You're sick," Charley spit out.

"I recall that you seemed unusually close to her. Is it possible I'm missing something? My gosh. I am, aren't I? You weren't lovers, were you?"

A silent beat passed before Charley declared, "We were."

"Yes, of course. I see it now. You and Ms. Rampton. You betrayed me for a lover. Delectable. That, I understand."

"Listen, folks," I said, sensing that things could soon turn ugly. "I hate to interrupt, but if no one here has the Dali, I'll just be scooting along."

Demos nodded at Karl who drew a gun, as did Flat Top. "I am truly sorry. But I cannot allow either of you to live. You"—he tilted his head at Charley—"I will miss. And you"—he tilted his head at me—"I won't even remember."

It was at that moment I decided this whole search-for-a-missing-Dali schtick was an ill-advised venture.

Time to make believe I was dead.

CHAPTER 48

"Here's a thought," I suggested. "Only whack Charley. I don't have any dirt on you, plus, fewer bodies to dispose of."

"Good to know you have my back," Charley said.

Demos said, "If either of you have the Dali, before our time tonight concludes, you will confess." He shrugged. "If you do not have it, then I'm afraid I have no choice." He looked at Karl. "You and Gregory take them to the basement. Be on alert for the Black man. I do not think he studies the Bible. Nor do I think he outsources revenge to God."

Before Karl and Gregory—a.k.a. Flat Top—could move, the door opened. One of the men who had briefly appeared earlier stepped into the room. "You rang, sir?"

I'd not seen Demos summon him.

"Yes, Alec," Demos said. "Tell our guests the party's over. And let Stephen know we have an uninvited guest. A Black man. Whereabouts unknown. I suggest you shoot first, ask questions later or not at all."

"What shall I say to our guests?"

"Empty the place," Demos commanded with irritation.

Alec left. Demos turned to me and Charley, who had maneuvered beside me. "If either of you knows where the Dali is, now is the time."

"Demos," Charley said. "We. Do. Not. Know. You've gone mad in your pursuit of something that can't be found."

"Mad?" he laughed. "It's *so* good to know you've been paying attention. The painting exists. I will—"

An electric whoosh shuttered the house. The room went dark. People shrieked from the pool area. The electricity was out.

I grabbed Charley by the arm. We dashed out the door. A generator kicked in. *Damn, that was fast.* Security lights blinked on. A gunshot splintered the air. A bullet ricocheted off the wall beside us.

"Duck," I yelled, which does a lot of good when the bullet's already past you. We slammed through the doors to the pool.

We jumped behind a shed that was likely used to house pool equipment. An eight-foot concrete wall surrounded the compound. The pool area was dark. The generator's effort was conserved for a few lights in the house and AC units, which rumbled back to life.

Garrett was beside me. I never saw him coming.

"You did the lights?" I said.

"Never saw the generator."

He handed me my gun and a knife with a strap. I placed the knife around my ankle.

"Got a gun for me?" Charley said to Garrett. She huddled close to me so that the three of us were shielded by the shed.

"No."

"How did you find out I worked for Shearson?" she asked, her breath in my ear.

"I called Gibson after I became suspicious. That bit about keeping tabs on Repose, meeting Carrie there. Was that all made up?"

"Not that simple. I did meet her there, but I knew what I was looking for."

I recalled her saying at The Tavern at Bayboro that she had a "contact" who had alerted her. Her phrasing had struck a dissonant chord at the time, but I couldn't resolve it.

"What about that line about facilitating the movement of rare art?"

"Just protecting my cover."

"You sold it well."

"Thank you."

"Did you have onions tonight?"

"Sorry," she said. "Damn things were strong."

"We have her. Carrie. Plucked her out of the water. You called the coast guard?"

"I did. She okay?"

"Yes."

"Thank God. He's a killer and will end a life without a second thought. Carrie doesn't get that. She makes a dumb blonde look smart. We've been tracking Demos for years. But we let him operate to find who he sells to. This time, we decided to bring him in."

"How's that going?"

"Not particularly well at the moment."

"A friend named Beatrice?"

"Jesus, was that stupid. Veronica Stafford gives some charity ten million if you find the Dali?"

"Close enough. Why's he so desperate?"

"He's run afoul of a pair of Russian brothers. He's in debt. Desperate for cash. He needs the Dali to keep hold of his businesses, or they'll seize everything he's got. Parker really snowed you, didn't he?"

"I'd rather not discuss it."

"I can understand why."

"Any leads on the—?"

"Business means nothing to Demos. The sole purpose of cash is to fund his extravagant lifestyle. But no matter how much money he has, his appetite always exceeds his bank account. No leads. You?"

"Veronica has a daughter," I said. "Jamie. Carrie said something about Nick finding an early buyer and keeping it in the family."

Charley swung her head. "That's news to me. I had no—

"Shhh," Garrett hissed.

"I'm Charley, by the way."

Garrett kept his eyes on the patio, where Karl, backlit by the security lights, marched onto the pool deck. Gregory was beside him. Alec and a man I assumed was Stephen were rounding up the guests and hustling them to the rear gate.

"Mr. Jake," Karl bellowed. "Let us talk. It is in the best interest of us both."

"If he leaves to search the house," Charley whispered, "let's hit the gate. We've got enough to bring the police in."

Well, that didn't sound like much fun. Not to mention Garrett would never sign off on it.

"Search the pool area first," Karl instructed the two men, which tanked Charley's run-away plan. Alec and Stephen fanned out in opposite directions circumferencing the pool deck. They would meet at our cozy shed. Karl and Gregory went back in the house.

"You got the north," Garrett said.

Charley whispered, "What do you—?"

"Shhh," I said.

"Stop shhhing me. They can't—"

"Shhh."

Alec, coming in Garrett's direction with purpose, was making better time than Stephen, who ambled toward Charley and me. Garrett and I would need to move together, which meant I had more ground to cover. Neither man had a gun drawn as they had no reason to believe we were armed. We needed to take them quietly so we still had a chance of surprising Karl and Gregory.

Garrett stood, wobbled, and started walking toward Alec, teetering as he went.

"I couldn't find a bathroom," Garrett slurred. "Those bushes were a little dry. I hope you don't mind."

"Let's go, buddy," Alec said, stepping in to him and grabbing his arm. "Time to haul your darky ass out of here."

Ouch. Poor Alec.

Garrett said, "Say that again."

Stephen, closing in on us, chirped, "Hey, you think he's the Black dude they're looking for?"

Just as Rambler appreciates it when a criminal leaves the victim's identification behind, it's always a pleasant surprise when your opposition is two bricks shy of a load. (I bet Melinda would like that one.)

Garrett punched Alec in his stomach. He bent over, struggling to breathe.

I sprang out and tackled Stephen. I wrapped one arm around his mouth to muzzle him. I coiled my other arm around his neck. Charley picked up a yard gnome and crashed it over Stephen's head. He went limp in my arms and slid to the ground.

"I had things under control," I said.

"You do thank you about as well as you do hello."

"Thank you."

"You're welcome."

Garrett, who had been searching Alec, found a gun and tossed it to Charley. We dragged both men behind the shed. We tied them with a hose and stuffed their mouths with a towel. Two men down. Three to go. Or was that two and a woman?

"Now what?" Charley said.

I nodded at her gun. "You know how to use that?"

"Bet your ass."

"We need to split," Garrett said. "I got the rear of the house." He looked at Charley. "Stay here. Don't move."

But Charley did. And at first, it was the right thing to do, but after that, nothing was the right thing to do. It's such a fine line between pretending to be dead and being dead.

CHAPTER 49
VERONICA

Present day

Everyone smile

They were due back in Florida tomorrow. Hopefully, the Dali would be waiting for them, Veronica's man, Travis, having done his job.

Six days ago, she'd insisted they drive. "Like we always do." Michael hadn't objected. They stopped overnight, as they would tonight. He'd selected a pair of boutique hotels. On the way north, Veronica's mind had been like an engine that conked out repeatedly every time it started. She'd been uncomfortable. Agitated. The boutique hotel was confusing. Everything was confusing.

They had hit the grocery store in Ellicottville on the way in. When Michael turned off the main road to the cabin, the crunch of tires on the gravel drive transported her back. She half expected to see their younger versions rushing out the door.

Now their last evening was upon them. Veronica thought

that should mean something, but meaning, along with memory, was slipping away at a wild and erratic pace. They planned to leave around noon and put about seven hours behind them before hitting their hotel.

Veronica was up first, her mind increasingly disinterested in sleep. She stepped out onto the deck overlooking the small lake and the unmatched pastoral woodlands. The Indian blanket, smelling of mothballs, cloaked her shoulders, and a mug of coffee warmed her hands. It was a crisp autumn morning in Ellicottville, New York, a rude northeast breeze firmly in charge. The fog ghost of summer wisped over the lake. The end season now close enough that you could feel its sharp breath. In the distance stood the ski slopes. Waiting for the heavy stillness of winter to bring out exuberant skiers who would streak down the hills in both gaiety and peril.

The deciduous trees were mostly bare, but the conifers soldiered on. Veronica knew they took no holiday. That even in the winter, their waxy needles still photosynthesized. She also knew in the subnivean layer, where the warm earth turned back the intruding cold, small mammals spent the winter months, scurrying in tunnels between dens and seed caches. She knew that while all snowflakes are different, they share the same hexagon structure. She remembered all that and more from her eighth-grade earth science teacher. It had been one of her favorite courses. Ever.

She thinks now: Who will carry these things? Does it even matter? Did it *ever* matter? She wants to believe that worthless knowledge is not worthless. It's hard. She's bone tired of it all. Her world has become a slow-motion bomb, all the little pieces floating away from each other. Tiny pictures of her life, fragments of her memories, forever expanding into dark, cold space.

"How long have you been out here?"

Startled, she turned to Michael.

Fifty years.

"Not long," she answered. "What time are we leaving today?"

"We'll shoot for around one. That gives us a leisurely morning. The fog should lift soon. It will be a beautiful day."

"Remember the first time we came? With Jamie? How we said we'd come back every year?"

"How could I forget?" he said. "Jamie loves the place. She'll take good care of it for the next generation."

"She got to be such a better skier than either of us," Veronica said. Her voice sounded more distant to her every day. Everything was melting in her mind. Day. Night. Dreams. Hexagons. Subnivean layer. Jamie. Dali. A face that looks like a smooth grain, *but whose?*

"I'm afraid I wasn't much competition there," he said. "The place looks nice."

"The man who used to take care of it? He passed away years ago. Now I pay his grandson. His wife cleans inside every month. I want it nice for when she comes here."

"Ready for a farmhouse breakfast?" Michael said.

"You bet I am."

Michael went inside, leaving Veronica to contemplate her future, for she had checked her phone that morning, and it was still there. The single word.

Die.

How strange to see the blank days that followed that entry. Numbers with white space under them. No gray dot indicating somewhere she was supposed to go, something she was supposed to do. With the swipe of a finger, she now scrolled forward into nothingness. Days void of all aspiration, of dreams and hopes. Anxiety. Laughter. Sorrow. Morning coffee. Folding warm towels, which she so loved to do. Books. Music. Thank you. Thank you all. You are now summarily dismissed of your duties.

That silver-bullet little word also cleansed her of her greatest fear. Obliterated it from the face of the earth.

She had pried it out of her doctor, the day he'd told her that her memory would become a cold breath. She wanted to make certain they were discussing the same thing. Needed to be crystal clear before her slide into decrepitude. She shuddered at the image of being trapped in her body for years, unable to speak or control her thoughts. Her only companion being that which she never wanted to remember.

Her mind again recollected her conversation with her doctor.

"If I have a memory that is blocked—no recall at all—might it surface because of the disease?"

"It's possible. We don't fully understand repressed memory. But it is highly unlikely your brain erased the memory. Rather, it's buried somewhere in your unconscious zone. And it may release it on its own accord."

Her doctor's words resulted in her simple choice to erase all possibility. A pill to cure all disease.

Die. It ceases all fears. Obliterates all disease. You just can't beat it.

Veronica pressed herself against the railing. The dream had returned last night. Crawling on the stone floor. Dragging her way to the sheet. With each new viewing, she got closer. She pulled the blanket tight around her neck. A wisp of coolness touched her cheek. The past seized her.

She had just stepped out of the shower, her body colliding with cooler air. Faye came in the steamy bathroom. She touched Veronica's cheek with her finger, tracing it down to the corner of her mouth. Down between her breasts. They did not speak. It had been twelve days since the world ended. Since she crawled on the floor. Toward the sheet. Twelve days since she'd felt anything, and she knew, in a drowning sort of manner, that she would never feel again.

Faye.

She had appeared at her door three weeks ago. No warning. The doorbell rang. Veronica answered it. They stood facing each other. This hit Veronica: *Oh, Faye! Look at us. We were young for so long, and now we are old.*

She hadn't told Michael. Faye didn't deserve to have Veronica's lips ever form her name again. Veronica couldn't remember what they discussed. *Did I mention the Dali?* After all, she had told her when she'd run back to her. That's what had killed it. Running back to her. Stupid. Stupid.

She went inside to escape her worrisome thoughts. Over breakfast, Veronica asked Michael what time they were leaving. Three times, she asked. Five times. Six. Michael responded each time with politeness. Never once saying, "I already told you, remember?" And certainly not a "We discussed this." At one point, Veronica asked him if she had previously asked him the question. He insisted that she had not and had promptly changed the subject.

THREE HOURS LATER, MICHAEL was packing up the last of his clothes. Veronica walked in the bedroom clutching a picture.

"Look," she said, proffering her hand. "It's from that day."

Michael reached out and took the picture. It was of the three of them at the Winter Park farmer's market. Jamie in her stroller. Michael holding the orchid. Veronica young. The picture was faded except for the orchid in Veronica's hand. Its colors were still vivid, like a cheap attempt to restore an old photo.

"What's it doing here?" Michael said, anxiety finally showing itself.

"I brought it with us. Faye took it. Remember?"

They'd run into her unexpectedly. Faye, holding a bag of cherry tomatoes and a loaf of bread she'd bought. Faye, dressed in tight jeans and a cream shirt with puffy sleeves, her long, untamed hair drowning her narrow shoulders. Faye, who had whipped out her Polaroid and insisted she take the picture. No, really. Allow me. How cute. A family. Everyone smile. Ready? One. Two. Three.

"It's a great picture of us," he said. "Jamie looks angelic."

Veronica cast her eyes up to his. She spoke with the silence of a white church. And while it was not her intention, no crueler words were ever uttered to Michael Fredericks.

"Did you change the light bulb, Michael?"

CHAPTER 50

I sprinted back inside the house just as the lights came on. A man and woman clumped down the stairs. Their clothing was askew, the woman's blouse partially unbuttoned.

"The heck is going on?" the man demanded of me.

"You need to leave. Now."

"No shit, man."

"My phone," the woman said. She had green eyes. I remembered later how they reflected the pale yellow of the Edison lights that were strung over the pool. Pretty, in a Dali sort of way. "I think I left it at the bar." She turned to the man. "Remember, we were looking at the drunk monkey videos."

"Forget it," I said. "Leave. Get out of here."

"Not without my phone." The woman started toward the pool. I snatched her arm.

"Hey, that hurts."

"You're not safe here," I said.

"Come on, babe," the man said.

"No. I'm getting my phone," she said, her eyes challenging mine.

"There's a gate on the pool deck," I said. "Get your phone. Leave through that gate."

"Come on, Kevin," she said. They dashed off to the pool.

"Kevin," I said to their backs. Kevin turned around. "Anyone else upstairs?"

"Not that I know, man. But"—he humped his shoulders—"pretty wild party, you know?"

I took the steps two at a time and did a quick search of four bedrooms and two baths, gun in my hand. I flew down the steps and headed to the rear of the house. The pool area, visible through the glass door, appeared deserted. I checked the room we'd been in earlier. Empty.

"Drop it," Karl said from behind me.

"Karl? Is that you?"

"Drop it."

I turned around and faced Karl, who was pointing a small cannon at me. There is nothing more demoralizing than going from one end of the gun to the other. I dropped my gun. Karl had likely heard me in the front hall arguing with the couple. I was ticked at myself. I should have assumed voices carried throughout the house.

"The Black man," he said. "Where is he?"

"Behind you."

"I don't think so."

"Struggling with the cynical themes of Ecclesiastes?"

"Walk out to the pool. Slow. Hands above your head."

I did as instructed. He waited until I was safely in front of him before bending over and picking up my gun. We ran into Kevin and the woman who had gone to get the phone.

"Hey," the woman said, eyeing Karl's gun. "What's with the gun?"

"Get out of here," Karl said.

"My wallet," Kevin said sheepishly. "I think it fell out of my pants. Upstairs."

Karl hesitated. "You can get it later. To the pool."

"How about if I—?"

Karl waved his gun. "The pool."

The woman said to Karl, "You just told us to get—"

"I changed my mind. The pool."

The woman gave an audible huff and we paraded back to the pool deck. Demos came out of the house along with Gregory.

"Where's Charley?" he asked me. His voice was pure Demos. No hint of Denise.

"She caught an Uber to the police station. You'll be surrounded within minutes."

"You never stop, do you?" He bobbed his head at Kevin and the green-eyed woman. "Let them go," he told Karl.

"Can I check the upstairs room for my wallet?" Kevin asked Demos.

"No. Come back in the morning. We'll have it for you."

"What time?" the man said.

But the green-eyed woman stood her ground. "Forget that. He's got a right to have it now. Besides, how do we know you'll give it back to him?"

"Leave, now," Demos said.

"It won't take him but a minute," I lobbied Demos. "Let the man get his wallet." But as I spoke, I questioned the reversal of my advice. I had previously urged them to leave which was in their best interest.

Taking my cue, the woman turned to her companion, whose face was draining of color. "Come on, Kevin. It's got to be by the bed. It always falls out when you drop your pants."

Demos hesitated and then said to Gregory, "Take them upstairs." He addressed the woman. "My apologies for the disruptive evening."

"Well, you can be sure I'm not leaving a good review."

She stomped off. Kevin and Gregory followed her.

Demos said to Karl, "The Black man?"

"We don't know."

"Ivan and Stephen?"

"They don't answer."

Demos approached me. "Where are they?"

"Ivan mentioned something about a neighborhood Parcheesi tournament. You know your gunshots will bring the police, right? Or are you too blinded by the Dali to think straight?"

"We're in Florida. I felt threatened. I stood my ground. I won't even be charged." He looked at Karl. "Search behind the shed."

Karl walked over to the shed and disappeared behind it. He came out on the other side.

"Nothing," he said.

Garrett must have moved them. But where are he and Charley?

Demos gave that a second. "Check the other side of the gate."

Karl went outside. A moment later he yelled, "They're here. Tied up."

Demos drew a gun. He walked over to the gate but pulled up short of walking through it. He glanced over his shoulder. Taken with what I can only assume was the sight of two of his men bound and gagged, he kept his eyes outside. I bent and grabbed the knife. I palmed it in my hand so as to hide it.

"How bad are they?" he said to Karl, who was out of my sight.

"They're fine," Karl said. "Stephen says the Black man is here. Charley is with him."

Gregory came back to the pool deck, Kevin and his girlfriend in front of him.

"It wasn't in the bedroom," Gregory said. "Now he wants to check the downstairs bathroom."

"No, really," the man said. "I'm fine without it."

"Oh, for God's sake, Kevin," the woman said. "You got the right to look for your frickin' wallet."

Demos strode back to where we were. "Get rid of them. Now."

Gregory started to nudge them toward the house. The woman planted herself in front of Demos. "Listen, you fairy freak, I don't know who you think you are. But . . ."

Demos pistol-whipped her in the face. She stumbled backward and fell in the pool. Kevin screamed. The woman in the pool started to sink.

Karl, sensing the turn of events, dashed in from the gate. I flung my knife at him. It planted itself in his stomach. He let out a loud grunt. The knife appeared to annoy him more than injure him. That's not good. A shot rang out from a second-floor balcony. Gregory went down. Charley dashed in through the open gate, her gun drawn. She hesitated. Karl spun and punched her in the face. Her gun fell to the ground a split second before she did. A sickening crack came from her head.

Garrett jumped down from the balcony.

Karl pulled the knife out of his body and tossed it to the ground, pesky gnat that it was. He bull-rushed me, tumbling us backward. I didn't want to wrestle the man. I rolled, sprang to my feet, and took two steps back. He came at me again. I took a quick step to the side, stuck my foot out, and tripped him. He started to get up. I smashed his face with my right foot. But like a Weebles toy that was round at the bottom, Karl refused to go down.

Only then did I realize that he had never released his gun. Karl was ambidextrous and had no problem smashing Charley with his other hand. He aimed his gun at me. I dove for his ankles, taking him down the same time Garrett shot him. But Karl got an errant round.

Demos grabbed a fistful of Charley's short hair. He yanked her up off the pool deck.

"Enough," he shouted. With his free hand, he pointed a gun at Charley's head. His eyes darted between Garrett and me. "Throw your guns down, or I kill her. Now."

That wasn't going to happen. Garrett also has two dictums. Garrett Dictum Number One: never surrender your weapon.

"I don't think so," Garrett said. He started walking toward Demos. He kept his gun loose at his side. He was about fifteen paces away. "We throw our guns down, we're dead. You kill her, you're dead."

"Stop. I'll kill her," Demos said.

"Go ahead," Garrett said.

I'm sure he didn't mean it. Right?

"Let her go, Demos," I pleaded. "It's the only way you get out alive."

I stole a glance at the pool. The green-eyed woman was floating face up. Her arms were agitating the water just enough to keep her mouth above the surface, her lips gaping like a half-dead fish. But her eyes were wide open as if she registered her predicament. She was trapped in a lucid dream unable to speak or escape.

Those wide open eyes locked on mine. Everything she had, all her tomorrows and all her yesterdays, she channeled to her lips.

Please. Please. Please.

CHAPTER 51

"I need to get her out of the pool," I said to nobody. "She'll drown."

"Let her drown." Demos wrapped his arm around Charley's neck and brought her body tight against his, using it as a shield. Charley's head bobbled side to side as she fought for consciousness.

Stephen, one of the two men we had tied, stumbled through the gate, his gun drawn. To this day, Garrett and I have no idea where he got his gun from. He must have had another on him, and, in a hurry, we didn't search him well enough. He got off an aimless shot before Garrett, who had instantly fallen to a crouched position, returned fire, hitting him in his legs.

From behind me, the woman in the pool gasped for air.

Demos had taken his eye off me when Stephen did his Lazarus number. I rushed him, reaching for his gun. It went off. I didn't feel anything, but Charley's body collapsed to the ground. We struggled for the gun. Demos squeezed it tight, trying to get the barrel pointed at me. Our faces were inches apart. I head butted him, cracking his nose. I did it again. His face blossomed into a bright stream of red.

Garrett rushed in, grabbed his arm, and snapped it behind his back. Demos howled and dropped his gun before crumpling to his knees.

"Kevin," I said to Garrett. For Kevin was slumped against the wall. His face draining of color. His shirt deathly red. Stephen's errant shot? Demos's? Sirens wailed in the night.

Garrett rushed to Kevin's side. He ripped off Kevin's shirt. He said some words to Kevin and started applying pressure to the wound. I jumped in the pool and, in one motion, gathered the woman with the green eyes. I hauled her out of the pool and laid her on the pool deck. I started to give her CPR but kept an eye on Demos.

Demos stood and stumbled toward the house.

Charley reached for Demos's gun. She struggled to her knees. She shot him, hitting him in the lower back.

"Charley?" he said, turning around. He sounded like Denise. He looked at his torso. "What have you done?"

"That is for Francis," Charley said.

"Oh, my dear," he said. Denise talking now. "Surely you know I never would have hurt her if I'd known."

Charley shot him again. But she was still woozy, and the bullet only grazed his side. Or maybe she wasn't a good shot. Or maybe she wanted him to die slowly.

Demos staggered. He flipped his Norma Desmond scarf over his shoulder. Did Demos want to die as Denise?

He spoke like a song, his voice sliding along a pentatonic scale. "It was fun, wasn't it, dear? The parties. The hot nights. The mindless pursuit of pleasure."

Charley shot him again. He staggered.

"Ohhh . . . that one hurt. Are you dying me, Charley? Are you dying me? You'd shoot a woman?"

"You did."

Charley steadied her hand. She hesitated. I wanted to tell her not to shoot Demos, that it wasn't worth killing him. That by doing so she would sentence herself to a life of nightmares, to lonely nights you shared with no one because you are too ashamed of what you have done and who you are, and—here's the real nut—that life in prison for Demos would be worse than death.

While the theme of Charley's future nightmares balanced on her finger, Demos melted to the ground. Charley lowered her gun. She dropped it.

As Garrett fought to keep Kevin breathing, I gave CPR to the green-eyed woman, but I was afraid I was too late, and it was all my fault. I should have walked away from Veronica Stafford. Nothing good had come from my efforts except I did like the painting of the four women, and that was such a stupid thing to think about at that moment, but there you have it.

PART III

THE GANGSTER OF LOVE

CHAPTER 52

Veronica Stafford sat in the same chair she had the first time I visited her. "The Windmills of Your Mind" played over the speakers. The steady click of the light timer methodically punctuated the air.

Lenin observed there were decades when nothing happens and weeks when decades happen. Veronica Stafford looked as if she'd just experienced the latter. Her eyes wary. Unfocused. Her hands clasped together, her fingers kneading each other. Her disease had advanced ten years in seven days.

"You did not find it?" she demanded.

I had just told her as much. We'd also discussed the death of her husband. She'd been notified by Wetzel. She'd shown little interest in discussing his demise.

"No."

"You certainly tried."

I didn't trust myself to answer her. Two nights ago, Detective Rambler had kept me up until sunrise, going over the details that led to the body bags being carted out of a house a few blocks from where I now sat. As far as I knew, Veronica was unaware of any of that. I'd cooperated with Rambler, although my memory might have been a bit foggy. Garrett reminded Rambler that he was a lawyer, knew his rights, and had nothing to say. Garrett's Second Dictum: never talk to the police. Every shot Garrett took was indisputably in self-defense—I think—but he'd put three men down that night. Not that anyone's counting. All three were expected to live. I believe that was by design, although I'd yet to discuss it with Garrett.

Veronica glanced at a piece of paper on the end table next to the chair. I adjusted my weight. I had eleven stitches in my right side where a bullet from Karl's gun had grazed me. I'd been performing CPR on the green-eyed woman when I noticed blood dripping onto her clothing.

"How close did you get?" she asked me.

"Tell me about your daughter."

Veronica stared at me as if someone was calling her name. But who?

"What does she have to do with this?" she demanded.

"Why didn't you tell me about her?"

"I didn't think it mattered."

It.

"Did you hire me to find the Dali or your daughter?"

A nervous laugh. "Whatever do you mean?"

"Answer the question," I said, my tone more hostile than intended.

"There's no need to be rude."

"The question."

"I hired you to find the Dali. I *certainly* know where my daughter is."

"Where is she?"

"She's in Europe. Paris, I assume."

"Give me the street she lives on."

"Oh, this is nonsense."

"Does she have the painting?"

"Whatever in the world are you talking about?"

"I think Nick sold, or gifted, the Dali before he died. I think your daughter was involved in that transaction."

"I hardly—well, that could be. But I doubt it."

"Who did you go to New York with?"

"Myself."

"No, you didn't."

"I beg your pardon."

I leaned forward in my chair, struggling to contain the events of the past forty-eight hours from splatting out on the floor.

I said, "You did not go to New York by yourself."

I knew that because Garrett and I had taken shifts outside her house. It was Garrett's turn when she returned with a man who, when I described him to Sally Herrington, she identified as Michael Fredericks. Veronica's first husband and father of their daughter.

"I went with a friend," Veronica said defensively.

"Michael Fredericks."

"How do you know of him?"

"You were married to him. Long ago."

"I asked you to find a missing Dali, not to spy on my life. Besides, how can any of this possibly matter?"

"Everything matters."

"Certainly, you have some leads."

"Where's your daughter?" I repeated.

"Oh, for heaven's sake. I assure you she does not have the Dali."

"Is she alive?"

"What a disgusting question."

"Do you have a good relationship with her?"

"Stop it. Of course I do."

"Would she do something behind your back?"

"Stop it. Please."

"Would she?"

299

"This is nonsense."

"Why?"

"Why? Because I say so. That's why."

"People died trying to get that painting. An innocent woman is fighting for her life in a hospital."

Her eyes flashed with uncertainty. As if she'd suddenly dropped in somewhere and didn't know where or why. I didn't mean to be cruel to her and felt bad about my last comment. Saint Augustine said never use the truth to injure. She had a disease, and I needed to be more delicate. I felt bad for my incessant questioning and was trying to think of something conciliatory to say when she spoke.

"I am sorry if it didn't go the . . ." She glanced at the paper. "Can I get you something to drink?"

"There's no pictures," I said softly.

"Of what?"

"Of her. In your house. There's no pictures of Jamie."

"You spoke her name," she intoned.

"Yes."

"I don't like pictures," she rallied and said defiantly. "All they do is take you out of the present."

A spooky silence settled over us as the song played on, having started over again. I decided not to press her further, for I feared I'd already hit her too hard.

"I met with Wayne Gibson at Rollins," I said. "He is conducting his own hunt. If he finds it, I believe he will keep your name clear."

"She might have it."

"Jamie?"

Veronica looked at me, bewildered by my presence.

"No. She."

"Who?"

She waved a hand in the air. "Oh, I don't know. It's just a silly painting."

"I know my seven days are up," I said, changing tack. "But I don't think you'd squabble if I were a day or two late. Where's Michael? I understand he's close to Jamie."

"Whatever gave you that impression?"

I saw no need to tell her that I'd met with Michael's ex-wife.

"Just an impression I got."

"He's . . . gone. He's not here."

"Do you mind if I talk to him?"

"You may do whatever you wish, Mr. Travis. Our deal was for you to find the Dali within seven days. It is unfortunate that you were unable to do so."

"How did you come into possession of the Dali?"

"You don't let up do you? I am not at liberty to discuss that."

"I think I earned as much."

"I think not."

"And Harbor House?"

"What of it?"

"Will you be gifting to it?"

"You know our deal."

"You will, won't you? You'd already decided to make the gift but then had the wicked idea of attaching a request to it. To make a game of it. Was it fun?"

That also came out crueler than intended, my belligerent tone foreign to me. The affairs of the last twenty-four hours were taking their toll. But that was no excuse.

"I hardly call this a game," Veronica said.

"I apologize if I've offended you. But what would you call it?"

"Theater, Mr. Travis." Veronica Stafford stood, stretching herself to her full height. "This stage of fools. I trust you can find your way out."

CHAPTER 53

VERONICA AND MICHAEL

Present Day

Dusty does it best

Michael waited until Jake Travis closed the door before stepping out of the study.

"He learned quite a bit in seven days," Michael said. "He found us. Jamie. But not the Dali. You'll do it anyway, won't you?"

"Do you think he knows I'll still do it?"

"I do," Michael said.

"I should have told him."

"He'll find out in time."

"I sounded rude."

"He was rude. You were fine."

"He had the right to be. It's just that he surprised me. All his questions about Jamie. I sounded so . . . mean."

"You were fine."

"What's happening to me, Michael?"

"You did great, Vee."

Michael moved behind Veronica. He wrapped his arms around her.

"Who is she?" he said.

"Who?"

"You told him 'she' might have it. Who is 'she'?"

She turned and faced him.

"Did I? I was confused. He threw me, talking about Jamie like that. I don't like it. Someone else talking about her. Now, Michael. There's no need to talk."

She broke his hold and strolled toward her bedroom. Michael hesitated, realizing the full measure of this speck of time. The moment he had steeled himself for, now upon him. He followed her. His feet moving without command, for they'd been rehearsing this moment for weeks.

At the threshold of the hall leading to her bedroom, Veronica turned and stole one last glance at her living room. The paintings. The exquisite glass sculptures. A nameless sadness washed over her.

"Remember Paris?" she said. "That little café? I can never remember its name. And Hawaii. Paris. The Tetons. We did it all, didn't we?"

"We did."

"And the movie, *Pillow Talk*. Remember we went out to dinner? We had a bottle of Italian wine, Badia a Coltibuono."

Good God, where did that come from? And if that meaningless debris is still around, will the rest—the horror—come gushing forward after years of repression? I lifted the sheet off her body. They told me I did. Said they had to pull me away. No, had to pull me "off," they said.

"I recall the dinner but not the wine," Michael said. "And our first trip to New York. How exciting it was."

"Your brother," Veronica said, fighting to subdue her nightmare, "what was his name? Ker-Chunk. Was that it?"

"How could I forget him?"

"He went to Yale, didn't he?"

"Stanford."

"No, Yale. I remember."

"You're right. It was Yale."

They were quiet for a moment. The living room in one direction. The bedroom in the other. Michael envisioned the last painting he would paint. It all made sense to him, and he was glad that at the end, it all made sense because nothing in between had.

"It's too bad the man, Travis, didn't find the Dali," he said.

"Whoever Nick sold it to will likely not sell it," Veronica said. "Even if they did, they would claim it a family heirloom of unknown origin. Rollins might contest that, but our name won't be involved."

"You left a letter with Wetzel?"

"Yes. He'll tell him."

"I wonder how he'll take it."

"What do you think Jamie's doing now?"

"Taking a vacation with her husband and children."

"We haven't talked much about the grandchildren, have we?"

"Jamie was enough for us," Michael said.

"You know Faye meant nothing to me, right? I was mad at the world. Not you."

"I know, Vee."

"I'm so sorry."

"Don't."

"Faye never should have allowed it. Letting me back like that."

"No. She should not have. She was not thinking of you. That was not love."

"I know that now."

It had been Veronica's sin, not the unspeakable tragedy, that had splintered their world. Placed an unbridgeable canyon between them. Although she never mentioned it to her doctor, Veronica believed her disease to be a direct result of years of stress. Her mind preying upon itself because of her past blunder. She'd never offered herself an olive branch, for she was not worthy. Did not deserve happiness. The world saw Veronica as a successful businesswoman. A pillar of the community. Little could they imagine that, on the self-esteem meter of life, Veronica Stafford registered mind-blowing lows.

The last thing to collapse is the surface.

After her world had crashed, and desperate to turn back the hands of time, she'd fled to Faye. To escape to a place where grief no longer consumed her. Where you smoked a joint to solve the world's insoluble problems. She'd long ago come to understand that her reaction to their immeasurable sorrow affronted Michael. Violated their trust. His act was the forgetfulness of a simple household task. Her act was a cruel reaction that torched the land. When she'd realized her miscalculation —he was gone. Michael had left, driven by guilt, crushed by her refusal to suffer with him. Jealous that she, in the moment of life's unbearable grief, found comfort in the arms of another.

Decades of silence followed.

When they finally reunited, Michael confessed that he wrote letters he never mailed. Writing was easy, he said. Therapeutic. Placing a stamp on the envelope? That's hard. That's commitment. The letters were an olive branch that, if refused, would shatter his dreams. And so, he labored on—dreamed on —penning words and stuffing them in a box, unwilling to take a chance.

A week after Michael learned he had inoperable cancer, which was three and a half years into Veronica's marriage to Nick Harris, he started writing *and* mailing her letters. Courage often appears when there is nothing to lose.

He wrote with brilliant and fearless strokes of the pen. Reminiscing about the pelican stuffy Jamie toted to her first day of preschool. Remember? Its beak was plastic, not soft. She loved it anyway. The time she skinned her forehead chasing a bunny as it scampered through a fence at Gettysburg on a day so hot Michael wondered if hell had broken free. The smile she flashed at them when she received her college diploma. Names of friends. The food she liked. Her travels. Postcards she'd sent. Not from the edge, but from the center. Choked with details.

We can't go back in time, but we can reconstruct it any way we wish.

She wrote him back.

Yes. I remember. I remember it all. He called her. Both of them, now tripping over each other's words. *I'm sorry. No, it was my fault. No, mine. Such a massive mistake. Oh God, I wanted to. But I didn't think you would ever forgive me. I never blamed you.*

They agreed to meet. He knew right away that something was off. By the distance in her eyes. The cadence of her speech. She told him. He didn't tell her. Didn't tell his ex-wife either. Michael Fredericks preferred to go quietly into that good night. That the opportunity arose to do so quickly was something he could not pass. Veronica guessed it. He denied it.

But Michael felt she knew and secretly approved. Just as the man, Travis, knew about the gift to Harbor House.

Veronica led them to the bedroom. Michael stared at the bed. "Our granddaughter will be getting married soon," he said, knowing he was stalling. "Having children. She'll be sending us refrigerator drawings."

Veronica placed a hand on his cheek. She could feel the maggots of death feasting on her mind, the final sunset of her life now upon her.

"Oh God, Michael. When I first got your letters, I came undone. I'm so sorry. Tell me you know that. Please, tell me again."

"I know. I knew before you."

He kissed the top of her head. She looked him in his eyes.

Time had been kind to him. His hair was a winter pasture of white and gray, his coiffured beard framing a still-youthful face.

"Did I come all the way back? Tell me yes, even if I didn't."

"You soared, Vee. We never lost her. She made us. She'll live forever."

"I'm ready. Dusty's singing now. She does it best."

She climbed into her bed. Michael followed, spooning his body next to hers.

"I love you, Vee," he whispered in her ear. "I can take care of you."

"No, Michael," she said, her face upward. "We've talked it through. It's hideous. Ugly. Destroying me by the minute. I will not allow it. You can do it. And afterward, your memories will be of me, of us. Not of some reduced form, boiled away until nothing is left. We always remember people at the end. The last pictures. The last words. If you don't do this, that is how you'll remember me. Mindless pounds of flesh. A gaping mouth with no words. You do it, or I will."

Veronica was impressed that she was able to get that all out. She knew it was the last hurrah of her intellect, and of that, she was proud. She smoothed out the white dress she'd selected. She reached into a drawer. She took out a gun. She handed it to Michael.

Michael took it, handling as if it was a putrid piece of flesh.

"You haven't asked me about the plane," she said.

"I assume it will be waiting for me."

"But you didn't ask. You're going, aren't you?"

"I am."

"To the plane. Not with me."

"I'll go to the plane."

"Promise me."

"I promise."

"Drop it in the water. When you leave, it will be dark. You parked a few blocks away, right?"

"I did."

"It was a good autumn, wasn't it? Early, like it was in a rush. I remember as a child going to the cabin, and the first snow would fall on colored leaves. I liked that. I used to think that every snowflake was an angel, picking out its favorite color to land on. Tell me again that you're going."

"I'm going."

"Not with me."

"No, not with you."

Veronica didn't know whether he was telling the truth or not. But talk at this point was dangerous. They'd discussed this over dinner at Dina's on their last night in Ellicottville. How, when the moment came, they would need to act quickly. With purpose and no hesitation. Michael had wondered what other couples in the restaurant were discussing.

Michael traced a finger over Veronica's cheek. Her lip. Her eyebrow. He ran his finger over the top of her forehead, brushing back her hair. He held her face in the palm of his hand, as if it were a freshly picked flower of indescribable glory. To look at her at seventy-two, to remember her at twenty-two, to love her more at the end—that was something no song, no painting, could ever touch. Michael Fredericks, at the end, knew that all art is failure.

Veronica said, "I love it when you hold my face in your hands. You asked me once, long ago, what I was thinking and it was that. I don't think I ever told you."

"You didn't need to." He paused. "It was a bird."

He didn't know whether to bring up the painting or that he had cancer. Or neither. But for some reason, he felt compelled to bring up one, and then it was so clear he was ashamed he'd not seen it earlier. The painting. Of course. The bookends of their lives.

"What was a bird?" Veronica said.

"The painting of mine. When we first met."

"I remember. The splash of colors in the center of a canvas. A feather sticking out. The gray background. Whatever became of it?"

"I sold it years ago," he lied.

"What was your inspiration for it?"

"A dead bird. I saw it in the middle of the road. The colors were so brilliant. So rainbowy. I couldn't imagine the bird being more attractive in life than it was in death. I picked up a feather and stuck it in the painting."

"A dead bird on a road was your magnum opus?"

"Afraid so."

"Well, that was hardly worth the wait," she said with a wry smile, humor not yet flushed from her mind. "I want to be on my stomach. It will be easier for both of us."

She rolled over. She turned her head on the pillow, away from him.

"Remember, while you're talking. You have such a beautiful voice. About what we talked about. Our script."

"I know."

She buried her head in her pillow.

Michael kissed the back of her head. He clasped her hand with his hand. Tight. Michael was not a big man. Not a strong man. Not a man who ever measured or considered the merits of physical stamina. He was not a man of religious beliefs. He did not know where Veronica was going, but he would not allow her to go there by herself.

Now. You are the gangster of love.

"We're sitting on the back deck," he said, reciting his lines. "Summer went so quickly this year. It's cold, and we fear the world when October goes. The trees are washed with color. Red. Yellow. Gold. Jamie is playing by the shore, chasing leaves. They are turning the color of her hair. See her run. See—"

Michael Fredericks shot his rainbow.

CHAPTER 54

MICHAEL

Present Day

The pharaoh's riddle

He vomited.

He'd purposely avoided imagining this part of it and was glad at least for that. Nothing could have prepared him for the carnage he'd created. Life was gone. In its place was a spattered, slimy, disfigured arrangement of flesh. The face he loved, that he'd just cradled in his hands, now annihilated. His destiny destroyed.

Oh God. What have I done?

His body shuddered in a dry heave.

Fuck me. Fuck me. Fuck me.

He took a deep breath. Another. He felt nothing, and he did not understand this. Philippe Aries's quote popped into his head: "A single person is missing from you, and the whole world is empty."

And now, my turn.

She had to know that he had no intention of ever again

seeing the winter woolen-gray sky. Not without her. Stroll through an art show. Not without her. Autumn. Not without her. Jamie. Not without her.

Jamie. Jamie. Jamie. He felt bad for never telling Sally about Jamie. *What a horrible husband. She deserved better than me. Oh well, too late now.*

He recalled his conversation with Veronica the last morning at the cabin. *Did she even know in the end?* And what will the man, Travis, think of it all? He had debated telling her that Travis had found him—hounded his voice mail—but he'd never returned his calls. He was glad he'd kept that to himself. It was of no good.

He resisted getting out of bed. Then what? A step here? A step there? Soon, he would be in another room. Away from her. For what? At best, another year? And what a swell year his doctors had lined up for him. He'd been through it a thousand times in his head. That's why he had two stiff drinks before coming over. Brushed his teeth to hide his timidity from her.

He'd created a persona, an alter ego, to get him through it. Fly above it all. He would become the marriage of love and violence. The joining of brutality and passion.

I am the gangster of love.

He stuck the gun in his mouth. The hardness of the metal startled him. A mad rush of poems seized his mind as if fearful they, too, would perish with him. Keats was first: *Here lies one whose name was writ with water.*

Then came the final torrent of Michael Fredericks.

Do it now. While she is still warm. Before her fingers turn white. Whatever became of Blue Monkey? I didn't see it on the shelf. Focus, man. Focus. Now. Before Hamlet's silence. Now. Like I did for her. Now. When the autumn leaves are the color of her hair. Now. The man will sort it out. He will make it all good. Now. Before my body eats itself. Now. Death be not proud. I am the gangster. Now. Under the wide and starry sky/Dig the grave and let me die. Now. Grow old along with me! The best is yet to be. Now. On this deck I will be fallen cold and dead. Stop it. Stop it. No more poems. Just one last painting. Paint it, man. Paint it!

For the second time in his life, Michael Fredericks, artist, poet, ardent gun hater, a man who wouldn't pluck a wing from a fly, a man who had just killed the only person he'd ever loved, squeezed the trigger and ended a human life. It was the seventy-fourth autumn of his years.

At midnight, in Saint Petersburg, Florida, all was quiet.

CHAPTER 55

I was about to enter the ramp to I-275 South when I did a U-turn.

Something that Veronica had said.

No.

Everything she'd said. About the way she referred to her daughter. How she took offense to my assertation that she didn't go to New York by herself. And what about Michael? I had every right to talk to Michael Fredericks. Either he was still part of her life or he wasn't. Gibson had admitted that the last time Rollins had inventory of the painting was "sometime in the early seventies." Michael was at Rollins then. Michael was an art student. He was family. *Did Nick sell it to Michael, who swiped it in the first place? And what's this baloney about a daughter?*

I had blood on my hands. Stitches in my body. I deserved to know more. To hell with Saint Augustine.

I pulled back onto her street just as the black curtain of night descended. I knocked on the door. Hit the doorbell. Knocked again. Maybe she was in the shower. I walked around to the back of the house. I peered into the garage. A car was inside. I continued walking around the house, surprised how dark it was. I would have thought there would be more lights on than just the one in the living room. I returned to the front door. I jabbed the doorbell again, pounded the door.

I tried the door knob. It was unlocked. I recalled hearing the snap of the deadlock when I'd left Veronica the first time we'd met. I'd heard no such sound that evening. I stepped inside.

"Hello? Veronica?"

Louder this time.

"Veronica? Sorry to disturb you but I had just a few more questions."

I stole into the sunroom, past the snow globe with no snow in it. The dining room. The study. A narrow hall off the living room led to a small half-bath.

No pictures. No Jamie. But who is "she," if not Jamie?

"Veronica?"

The hall continued to a bedroom, for I could see the foot of the bed in the dim light.

I went into the bedroom.

Veronica and Michael lay together. At least what was left of a man I recognized from pictures of Michael Fredericks. It was not a painting I wish to explain. I collapsed in a chair, my legs leaving me. I sat there a long, long time. Several times I thought I should rise, but a tidal force not of this world pressed me to the chair.

I finally went to the living room. Like a child who knows his assigned seat, I sat in the same chair I'd sat in when talking with Veronica. I called Detective Rambler. Only after we disconnected did I hear the song, and I wondered why I hadn't heard it when I'd come in, and I got up and went to the bookcases and turned the music off, and that just left the ticking of a light timer, and that grew so annoyingly loud that I yanked it out of the wall and then sat in the dark.

CHAPTER 56

In New Orleans, they bury the dead above ground. They say it's because of the water level, but I don't buy that. I think the dead don't want to leave. And the living aren't that alive. They creep in the city heat, eyes hollow, steps small, equally as dead as alive.

That's how I felt when I walked into R. Wetzel Brookings's office. Equally dead as alive. A real tug-of-war. I'd done my morning run. Punched and kicked the bag. Went out to breakfast. Ate bacon off a scratched plate. Smeared butter on toast before bathing it with jelly. Drank coffee and breathed in salt air. But the endorphins just weren't there. Must have called in sick.

Wetzel rose to greet me. We again took seats under the curve of his deceased wife's back. I had been the one who notified him of Veronica's and Michael's deaths. Rambler had confirmed that Michael Fredericks had shot Veronica first and then turned the gun on himself. He also added that he wished I would move out of his jurisdiction. I'm sure he was just kidding.

"They planned it all along," Wetzel said with too much admiration for my taste. "You know she was not well."

"I believe you lied to me on that point."

He adjusted his weight. "I didn't want to—"

"She was confused on dates. She relied on notes to keep her conversation on course. Early dementia?"

"I'm afraid early sailed some time ago. It was progressing rapidly. Apparently, she chose to meet it on the field. After all, by dying, she also killed the disease. Is that not victory? She was a woman, as I believe I explained when we first met, who dictated life on her terms. As for Mr. Fredericks, her first husband, I did not know the man."

I asked if he thought Veronica knew that Michael would follow her.

"A question for the ages." He stood and walked over to the window, his body casting a shadow on the floor. He spoke facing Tampa Bay, his back toward me. R. Wetzel Brookings was a man who spent considerable time staring over open water. "She confided a great many things in me. But that is not the same as confiding everything in me."

I told him that Nick Harris told Carrie, or at least gave the impression, that he was close to a fast deal to move the Dali. That it involved someone close to Veronica. Possibly related to her. I explained how I'd come to learn about their daughter, Jamie, but had been unable to locate her and that Veronica was of no help.

"It's time for the second letter Veronica prepared for you," he said. "Recall, in the first letter she—"

The second letter.

A sense of déjà vu flooded me. Years ago, while searching for a lost letter from a CIA operative, I'd stumbled across a second letter. I assumed the letter concerned national security. Instead, it was a love letter. It had changed the trajectory of my life. Was *I* trapped in Veronica's song, going around and around? Is all we—?

"Mr. Travis?"

"Yes?"

"I inquired if you recalled that in the first letter, she mentioned a small favor in which she didn't feel you would object to."

"Jamie's made up, isn't she? She's not even real."

"Oh, she's very real. But perhaps in ways beyond our comprehension."

He walked over to his desk. He opened a drawer and withdrew an envelope. As with the first one he'd presented to me, my name was written on it.

I withdrew the letter.

Dear Mr. Travis,

Foremost, allow me to thank you for your effort in searching for The Lost Body. Successful or not, I have no doubt you did your best.

I, of course, fully intend to donate the ten million to Harbor House. That such a meaningful gift rests on something so trivial as a missing painting of a madman was never in question. Forgive me if you feel I freeloaded off your efforts.

If you recall my previous letter to you, I mentioned "one small favor."

I would like naming privileges for my gift. I'm sure you understand that is the way these things work. I have no desire to erase Walter MacDonald's name from the property. I do request that my daughter's name be added.

I suggest The Walter MacDonald, Jamie Fredericks Harbor House.

I do this for selfish reasons. We gain immortality through our children, Mr. Travis. I wish to be immortal.

Respectively submitted,

Veronica Stafford

I stood. Wetzel's eyes were hard on mine.

"I get the money?"

"You do."

"She's a son of a bitch."

"I understand it . . . got more violent than anticipated."

"You don't understand a thing."

"I am the messenger here. There's another ten."

"Pardon?"

"She had allocated ten million to buy the Dali. By failing, and I mean no disrespect, you double what Harbor House gets. Her estate will be bequeathing twenty million dollars. Perhaps even more once the estate is settled, as she instructed all residual amounts also be gifted. Originally, she and I did not calculate that to be a meaningful sum. But as her husband died intestate, his estate is now included in hers. We are still unraveling his estate. It has proven more difficult than one would expect. That is by design, I believe."

"You didn't answer my question about their daughter, Jamie. What did they do? Make her up after having an abortion years ago? A miscarriage?"

Wetzel gazed up at the painting of his wife. "She comes to me in my dreams. Speaks to me. I speak to her. In those dreams, she is as real as she ever was when her heart beat." He leveled his eyes at me. "Who's to judge what is real and what is not? The wilderness of our illusions are never cleared. Jamie Fredericks, Mr. Travis, is very real. It has, however, been forty-eight years since her last breath."

CHAPTER 57

VERONICA

1975

In the park across the street

They'd gone to a different restaurant than they told her mother. Veronica liked Billy Joel's song "Scenes from an Italian Restaurant." What mood was she in? A bottle of white? A bottle of red? At the last minute, she decided on steak.

That is why the two officers sent out to retrieve them came back empty. It was a nasty assignment, and both men, Bruce Bernard and Phil Martinson—Martinson had a two-year-old at home—were relieved when they couldn't locate Veronica and Michael. They lied the next day when their supervisor asked if they searched other restaurants as well, using the description Veronica's mother had provided the police. The supervisor, twenty-eight-year veteran Phil Stapleton, hadn't wanted the young couple to go home on their own.

Veronica and Michael had just ordered dessert. Michael told Veronica that the torched sugar topping of the crème brulée resembled the color of dry leaves on a walking path.

"You're right," Veronica said, thinking it was a perfect description of not only the color but the texture as well.

Michael tapped the glassy surface with the edge of his spoon. "A tad longer with the torch would have brought out even more colors."

"But it's still good, isn't it?" Veronica said, worried that an imperfect crème brulée might stain the evening. Ever since Jamie's birth, they'd had so few evenings for just the two of them.

Michael poked through the crunchy top with his spoon and took a bite.

"Pure heaven."

They battled each other for the final scoops, their spoons lunging and parrying. They debated getting another but opted not to. Dining out, after all, was an expensive treat.

They strolled hand in hand back to their apartment. They talked of the things to do, of places to go. Bills to be paid. Career dreams. Veronica's left foot hurt. Her shoes were new, and the left shoe didn't want to break in as easy as the right.

Two blocks away, they spotted the ambulance in front of their apartment complex.

One block away, Veronica broke into a run.

Michael did not catch her in time. He was, as he'd admitted the summer evening when they first met, a clumsy runner. Officer Martinson stood at the entrance of their opened front door. He tried to wrap Veronica in his arms. She shoved him aside. Her mother was slumped on the floor at the bottom of the dark steps. She stared at Veronica with haunted, godless eyes. A man squatted next to her, tending to her leg. Veronica's mind seized the inconsequential. *Who cares about her leg?* On the floor, next to her mother, lay a lumpy sheet.

Veronica collapsed. She crawled to the sheet. Her memory ends here. She woke the next morning from a drug-induced sleep to a clear and cloudless Sunday. The air pealed with church bells and the squealing of the twins playing in the park across the street.

CHAPTER 58

K athleen, Morgan, and I sat on the screened porch on a smoky saxophone evening. The rising moon bleached the bay, and Kathleen's solitary candle flickered in the breeze. I got up, went inside, grabbed a blanket, and returned to the porch. I draped it over Kathleen's shoulders. She took it in both hands and tightened it around her neck.

No one had spoken for some time. The three of us have no problem sitting in silence, for it is an adhesive element that binds us together.

Kathleen broke that sacred quietude "She'll be all right?"

We'd previously been discussing Charley. She'd been released from the hospital earlier that day.

"She will," I replied. "It was nip and tuck with her blood loss, but she pulled through."

"And she got her revenge."

"For whatever that's worth."

I'd told Kathleen and Morgan that, while I was visiting her in the hospital, Charley told me she'd been stalking Demos ever since he had her lover, Francis Rampton, killed for accusing him of manufacturing fake prints. She hadn't wanted

Demos to die, but rather to spend the remainder of his life incarcerated. A sentence, she felt, far worse than the chair. She got her wish as, inexplicably, Demos had survived. When I asked her why she'd repeatedly shot Demos if she wanted him to live, she'd just looked past me.

I glanced at Morgan. "Charley wants to drop by Harbor House tomorrow. See what all the fuss was about. I told her you'd be there all day."

"I will be," Morgan said. "I'm interviewing for the position of director. But that person will need to be able to teach classes, cook. Everything. I don't want the money to breed bureaucracy."

I remained silent.

"The money will make an incalculable difference," Morgan said. It was kind of him to say that.

A great blue heron squawked and took flight, the whoosh of its wings breaking the silence. Something must have infringed on its territory, or else it would have taken to the air silently.

Morgan stood. "It's been a long day. There is a strong tide Tuesday morning during the full moon. Care to join me?"

"Absolutely."

He strolled out the side door and across the yard, his figure interrupting the wide highway of moonlight a breeze blew across the water.

"What did Rambler say about Demos?" Kathleen asked.

"They got enough to stick him away. Parker, his accountant, ended up cutting a deal."

"And the murder of Nick Harris?"

"They can't pin it on him."

"He'll get away with it?"

"Looks like it."

"Terrible. And the woman? Anna, right?" Kathleen said.

Anna. The green-eyed woman in the pool. *Please. Please. Pl—*

"Babe?"

"Pardon?"

"How is Anna?"

"Still in a coma."

"Garrett told me the medics said you kept her alive. Breathed into her until they came. That they had to pull you off."

"She's in a coma," I repeated.

"She'll be fine."

"They have no way of assessing brain damage until she comes out. If she comes out."

"She will. And her boyfriend, Kevin?"

"He pulled through."

"And you?"

"Never better."

"I got—hey, look at me. I'm talking to you."

I did as instructed, for my gaze had wandered over the water. She stood, took a step, and plopped on my lap. (Reason 3. Remember?)

"She'll be fine. Hear me?"

"I do."

"I got an offer on my condo."

"When?"

"Yesterday. Your plate was full. Stacey's thrilled. It was a quick sell, and she's already picked up two new listings. We close in thirty days. Know what that means? You owe me an addition, mister. A seaside library."

"Do I, now?"

"Yes sirree. In the meantime, I'm renting a storage unit. Morgan, by the way, is beyond thrilled. To be able to teach every day and not be burdened with all that other stuff."

"Speaking of teaching, do you miss your classes?"

She ran her hand through my hair. "Thought I would. Thought wrong. When I take the girls out? To the store or to the children's art class I told you about? I swear, I don't know if it's just them discovering life for the first time or me as well."

"Why not both?"

"Why not?"

THAT NIGHT, AS KATHLEEN slept next to me, it wasn't the eyes of a man learning to beg that came to me. Or a woman with one earring. Or my daughter winking at me from inside our house.

That night, as Kathleen nestled next to me, those babbling images and shards of memory had no chance. For in the boneyard of my mind floated a woman with green eyes. Trapped in purgatory, unable to help herself, yet knowing she was in trouble. She looked at me. Garrett said we saved Charley. Kevin. Ourselves. Maybe Anna. Maybe not. Can't win them all, he reminded me.

But she hadn't looked at him. Anna had looked at me. Moved her lips.

Please. Please. Please.

She was there because of me. My foolish games.

TWO WEEKS LATER, WHILE running on the dark beach, I realized I never talked to the neighbor to the immediate right of Veronica. The one who had lived in the neighborhood the longest. I recalled her name from when I first researched the house. Barbara Langford. She was never home when I knocked.

I rang her doorbell at nine that morning.

CHAPTER 59

The first floor of the house was two steps above me, which put the woman who opened it at eye level. I introduced myself and asked if she was Barbara Langford. She confirmed she was. I explained that I was an acquittance of Veronica Stafford. That I would appreciate a few minutes of her time.

She wore jeans and a yellow and blue willow pattern blouse with the sleeves partially rolled up. A collection of bracelets garnished her right wrist. Her eyes were curious, like someone amazed with every day.

"She passed away," she said. Her voice conveyed the sadness of her words, not the declarative fact.

"I'm aware of that."

"What is this regarding?"

"Something she hired me to do for her."

"Find the missing Dali?"

"You know about it?"

"I'm surprised you didn't drop by earlier."

"You weren't home on numerous occasions."

"I am now."

"May I come on in?"

She stepped back. As I entered her house a whiff of lavender died in my senses.

"Would you like some coffee?" she said as she walked in front of me.

"If it's not too much bother."

"It's a Keurig machine. Could hardly be easier."

We entered a side sunroom, similar to Veronica's. Her house now had a FOR SALE sign staked in the front yard. Barbara pointed to the Keurig. "Help yourself." I selected a dark roast and a coffee mug with Vincent Van Gogh's *Almond Blossoms* on it. After the machine had hissed out its last drop, I settled in a chair-and-a-half across from her. The comfort and spaciousness impressed me. I made a note to surprise Kathleen with one for her study.

Barbara Langford had been a neighbor of Veronica's "since the year we both bought our houses, and please, don't ask me when that was. It seems like only yesterday, but we both know that only yesterday was a long time ago."

"We were friends," she continued. "Friends who always had each other's back. Do you know what I mean, Mr. Travis?"

"Jake."

"Do you know what I mean?"

She had an innocent yet confident transparency to her voice. As if she'd reached that point in life where pretenses were an intrusion, and she retained little patience for the peripheral.

"I do."

"I doubt it. Nothing personal, but I don't think men are capable of understanding a woman's need of friendship with another woman."

Bonita's comments along the same lines squatted in my head. My thoughts, as they'd been prone to the past week, wandered. Do women have some secret club they all belong to?

They often seem so comfortable in each other's company
that I—

"Mr. Travis?"

"I'm sorry."

"I said, did you find it? The Dali?"

"I did not."

Her face registered disappointment. "What a shame.
Veronica wanted that painting returned to Rollins more than
anything else in the world."

"What did she tell you about it?"

Before answering, she took a sip of coffee. When finished,
she kept the mug cupped in her hands on her lap. "What do
you know of Veronica?"

I explained that I knew she'd once been married to Michael
Fredericks, the man who had killed her before turning the gun
on himself. I was about to start in on Jamie, but something in
Barbara's eyes paused me.

"Michael," she said, as if his name evoked something from
beyond. "Veronica and I talked deep into many nights about
him. Them. He wrote her after she married Nick Harris—a
mistake she willingly walked into. If that first letter from
Michael had come a few years earlier, there would be no Nick
Harris. I think she wanted to suffer. To feel emotional pain.
Sometimes, Jake, we need to pinch ourselves to make sure we're
still here. That was Veronica, in the end. You know she had
Alzheimer's, right? Or some sort of dementia. Timing was
never my friend's friend."

She was quiet for a moment before coming back in.

"It's a terrible disease. By the time they diagnose it, lord
knows how long it's been lurking in someone's mind. Playing
tricks with their world."

I asked her if Veronica shared the secret of the Dali with
her. It was my second pass at the question. It did not
escape her.

"I wanted to make sure first that we're on the same page. She asked my advice on getting it back. Not an easy task as she ruled out going to the police. I gave her your name."

"Pardon?"

"Elizabeth Walker was a friend of mine. I hired her for her first banking job. We kept in touch over the years. Before she died, she told me of the work you did for her. How she relied on you to find *her* daughter. It was I who passed your name on to Veronica. I'm sure you see the similarities."

I had wondered where Veronica got my name. I initially thought she'd been referred to me by Yankee Conrad or his wife, Constance. I'd questioned Wetzel, but he'd claimed he didn't know. Like the sun blazing free of a pesky cloud, I felt the similarities, the parallel universe, between the Elizabeth Walker affair and Veronica. Both women had met their soulmates in college. Both had daughters. *Four women.* Both had suffered immeasurable tragedies that had torn their lives asunder. Both reconciled but too late. The song that Veronica played over and over. Is it that simple? Do we—?

"Mr. Travis?" Barbara said.

"Pardon?"

"You seem . . . distracted. I said it was I who gave her your name. I hope you didn't mind."

"Not in the least. Do you know how she came to be in possession of the painting?"

"I do. Michael, swiped it from a hallway in college before they were married. He claimed he didn't know what he had taken until he got back to his apartment. One thing led to another, and he never returned it."

That didn't surprise me. Michael was always the crowd favorite to have swiped the Dali.

"She had a child," I said. "A daughter."

"I am aware."

"She died nearly fifty years ago."

"Tragic. Do you know how?"

I'd asked Wetzel, and he said Veronica had never confided that to him.

"I do not."

She told me. As she talked, I imagined coming home with Kathleen from a night out. Perhaps a half-full second bottle of wine from the restaurant in our hands. We don't have stairs. Maybe the pool. The seawall. Because this dumb oyster didn't listen to his wife and put a fence in. But we have two. Which one? A Sophie's choice. My body tingled.

I spoke, rushing to get ahead of my mind as it envisioned the unimaginable.

"Did Veronica, at the end, know that her daughter predeceased her?"

She crossed her legs. Outside, a lawn mower fired up.

"Does it matter?"

I would think so. After all, that's more than a few degrees off reality. Or is it?

I passed on her question and said, "I got the impression that Nick Harris sold the Dali to someone related to Veronica. Would someone have tried to impersonate her daughter? Take advantage of Veronica?"

Barbara took another sip of coffee. The lawn mower must have gone behind a house, for its sound diminished by half.

"She had a visitor. A few weeks ago."

She paused.

"Go on," I prodded her.

"Someone from her past. Veronica said she hadn't seen the woman in years. Since college. She was afraid that she told the woman too much."

I leaned forward in the chair. "Too much of what?"

"About the Dali. Veronica told me she was afraid she rambled. Spilled the painting. That she wished the woman had never come by. Veronica was a strong woman, but she knew she was weakening by the day. That her mind was deserting her."

"Did she give you the name of her visitor?"

"No."

"You said you were close."

"She told me she never wanted to hear the woman's name again. That the woman had taken advantage of her. Ruined it for her and Michael."

"Did you see the other woman?"

"I saw her leaving the house. I was sitting where I am now."

I asked her to describe her to me, although I already knew who she was.

"Tall. Thin. Money on heels. The type of woman who never says thank you when someone opens a door for her."

CHAPTER 60

I had one stop to make before driving to Winter Park. Just to make sure—going forward—that I had it right. But I knew. And I should have known earlier. It's always like that at the end, isn't it?

You finally catch those answers, and they're so simple you wonder why you ran so hard.

Melinda Varker's car was in the parking lot when I pulled into Nick Harris's office.

"Well, hug a porcupine," she said when I burst through the door. "Can't say I expected to see you again."

"How's the annuity business?"

"Keeps me running around like a bunny with a bottle rocket up its ass."

There's an image for you.

She continued. "I've been darn near living here, putting in twelve-hour shifts. But I like it. It's invigorating. I scheduled my tests. Sent out new cards, the whole kit and caboodle. I got a knack for this business. I like people, and that's half the battle. What can I do for you? Still searching for your Degas?"

"Dali."

"Right. Dali. How come I can't get that right? Hey, I went to that museum after you dropped by. Never been before. He did some weird stuff. Can't say I'm a fan of ants, though."

"Do you remember a woman coming by, likely no appointment, three, four weeks ago? She would have been tall. Dressed in expensive clothes designed to make her seventy years look like fifty. She might—"

Melinda held up a calvary-halt hand.

"Hold it right there. I know exactly who you're talking about. She marched in maybe three weeks ago? Wanted to see Nick. Lucky for her, he was in."

"Her name?"

"I asked. She never gave it. Said just to tell Nick that a friend of Veronica's was here to see him."

"What did they discuss?"

"They were in his office the entire time."

"You certainly asked him."

"Certainly did."

"And?"

She zipped a finger across her lips. "He wouldn't say. I let it go. Why the Q and A? Who was she?"

I explained that she was an old friend of Veronica Stafford. That I had reason to believe they discussed the Dali.

"She's dead, you know that, right? A murder-suicide with her first husband."

"I do. Do you have access to Nick's accounts? Cash in and out? Wire receipts?"

"You need a POA for that. Veronica's attorney has been in contact with me."

"R. Wetzel Brookings?"

Melinda canted her eyebrows. "'Please, call me Wetzel.' Nick died without a will. He was in the process of drafting a new one, getting a divorce and all, but never got around to it."

I said, "Nick and Veronica were still married when he

predeceased her. Under such circumstances, in the state of Florida, the property goes to the surviving spouse. Anything Nick received for the painting would belong to Veronica's estate."

"If you say so. But I can't allow you to look at his accounts without—"

"Wetzel has authority over Nick's estate," I interrupted her. "I'll get him on the line."

I explained to Wetzel where I was and what I needed. He asked to speak to Melinda. I handed her my phone. She listened, chirped a perky "Okey dokey," hung up, and handed my phone back.

"All right, captain," she said, her fingers dancing on her keyboard. "You're cleared for takeoff. Let's see what trouble we can find."

I walked around behind her so I could look over her shoulder.

"This was Nick's main checking account," she said, dipping her head toward the monitor. "We're looking at all activity in the past thirty days. We can go back further if you wish. I don't see anything unusual here. Automatic debits. Cable. Utilities. Certainly nothing to raise concern."

I asked her if he had other accounts. Something she wouldn't have access to.

"I would assume, but I can't say for sure. He did all his checking and ACH payments from this account. Those I know about, of course."

"You said Carrie took care of that for him."

"She did."

"If he wanted to do a financial transaction without her knowledge, he would need to do so at a different financial institution. Most people have more than one checking account."

"I don't know where to—"

"Let's go to his office," I said, straightening up, for I'd been bent over studying the monitor. "I'd like to look around."

"Follow me."

I trailed her into Nick's office. I asked her if I could take a swing at his desk. I slipped past her and took a seat. I soon got the rhythm of his system: product brochures in the right drawers, client information in the left. The long middle drawer was a hodgepodge of ibuprofen, tissue, loose change, notepads, and an assortment of pens and yellow markers. I pulled the drawer out as far as it would go. Photos of golfing foursomes. A collection of business cards held together by a rubber band. Blue Post-it Notes. A blank legal pad. Underneath the legal pad was a single piece of paper. Written in ink on that pad were internet sites and passwords.

"Whatja got there?" Melinda said, for it was her turn to peer over my shoulder.

"Passwords. They'll be helpful to Wetzel, but I don't see any banks or financial institutions."

She pointed to an entry. "Take a look at this?"

"The First Furniture Store? What about it?"

"I write down passwords, who doesn't? But I always disguise the site so if anyone finds my list, it'll make no sense to them."

"Good thinking. What do you make of First Furniture?"

"A password for a furniture store? God help us. But there is a First Federal Savings two blocks from here."

The monitor on the desk was off. I turned it on, but it was still blank.

"Let me in there," Melinda said. "That one's a bit finicky."

We switched positions. She fiddled with the monitor, and it sprang to life. She hit the mouse a few times and brought up the log-in page for First Federal Savings. She entered Nick's email address.

"Read me that password," she said.

"Gators2009. Initial cap."

"Makes sense. That man loved college football, and that was his alma mater."

"But he didn't graduate then."

"We went undefeated that year, but the Tide got us in the SEC championship. We beat them the year before, in '08, for the national title."

"Why wouldn't he use the victory year?"

"A password, right? You remember the losses, not the wins. Bingo. We're in. Same thing? Money in and out?"

"The last thirty days."

She leaned into the monitor. "Hmm, let's see." She scrolled down the screen, then back to the top. "Holy shitsky. He's got close to six mill here. Let's look at the activity." She clicked the mouse. "Here we go. My, my. Just look at those zeros. One, two, three, four, five, six. Nick received a wire for five million dollars about two weeks ago." She let out a low whistle. "I bet our friend R. Wetzel Brookings will want to know about that."

I squinted at the monitor. "Where did it come from?"

"Let's see . . . Hmm, Storage Queen Properties. Mean anything to you?"

CHAPTER 61

The Dali, like Dali himself, never escaped itself. It was a hostage to its origins. Doomed to return to the womb.

Wetzel confirmed what I thought. The money used to purchase the Dali would, as a residual of Veronica Stafford's estate as her husband died intestate, be gifted to Harbor House. That brought the total to twenty-five million. Three point six a day. How come I didn't feel good about that?

It was dark by the time I located the house. I'd spent the two-hour drive chastising myself for not seeing it all sooner, replaying in my head my conversation with Veronica.

"She might have it."

"Jamie?"

"No. She."

We'd been discussing her daughter, Jamie. But Veronica's mind had switched tracks. Mine had not.

I swung my truck into the middle of the circular paver-brick driveway and climbed out. The cold front that had been threatening for the past week was pushing through bringing conflicted air. It was muggy, like the dying gasp of summer, yet in the next breath it carried the chill of winter. A pestering rain that had chaperoned my drive got serious, the water bucketing down as I sprinted up the four brick steps to the front. I pushed the doorbell. The Westminster chimes rang inside the house. I stepped closer to the door to shelter myself from the rain, and, without prompt, it flooded back to me.

My foolish game.

Demos had told Kevin and Anna to leave. Then Kevin wanted to go upstairs to look for his wallet. In a meaningless attempt to irritate Demos, I'd reversed my earlier command that Kevin and Anna leave. I put the couple in harm's way. I was just trying to needle Demos, and look what came of it. Anna was still in a coma. Her family keeping vigil. The blank page of fate awaiting instructions. Me and my stupid games. My cavalier attitude. Dancing with other people's lives and—

The door opened.

"Well," Faye Wilkinson said. "It took you long enough."

"May I come in?" I said, my thoughts deserting me, but I knew they wouldn't wander far.

"What if I say no?"

I brushed past her into her house.

"Just walk right in," she said from behind me.

The marble foyer opened into several other rooms.

"Where is it?" I said.

"You interrupted my evening glass of wine."

She strolled past me and into a large living room. I followed. It had high windows that overlooked Lake Virginia. Landscape lights around a pool glistened in the rain. The room had a fireplace at one end and a sunken bar along a wall. She walked around the bar and refilled a glass of red wine.

"Care for anything?" she said.

"No," I said, my eyes stuck on the painting above the fireplace.

"Must it be this way?"

I turned to her. "People died."

"And I'm sure my glass of wine won't bring them back."

"She told you, didn't she? When you went to see her a few weeks ago."

"She did."

"Why did you go to her?"

She took a patient sip of wine. "Would you believe me if I said I was in town and just decided to drop by? It'd been fifty years. We don't have another fifty."

"She told you about the Dali."

"She rambled a bit."

"She had dementia. You certainly saw that."

"Don't tell me what I saw. I—"

"And you didn't just happen to drop by."

Faye plopped her glass of wine on the bar.

"Fine. You want the damn truth? I went to tell her that I loved her. That I've always loved her. I went there to tell her before our time ran out. That's what happens when you get to be my age. You'll get there one day. Would you like to know what she said?"

Faye waited for me, as if incapable of proceeding without affirmation that she at least had an audience of one.

"Go on."

"I assume you unearthed the Jamie story?"

"I have."

"After Jamie died, Ronnie came to me for comfort. To my bed. My pillow. When I told her I loved her a few weeks ago? She told me she blamed me for ruining her life. That I should have told her to stay with Michael. Not taken her in. She said she hated me. That true love is sacrifice, not self-indulgence. She accused me of using Jamie's death for my own selfish reasons."

"She knew you well. Why—"

"Screw you."

"—the Dali?"

She took a moment before answering.

"When she said she hated me? It took my life away. Made a fool of all my passions. It hurt. Hurts. I decided right there to hit her back. If she cared so much for some damn painting, then I wanted it."

My gaze returned to the painting above the fireplace.

When I turned back to her, her eyes were waiting for me. Eyes that, when I first met her, didn't believe in truth. Eyes that I now realized had lost all sense of morality, and I wondered if that pesky trait had ever been part of her DNA.

"But you didn't want her to know you had it," I said.

"I might have told her one day, if the smugness of having it without her knowledge ever wore off. But that's a moot point now that Romeo blew them both away."

"You're a real bitch."

"Don't be getting any thoughts in your head, or you'll discover just how mean this real bitch can be."

I walked to a sofa that had a blanket draped over it. I picked up the blanket. I walked to the fireplace and glanced up at the painting.

The woman's curved neck was too long. Her face seemed out of place with the rest of the painting, which was photograph real. She was void of color, except for her lips, and they were the shade of a dead red rose, of tired sex. Half her face was dark, never to be seen. Whatever you wanted to see, to feel, to believe, you saw in half her face. I recalled Veronica telling me it was a face you would never forget. She was right. On the road between impressionism and surrealism, Dali had painted a face to reflect the vulnerabilities of whoever viewed his painting. Did he set out to do that, or, as our favorite Roman orator foretold, had he stumbled upon it accidentally?

On the mantel, under the painting, was a black-and-white photograph of Veronica when she was young. The right side of her face lost in darkness, her left eye staring out at me, her lips parted. I glanced up at the painting. There was the eerie similarity between the face in Dali's painting and the photograph. Had Faye displayed the photograph of her college lover for fifty years?

I turned away from the fireplace and moved a picture book of 1950s Florida off a square glass coffee table. I unfolded the blanket. I spread it out evenly over the glass table. It was blue with *ROLLINS* in white with the crown of a yellow sun above the name.

"I'll call the police. It's my town. My house. You broke in. Touched me. Threatened me."

"Go ahead," I said, smoothing out the blanket. "Make your call."

"I'm not joking. You'll leave here in cuffs."

I reached up, carefully took the painting by its two lower corners, and lifted it off the wall.

"How did you plan to explain that you have a Dali in your house?"

"You mean that worthless reproduction you're holding?"

I placed the painting on the blanket. It was a nice touch that Gibson would receive it wrapped in a college blanket.

"Tell me about Nick Harris," I said. "How did you know he was trying to fence it?"

It was a loose end that still eluded me.

"You're not even close," she said in the voice of a sinner who wanted to be caught. Wanted the world to see her transgression. I stopped wrapping the painting, my body frozen by the apparition of that which had been so muddled, now so clear.

"You approached Harris, didn't you?" I said. "Sought him out. He never had any intention of selling the Dali until you poisoned his ear."

Faye Wilkinson hung herself with silence before answering.

"Bravo for you. After Ronnie spilled her life-ending desire that the Dali be returned to Rollins I dropped by Nick's office. I told him I knew the Dali was in the house. He didn't want to steal it from Ronnie. Five million dollars convinced him otherwise. He said Ronnie was leaving him. That Magic Mike had reappeared in her life. He needed money."

She continued, as if recalling her moment of glory.

"He swiped it and moved it to his office. But before we consummated the deal, and in a total failure of sound judgment, he blabbered to his girlfriend, some eager twit who wanted to shop it around. Problem is Nick Harris never told her that he'd already made a handshake deal to sell the Dali. He came back to me and said he was having thoughts, that five million was too low. I wired him the money."

"After he said he was going to shop it around?" I said.

"I thought that by seeing the money in his account, he would come to his senses. Not be blinded by greed. It didn't work. He said if he got over five for it, he'd wire my money back, or I could double down. But we'd made a deal. I couldn't have that."

"Carrie didn't know, did she?"

"Carrie?"

"Eager-twit girlfriend. She claims that Nick never told her about another buyer. Said she got some sense of a family member being interested in the Dali but nothing more specific than that."

Faye was quiet. I wondered what I'd said that had caused her to pause. My mind went blank, and in that suspended moment, Faye's words came back to me.

I couldn't have that.

Demos, to the end, had insisted he had nothing to do with the death of Nick Harris. I'd refused to believe him. That pigheadedness had prevented me from considering other possibilities. From seeing the obvious: Demos had admitted to killing Charley's lover, Francis Rampton. So why did he continuously deny killing Harris?

Because he didn't.

"You killed Nick Harris," I said. "Hired the job out."

Faye's cool eyes rested on mine. Baiting me.

"I haven't a clue what you're talking about," she said in a voice that conveyed the opposite of her words.

"The key to the closet. How did you get it?"

"Here's what I know about men: they keep their dicks in their hand and their keys in their pockets."

I thought that Carrie, by telling Demos about Nick wanting to shop the Dali around, had sealed Nick's fate. That wasn't the case. Harris told Carrie about the painting, and she told Charley, who contacted Demos. And down the hill went the rolling boulder. While that was going on, Nick did a deal with Faye and then tried to alter the deed. Faye, in no mood to engage in a bidding war for the Dali or to allow a neophyte to double-cross her, put a hit on Harris and snatched the Dali.

"How did you know he hadn't moved it?" I said.

Faye just smiled at me. Me, another neophyte. Another toy. Of course. Harris talked before he died. It had been nothing other than a baseless assumption that he had not. I had more questions—I wondered if whoever Faye hired to kill Harris told her that he died of a heart attack—but they plummeted from the sky. I no longer cared. I was done reconstructing the past. Done trying to figure out where I'd gone wrong. But mostly I was done with Faye Wilkinson. Treacherous. Vindictive. Murderous Faye Wilkinson.

I resumed folding the blanket around the picture.

Faye said, "After Ronnie came back to me? She left again. Said she didn't love me. You think I used her? Bullshit. She used me. I knew I'd get back someday. What will you tell them?"

"Don't flatter yourself. No one ever wants to hear your name again."

I was a few feet from the door, Nick Harris on the fading

horizon of my conscious. How he wasn't the dishonorable person Veronica thought him to be. From beyond, Nick Harris must have been channeling his thoughts across the universe. That's the only way I can explain the convulsion in my mind that again exposed Faye's lies.

Carrie had confirmed that Harris thought he'd made a mistake. My assumption was that his mistake was not holding on to the Dali for a higher price. But was that really who Nick Harris was? Melinda told me Nick was a sweet man. And Veronica? I'd always had trouble seeing her as someone who got suckered into a bad marriage. While she didn't act surprised that he'd taken the painting, she was not of sound mind.

I spun around to Faye.

"You never stop, do you?"

"Stop what?"

"Lying. You made that up. The part about Nick Harris trying to get more money from you. That's not what happened, is it? He took your blood money, then felt guilty. His sin wasn't wanting more money. His sin was that he wanted to *return* your money. Give the Dali back to Veronica. He didn't have the stomach for what he was doing. That wasn't him. Your tall tale that he wanted more money? That was to make you feel better. Elevate you from the killer of a man who wanted to do the right thing to a killer of a man trying to renege on a business deal."

A smile formed on her rotten-strawberry lips.

"Poor, poor little mustard man. You'll never know, will you?"

I looked at her, a species I'd never encountered. A heart not of this world.

I said, "Incurable, in each, the wounds they make."

"Pardon?"

"The rest of the Euripides quote that you wrote on the chalkboard. The part you left out. 'Stronger than lover's love is lover's hate. Incurable, in each, the wounds they make.' But you know that. You set out to hurt her. To wound her. You never loved her."

"Of course we loved each other. How else could we have wounded each other so badly?"

I marched out the front door and into the rain. I put the painting in the back seat of the truck. I took out my phone and made the call.

"Good evening, Mr. Travis," Wayne Gibson said.

"I wonder if I might have your address, Mr. Gibson. I have something that belongs to you."

After I left Gibson's house, he promised, going forward, the college would do a better job of inventory management, I got back in my truck and headed home. As the wipers did their mindless job, I drove back to the green spot of my life, back to dolphins surfacing at the end of the dock, back to four women, back to Morgan touching one person a fingertip at a time, back to Joy and Sophia living in the round-tower of my heart, and back to Kathleen and Kathleen and forever Kathleen.

Before I got on I-4 West, I spotted a drugstore. I pulled in and bought a large bottle of shampoo. I also picked up a pair of nice beach towels to keep on the boat. In my line of work, you never know when you're going to pluck a naked woman out of the Gulf of Mexico.

ABOUT THE AUTHOR

 Robert Lane is the author of the Jake Travis stand-alone novels. *Florida Weekly* calls Jake Travis a "richly textured creation; one of the best leading men to take the thriller fiction stage in years." Lane's debut novel, *The Second Letter*, won the Gold Medal in the Independent Book Publishers Association's (IBPA) 2015 Benjamin Franklin Awards for Best New Voice: Fiction. He is also the recipient of the Eric Hoffer Award for Best Mystery. Lane resides on the west coast of Florida. Learn more at Robertlanebooks.com.

Receive a free copy of the Jake Travis series prequel, *Midnight on the Water*.

As much mystery as love story, *Midnight on the Water* is the saga of how Jake and Kathleen met, tumbled into love, and the drastic measures Jake, Morgan, and Garrett take to save Kathleen's life—and grant her a new identity. *Midnight on the Water* is available only to those on Robert Lane's mailing list. The newsletter contains reviews of books, music, and television shows across a wide range of genres. It also includes updates from the next Jake Travis novel.

Enjoy *Midnight on the Water*.

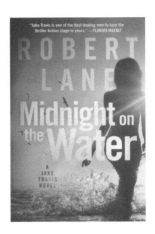

Also be sure to read these other standalone Jake Travis novels:

The Second Letter

Cooler Than Blood

The Cardinal's Sin

The Gail Force

Naked We Came

A Beautiful Voice

The Elizabeth Walker Affair

A Different Way to Die

The Easy Way Out

Visit Robert Lane's author page on Amazon.com: https://www.amazon.com/Robert-Lane/e/B00HZ2254A

Follow Robert Lane on:

Facebook: https://www.facebook.com/RobertLaneBooks

Goodreads: https://www.goodreads.com/author/show/7790754.Robert_Lane

BookBub: https://www.bookbub.com/profile/robert-lane?list=about

Learn more and receive your free copy of *Midnight on The Water* at http://robertlanebooks.com.

Made in United States
Troutdale, OR
08/09/2024

21879434R00224